P9-ELU-123

SUN DOGS

By Robert Olen Butler

The Alleys of Eden

Sun Dogs

Countrymen of Bones

On Distant Ground

Wabash

The Deuce

*A Good Scent from
a Strange Mountain* (stories)

They Whisper

SUN DOGS

◇

A NOVEL BY

Robert Olen Butler

Henry Holt and Company
New York

For Joshua

Henry Holt and Company, Inc.
Publishers since 1866
115 West 18th Street
New York, New York 10011

Henry Holt® is a registered trademark
of Henry Holt and Company, Inc.

Copyright © 1982 by Robert Olen Butler
All rights reserved.
Published in Canada by Fitzhenry & Whiteside Ltd.,
195 Allstate Parkway, Markham, Ontario L3R 4T8.
Originally published in hardcover in 1982 by Horizon Press.
Reissued in cloth and paper in 1994 by Henry Holt and Company.

Library of Congress Cataloging-in-Publication Data
Butler, Robert Olen.
Sun dogs / Robert Olen Butler.—1st Owl book ed.
p.   cm.
1. Vietnamese Conflict, 1961–1975—Veterans—Alaska—Fiction.
2. Man-woman relationships—Alaska—Fiction.   3. Private
investigators—Alaska—Fiction.   4. Widowers—Alaska—Fiction.
I. Title.
PS3552.U8278S9   1994   93-34670
813'.54—dc20   CIP

ISBN 0-8050-3201-0
ISBN 0-8050-3143-X (An Owl Book: pbk.)

Henry Holt books are available for special promotions and
premiums. For details contact: Director, Special Markets.

Printed in the United States of America
All first editions are printed on acid-free paper.∞

1   3   5   7   9   10   8   6   4   2
1   3   5   7   9   10   8   6   4   2
pbk.

This novel is a work of fiction. Names, characters, places,
and incidents are either the product of the author's imagination
or are used fictitiously. Any resemblance to actual events
or locales or persons, living or dead, is entirely coincidental.

And when the sun is down, he shall be clean.

—Leviticus 22:7

Life itself is but the shadow of death, and
souls departed but the shadows of the living.
All things fall under this name. The sun itself
is but the dark simulacrum, and light but the
shadow of God.

—Sir Thomas Browne

1.

The office was stripped. Wilson stood in the center of the floor and he suddenly feared he was going to flash back. The room was empty, all trace of his life was gone from it now, and he knew that somewhere inside him this office was starting to ratchet into a memory—a room in a village in a distant place, stripped, too, silent.

He moved to the phone coiled in a corner. He crouched beside it and picked up the receiver. It was still connected. He dialed his service and looked toward the door. The frosted glass held his name and the word "Investigations." A shadow rippled through the glass and passed on. Wilson was all right now as the woman answered.

"Wilson Hand," he said.

"Just a moment," the woman's voice said.

Wilson focused on the backward crawl of the letters of his name through the white flare of light from the hallway.

"One message," the woman said. "Mr. Grevey called from Royal Petroleum. He said your tickets for Anchorage will be waiting at the Northwest Orient ticket counter at JFK. Your flight is at ten o'clock tomorrow morning."

Wilson touched the disconnect button and then dialed Beth.

"Yes?" Her voice was tight, sucked in.

"Beth. It's Wilson."

"Yes," she said but there seemed to be no comprehension behind the word.

"Beth. Are you taking something?"

"No."

"It's Wilson."

"I know it is," she said, still flat. Then abruptly her voice bloated with feeling. "I should know goddam well...What do you want from me? Do you know how many men I've fucked in the past five years? It is five, isn't it?"

"It's five."

"Do you know how many men have wanted me? In my whole life, I mean?"

"Beth, I want to come over there now. Can I do that now? Will you stay there for just another thirty minutes?"

"What do you want from me, Wilson?"

"I'm going away."

"You went away a long time ago."

"I'm leaving New York City. I'm going to Alaska. I'm giving up the business here. I've got an assignment in Alaska."

"Alaska? Jesus." She sounded as if this were the first time she'd heard about his plans. He'd said the very same words to her on the phone yesterday. Briefly he hesitated. Maybe this was the wrong thing to do. They'd been married two years and she'd haunted him for the following five. But he hadn't seen her often since the divorce. It had been over a year now since the last time. But he was going far away. And, oddly, he felt the drive to go—and the desire to see her—flowing from the same source; he felt this clearly even though he could not identify what that source was.

"I want to see you," he said. "I'm leaving New York for good and I just want to see you one more time...Will you be there for another thirty minutes?"

"Where the fuck is there to go?"

"Okay. Good. I'll be there." He laid the receiver gently in its cradle. He rose and the silence thrummed in his head and he strode across the floor.

In the street he passed the cast iron buildings, the columns and pilasters, the terra-cotta faces of Chelsea, without seeing anything.

She was going mad. Maybe that was what was drawing him to

her. Not the madness itself, but its intensity, its extremity. There was something pure and barren about her. And so he'd go and sit and watch her restless hands for a time before he left all this.

Wilson was drawn to a poster on the subway platform. Oil drums were growing on trees and a man gazed up at them, just out of reach, from the ground below. "We've got all we need..." the poster said in large lettering. Wilson skipped the small-print text and looked at the President's signature at the bottom and the broken-chain symbol of the President's Energy Independence campaign. Wilson thought his new employer must be very pleased with all this.

The platform filled suddenly with the dank, artificial wind of an approaching train and Wilson turned and moved toward the tracks. A crescent of people shaped behind him and when the train stopped and the doors opened the crescent contracted and carried him forward into the already crowded car.

Wilson was bound tight on all sides by bodies and he was pressed forward immobile against a young woman holding on to a central pole. The train began to move and all around him faces that had tightened slightly at the paroxysm of new riders grew slack again.

From knee to chest his body touched the woman with the even, insistent pressure of a lover. She was turned at an angle and his chest lay against her shoulder, his crotch fit into the top of her hip. He tried to adjust himself into a less intimate position, but he quickly knew it would only make matters worse. He could not move.

For a time he was more aware of the heat in the car, the thick, sweaty air and the grinding of metal, wheel against rail, than he was of the woman. But soon he was watching her. With no sexual intent, just casually. Her fine brown hair was swirled up from the back of her neck and clipped at the side. Her profile was timid, a small nose and chin, and she had large, nearly black eyes.

But inevitably his genitals began to stir, and when he felt the nibbling there of sexual arousal, he was very conscious of what had finally moved him in this way. It was not the touch of their bodies, her warmth, the curve of her chin. The moment came as he looked at the clasp on the thin gold chain she wore around her neck. It was this that aroused him—this tiny clasp and the vision of her fumbling at it, fastening it, putting this thin little chain around her neck to make herself pretty. The vision of this swelled him at once with a feeling of tenderness for the woman. The clasp and now her barrette, holding her hair in its swirl. The barrette had a tiny, blue, four-petaled flower in its center. He thought of the woman choosing the barrette for herself, touching the flower with her fingertip and wanting it in her hair. This was what stirred Wilson, made his penis swell now against the woman's hip. And the fingernail polish on her hand. The fingers were curled around the silver metal bar and he looked at the paintbrush strokes in her pink polish. He saw her in a quiet room carefully moving the brush. These little things ravished him, made his chest tighten, these little things, the clasp on her chain, and then Wilson felt himself slipping back.

It rushed on him, this flashback, as if he'd just come on the woman, as if her falling away from him now was from his own physical release, the in-turning of an orgasm. But instead it was a recollection so strong that not only the woman vanished but all the other bodies around him as well and he was in a small, bare room and the smells were of dust and poultry and linseed oil. Across the room one of his captors had torn down his rifle and was oiling the parts. Another man crouched in that flat-footed Vietnamese way and his rifle was laid across his chest. Wilson could hear the tiniest sounds of the metal parts. He closed his eyes and he heard the faint thunk of a part placed on the floor, the flex of a spring, even the wood-scrape and then silence of a piece lifted up from the floor, the silence that followed a clear, distinct sound. The dust floated into his lungs. He felt the dust go in and then come out. A chicken clucked somewhere outside. He opened his eyes and through the window a palm frond moved against the sky. His chest began to heave. His right arm ached, the arm that had been broken, his arm ached and he couldn't draw a breath, the air burned in his lungs, he gasped in and out, in and out.

Voices grew loud. He could not draw a breath. Voices grew loud.

"You creep you pervert you fucker you...Trainman! Somebody get the trainman!"

The young woman's face was full on Wilson. He heard his own breathing, panting, he still could not breathe. One last moment in the room, one more dip of the palm frond, and then he could see the young woman with the thin gold chain, her black eyes burning at him, her hands on his chest, pushing him back. He heard his own breathing now, still heavy, and he understood what had happened. What she thought.

The train was slowing. The woman yelled on, for a trainman, for a policeman, for someone to do something.

The train stopped and Wilson heard the doors open behind him. He turned and put his elbow out and wedged between two women.

"Stop him. He was touching me, making sounds."

Wilson pushed hard. A man's face intervened and Wilson lowered his shoulder and the body yielded and he was out the doors and on the platform. People pressed at him, pressed him back toward the train. His arms flailed. "Shit," someone said. "You fucker," said another voice.

Wilson was running. Down the platform, up steps, two at a time, through the exit doors, bars there, past the token booth, more steps, a crowded street, all the people coming this way, he turned sideways, edged against the storefronts, quickly, around the corner.

He was panting from the exertion, the memories threatened again, they crawled along this link, this breathing. He wrenched at his mind, fixed on the fear. Was someone following him from the train? He went out into the street, clear of the people. He ran to the end of the block along the verge of the traffic and he stopped and leaned against a streetlight. There was no one following him; his breathing slowed.

And then his mood swung abruptly around and Wilson began to laugh. The way it had all happened on the train—the clasp of her necklace, a hut in a village ten thousand miles and almost a decade away, and he suddenly seemed a wild pervert, roused and panting—Wilson leaned forward sharply in laughter. He held his sides as they started to ache and he laughed on, even as passersby began to arc wide to avoid him.

Beth's buff-colored brick building stood on a three block stretch of apartments on Columbus Avenue, buildings that huddled large and defenseless in streets stalked by junkies. Wilson stopped on the sidewalk and counted up fourteen floors and over three balconies and he saw a figure there, briefly, disappearing into the darkness of the open balcony doors. Had she been watching for him?

It took a long while for her to buzz him in through the downstairs doors and a long time again for her to answer his knock at her apartment. Finally the door opened and Beth stood there. Her hair—still the color of a seal pelt—slashed down across her face, but her grey eyes seemed clear, her mouth looked freshly made up with pale pink lipstick. She stood with one shoulder hunched slightly up and the fingertips of one hand resting in the spot between her breasts. She'd stood this way the night he'd picked her up for their first date. She'd stood this way before him countless times, always in her calm moments. But the pose did not renew any of his old sexual feelings for her, in spite of the dark disks of her nipples faintly showing through the cloth of her blouse. Instead, her standing like this made him intensely interested in her, interested in a way he'd never been when they were married, interested in a way that was intensified by not including the desire to touch her, interested in the way that he was interested in the trip ahead of him. He was interested in the intensity that she gave off even now, an intensity that dazzled him like ice-blink.

"I don't know what you want to do this for," Beth said, but

her voice was gentle.

"I told you..."

"I know. All right. Come in. I have a few minutes." She turned and padded ahead of him. Her feet were bare and still Wilson did not respond to her sexually. He passed behind her through the hallway stacked on both sides with boxes. They were new boxes, original cartons for earthenware, food processors, vacuum cleaners, an encyclopedia. Some had been opened but many had not, and even the ones that were open still held their contents capped or clutched by styrofoam shapes.

She led him to her living room where the balcony doors were open. The room was filled with objects. There were two couches, both new, one with a showroom label still on it. A table held three digital clocks, two with radios; there were piles of books in fresh dust jackets, piles of records; two lamps sat side by side on a table, two more side by side on the floor; perhaps a dozen collapsed director's chairs were stacked against the wall; and art prints—Kandinskys, Klees, O'Keeffes, American primitives—all in aluminum frames, were hung in massive, crowded patchworks on the walls.

Beth sat on the couch with the label, her back to the open balcony doors, her feet tucked under her. Wilson recognized an overstuffed chair from their married days and sat in it.

Beth's hands were folded in her lap and she seemed to be waiting for Wilson, seemed to be calmly waiting. It was Wilson who fretted, whose hands would not hold still. He rubbed at the nap of the chair's arms.

"I'm sorry to just drop in on you like this," Wilson said.

"No," Beth said. "I'm the sorry one. I gave you the wrong impression on the phone. It sounded like I think about you a lot, like these past five years I've been regretting everything, getting angry at it. In fact I haven't thought about you in a long time. And the times I do, it's very brief and something trivial. Believe me. That's true."

"I just wanted to see you again before..."

"Believe me, Wilson. Tell me you understand what I just

said.'' Her hands still had not left her lap. She was insistent now, but she seemed very calm.

"I understand. I believe you," Wilson said.

"Good. It's true."

"So then you don't mind my being here."

"No," she said, suddenly sounding very tired, turning her profile to the open balcony. The morning light glinting from windows across the way lit her face with a faint penumbra. He saw her mouth draw in, the lips tighten.

"I'm going to work for an oil company," Wilson said. "They're sending me to Alaska." He was aware that he'd already told her these things. It wasn't words he was here for. But it wasn't her touch either. He was here just to be near her. He wanted to watch her. He would have preferred to come here invisibly, to watch her moving through her life without his own presence influencing her. But he knew she expected him to talk. Without words he could not justify staying.

"I'm going to do some investigative work for them," Wilson said. She did not turn her face. He felt her silence as a demand on him. His mind knew it was foolish, but he had the feeling that she was demanding more than small talk, that she wanted him to say something revealing. Otherwise he'd have to leave.

"It's not just the work I'm going for," he said. "I'm tired here. The city's full of clutter." Speaking the word made him conscious of Beth's apartment. "You've been doing some shopping," he blurted, not meaning to speak the thought.

But this leap brought her back. She looked at him. "They see me coming," she said. "'How was that food processor you bought last week?' they say. 'Terrific. Give me another,' I say." Beth stopped and laughed.

Wilson laughed with her. "If you have enough people over to fill your two couches and..." He looked toward the stack of director's chairs. "...twelve chairs, you'd probably need two processors going at once to make enough dip."

"Four."

"Four?"

"I've got four processors," she said, starting to laugh again.

Wilson looked around at the digital clocks and lamps and window fans and television sets. "All you need is a teller's cage and you could open a bank."

"Free gifts for deposit," she said through her laughter. "Yes. I'm ready."

She pounded her forehead with the palm of her hand as she laughed and Wilson grew alarmed. "It feels good to buy things," he said lamely, wanting her to stop.

"They've all got different features," she said, her laughter winding down.

"What?"

"The processors. The four are not identical. It's good to know I've got..." She began to laugh again. "...options...It's crazy, isn't it? But you're right. It feels damn good. I don't mind the clutter. Not like you. We never did see eye to eye on that sort of thing. On a lot of things. I like the clutter. I don't want gaps that I have to fill in. I want these things. They all have a function. Even the things out there in the hall that I haven't gotten to. There are *possibilities* out there in the hall. Each time I go out or come in, there are *possibilities*. You don't think Alaska's cluttered?"

The question came abruptly, her eyes fixed on Wilson, and she waited. He stammered. "No...No it's not," he said. "I just want to get away from here...I'm having these spells. You remember my spells."

"Your flashbacks."

"Yes."

"Still to that week you spent as a prisoner?"

"Yes."

"You really are crazy, you know, Wilson. You're nuts. Bonkers. Off the wall." She said this quietly, earnestly, her eyes narrowing.

Wilson felt her madness, felt her burning there on the couch, but burning with a cold fire, a fire reflected from some source out of sight, the same source, perhaps, that touched him. She burned coldly, a full moon pulling at him as if he were a tide, his body lifting, following, but, like the sea with the moon, not drawn high enough to touch this object of attraction. But she did draw out more words.

"Why is it I'm driven back to my captivity?" he said. "There's something there. Not just a time of terror that I'm trying to exorcise. I'm not just picking at a scab. There's something. I don't know. And I feel dead in this city...You like all the clutter. But me, I look around this room and I feel like some twentieth century Tut in his tomb. I'm buried with all the necessities of my life on earth. I'm floating to God on a Castro Convertible, my whirring little slaves in attendance juicing my carrots and telling me the time on my trip through the afterlife. And it's not just in your apartment. I felt that way in my office, and out in the street...But I don't believe in it. I'm not going to get to God this way. I'm going to end up in a glass case somewhere, mummified in my Fruit-of-the-Loom."

"Look," Beth said, "I like all this shit I've bought..."

"Didn't you ask me about Alaska?"

"I don't want to argue with you."

"I'm just explaining."

Her profile again. "I'm calm today. For once."

Wilson stopped and considered this. She did seem much calmer than usual. Her hands were back in her lap. All this buying she'd been doing was very odd, but she seemed to realize it; she'd laughed at it herself. "You've never bored me," Wilson said.

She looked at him for a long moment and then said quietly, "Why don't we leave it at that?"

Her calmness now seemed to be eating away at his ties to her. He was suddenly very conscious of all the objects in the room; he felt them as a crawling on the surface of his skin. He had to go. "Yes," he said. "We'll leave it at that."

He rose but she did not. She turned her face away. He felt his own face grow warm, his eyes fill—from what, he did not know. He expected to feel pity for her, but if it was there he could not disentangle it from other things. He moved to her and bent near and kissed her on the hair, awkwardly, almost losing his balance. He drew back and her face remained averted and he moved past her sealed boxes and out the door.

Wilson went to the hotel that he'd checked into the night before; his apartment lease had expired, his possessions had been disposed of, his life had collapsed into a large bag. Because his business had been slack and he was still a day away from an expense account, the hotel was cheap. It was just north of Times Square and a whore with a scar from jugular to jugular said something low to him as he entered the lobby. The din from the traffic, the blare of neon, the shuffle of people, made his jaw ache with impatience to leave. At the front desk, he found the same message from Grevey at Royal Petroleum. His ticket to Alaska was waiting at JFK. Even now.

This held Wilson till he was in his room. The room's bareness soothed him. He crossed to the window and, though the mid-October day was hot, he closed the window without looking. The room smelled of old cigarette smoke and German roaches and he lay down on the bed in his clothes.

The traffic was muffled; it was better than silence, really, because he felt more clearly that he was cut off from all that. As sleep came, he thought about the incident on the train. It didn't seem as funny, in half-sleep, as it had before. It puzzled him. On a crowded subway, focused on that woman—what was the link? His mind blurred and before he could shape the question again he was asleep.

He woke in a sweat. The room was dim. He sat on the side of the bed and his head felt cushioned in styrofoam and shut up in a cardboard box. Trapped in his head were a handful of words. They tumbled around: You never bored me. Wilson wanted to go out. Eat some food, walk around until he could sleep again. Perhaps go to the airport early. In the middle of the night, even. He couldn't take the city for much longer.

Crossing the room he was startled by his own reflection in the

17

mirror over the dresser. He stopped. His face, long-jawed anyway, seemed gaunt to him. He was thinner than he'd felt. His shirt collar looked too large. His dark hair cut across his forehead evenly, like a bad toupee. He pushed his hair back and straightened his tie, but he was distanced, still, from this image of himself and he could not suppress the thought that this face looked like it belonged in the streets of New York. You never bored me. He didn't want to leave it at that. He didn't know what he would say, but he had to say more to Beth. He crossed to the nightstand and dialed her apartment.

The phone rang half a dozen times and he cursed softly. She was out. He'd call again from the airport. Then a man answered. "Yes?"

Wilson drew back. He thought simply to hang up. Another of Beth's lovers. But he felt a rush of resentment. The man couldn't keep him from her. "I'd like to talk to Beth."

"Who are you?" the voice said. Wilson imagined a young man from the voice, burly.

"I'm...Look, tell her it's Wilson. Don't hassle me, okay?"

"I'm Officer Park, New York City Police. Are you a relative of Elizabeth Hand?"

"I'm her ex-husband. What is it?"

"She went over the balcony early this afternoon."

"What?" Wilson felt a tumbling in his chest. Something broken loose.

"I mean she's dead. She...ah...killed herself...We're finishing up here...Listen, I'm new at this. I'm sorry how I put it, just now. She did...ah...jump. This all happened four or five hours ago. One thing I should do is warn you to avoid reading *The Post* tonight. They've got a photo. You know how they are...I'm sorry the way I broke the news to you...Can you give me a little information now about..."

Wilson hung up the phone and he left the room. In the street he found it was dusk. He'd slept at least seven hours. The tumbling had stopped; his chest had compacted; he felt stiff. He walked away from Times Square, going uptown instead. The shops on up were closed or closing and the crowds would be thinner. At the corner a city bus passed with an Energy Independence poster on its side: "We've got all we need..."

Now Wilson wanted to get out of the street. He saw a Horn and Hardart on the next corner. A cup of coffee. She was dead. Avoid the *Post*. He approached a newsstand and he stopped. Beth was there, he knew. He could not pass her by. He moved to the stand and the tabloid had a front page headline about a tenement fire in the Bronx.

But the photo. Large. Filling half the page. The photo was a tight shot from over the front of the hood of a car. It showed a woman's bare feet thrust out of the window toward the camera and the woman's body folded sideways in the car's seat. The woman's eyes were open, her stare was vague, disconcerted. It was Beth.

LEAPER DIES, the photo caption said. "Elizabeth Hand, 34, of 710 Columbus Avenue, lies fatally injured after jumping from her fourteenth floor apartment balcony. Miss Hand initially survived the jump when she landed on a car parked below. Hours later, however, she died of her injuries at..."

Wilson felt dizzy, but it was a purely physical feeling. He fumbled through the pile of change in his palm and bought a copy of the paper and he folded it under his arm and walked away. He went to the end of the block, past the Horn and Hardart, he crossed the street and finally slowed and stepped into the doorway of a darkened bank.

He unfolded the newspaper. He did not finish reading the caption. He stared at the picture. Beth's bare feet were thrust from the window, her high arch, her slender toes, the little toe on her left foot separated just slightly. Wilson began to cry. He'd loved her feet.

The lake below was vinyl, rigid to Wilson's eyes. To fall here the broken wings of the jet would find no yielding; they would carom across the lake's surface, bounding high, shards of steel breaking apart in air and falling heavily on a dustless plain. He thought this calmly, watching the wings fall in silence.

He picked up the plastic spoon on his tray-table and began to stir his coffee. She's dead. Only words. The tap and scrape of plastic defined his place in the seat, and against the tiny sound near his hands the window showed a gasp of sky. He heard the faint tracking of his spoon, the sound of his own breath; and the tightness of this little circle played against the vastness beyond the window. Then the plane entered a cloud. The circle was broken and a low chatter, a creaking, a flapping of a magazine's page began to crowd into his mind. A woman laughed a few rows up.

Wilson closed his eyes: Beth laughed loudly—she veritably shouted in laughter—as she and Wilson stood beneath an almond tree along the road that flew without turning into the Atlas Mountains. Their cheap rented French car steamed beside them and the billows obscured Beth's face even as her laugh roared on.

Wilson opened his eyes and the grey outside persisted for a moment and then it vanished. The sky filled his sight once more and immediately the plane's wing rose slightly. Wilson felt the jet move almost imperceptibly into a shallow bank to the right. Then, not two hundred feet off and slightly above the left wing, a small twin-engined prop plane passed by tail first. Wilson put his face to the window and he saw the spinning props for a moment as the jet passed on.

He turned to look into the cabin. Not another face was pressed to the window. There was no stir. None of the other passengers had seen what he had. None of them knew how close they'd all just come to dying. The tops of the heads stretching before him remained motionless, curls of smoke rising here and there above them. He heard a faint laugh somewhere and the snapping of a newspaper page. He sat back in his seat and closed his eyes. In his mind the cloud disappeared again and the jet banked immediately. The turn had been so deceptively mild.

What did Beth know? Right now. Right this moment. He was calm. She knew the answer. Uncluttered. The steam from their car swirled about her head and it had seemed to Wilson at the time that she'd just died; her face had disappeared suddenly, like the moment of death, and still he had heard her laughter. Now, Wilson thought. Now. He strained to hear Beth now that she was really dead. Whisper to me. Moments before, he'd almost learned what she already knew. A face drew near his. But it was a man, dark-skinned, almond-eyed. He said something in Vietnamese and although he was looking straight at Wilson, the words clearly were meant for the other man in the room, out of Wilson's sight. Wilson gripped hard at the armrests of the plane's seat. One thing clearly struck him. He had not hated his captors. At no time, even when they hurt him, did he hate the Viet Cong who held him captive in that village hut. The man's face had an oval bluish spot high on the cheek. Wilson wondered if it was cancer.

A voice was speaking overhead. "The captain has turned on the seatbelt sign..." The stewardess' voice. The plane dipped minutely, wobbled in choppy air, began very slightly to descend. The voice went on and Wilson turned his face to the window. Ahead were dark, jagged, huddled mountains. Wilson was drawn forward, his face leaned against the window. Immediately below was a plain—wide, flat, striated in red and yellow and white, like the face of Jupiter—not a plain, a glacier—its surface wrinkled, whirling around a vortex. Then all the color was gone and they were over a grey, cratered area, the place from which the glacier had withdrawn. Its cold body had pressed like a selfish lover against the earth and then left it ravaged, dead. Or maybe the earth was dead to start—it had pulled the ice to it with its emptiness.

The mountains jumbled in now, filled Wilson's sight. And he remembered—a controlled memory, this, not a flashback—he remembered the long flight to Vietnam. Very late at night. The pilot woke up all the sleeping GIs. Wake up, he'd called over the loudspeaker. Have a last look at home, boys. And they'd all looked out into the phosphorescent night and they saw perhaps these very mountains—uniform, barren, a wasteland the man was telling them was home. Wilson tried to remember his feeling at that. Bullshit, someone had said. Others said it, too, laughed. Some, Wilson guessed, had believed what the pilot said—for this land was echoing their own minds at that moment; their fears, which were their new homes. But Wilson thought he himself had been oddly accepting; this was a vision of home that had no fear in it. Perhaps I'm just projecting backwards, he thought now. For he liked these mountains that packed tight and grazed an earth as stark as themselves.

He lifted his eyes and in the clear sky he saw three suns. Two were sun dogs, he knew. Out beyond the edge of the mountains, where the sea was, the true sun burned. And just below it, on each side, were two lights, somewhat smaller but nearly as bright. These two pursuers of the sun, two companions, seemed to give off their own heat and light; but they were cold, they were reflections of ice in the high, thin air. In this country sun dogs could suddenly appear and run with the sun, mock it, speak to it of things unseen, things that claimed a special knowledge, that could take on the sun's very light.

Wilson found he was breathing hard. He sat back in his seat, closed his eyes, as the jet descended.

2.

From the back seat of the taxi Wilson felt a knot of panic in his chest as he watched Anchorage. The first sight of the city as the plane had come down over the Chugach Mountains and into the Cook Inlet basin had prickled his skin with a schoolboy joy. The city had seemed to lie compactly on the edge of the inlet, a huddling of shapes overwhelmed by the vast, simple elements—sharp-edged mountains and flat basin and sun-scraped thrust of water. But here, on the ground, Anchorage was a sprawl of mobile homes and cheap clapboard houses and cyclone-fenced collections of concrete pipes or trailer-beds or heavy machinery. There were runs of fast-food shops and auto repair shops; a light plane sat up on blocks with its engine wrapped and there were propane dealers with tanks in their yards. The city was like the basement of a disorganized handyman. The clutter stuffed itself into Wilson's head and he turned to look over his shoulder at the Chugach Mountains.

They seemed very close, their flanks streaked with black spruce, their peaks white. But a pickup truck raised far off the ground on oversize tires came up behind the taxi and blocked Wilson's sight and he had to turn away. His limbs wanted to thrash around. This clutter again—tract houses, rows of them, a cinderblock church. Then the shops began to cluster closer together. Pawn shops now, a laundromat, a Mexican-Chinese restaurant, a street of bars with Eskimos hunched on the stoops, a massage parlor, another bar, this one with "Live Nudes upstairs."

This can't go on, he thought. He was seeing Royal Petroleum's Anchorage man yet this afternoon and he would tell the man that he had to get out of Anchorage as soon as possible.

Gordon James sat with his back to the west window. Beyond him, blocking the view of the late-day sun and the inlet, was another petroleum company's office building done in bronze glass almost identical to Royal's. The window which looked to the south, no doubt with an unhindered view toward the Chugach Mountains, had its beige curtains drawn across it.

Gordon James was a short man, but Wilson imagined that he'd once been six inches taller. James's neck was stumpy and, although he was not a heavy man, Wilson felt a terrible sense of weight about him. It was as if his head were receding into his chest, his chest into his abdomen, his abdomen into his hips. His pallor looked brittle, squeezed dry. He was very formal in manner and on his lapel was a tiny gold pin—the broken chain symbol of the Energy Independence campaign. James's title was vice-president of internal operations and all Wilson knew was that Grevey, the New York contact, reported to him. So Wilson in fact worked for this man. James spoke in a voice that was strong but as brittle as his face, as if it too were being squeezed tight by the pressure of James' compacted body. So far all he'd talked about was Royal Petroleum's high purpose.

"The President has talked personally to our division executive v.p. up here. He knows the importance of our freeing ourselves from the shackles of foreign oil dependence. 'We've got all we need...' That's what the President wants the country to understand. And we've got to find what's there—*we* are the 'we' in that slogan. Royal Petroleum...You and I."

"Who put theirs up first?" Wilson said and he opened the knot of his tie just a little bit and crossed his leg. This man was holding something in. Wilson had seen it over and over in his work and he decided to break the flow abruptly to find out what would happen.

"What? What's that?" the man said, though his monolithic physical reserve was undisturbed. Wilson thought he saw signs of a righteous middle-management wrath beginning to build.

Wilson flipped his chin up to indicate the building behind James. "United Oil over there. Who put up their bronze building first?"

James's eyes widened. "I don't see what this has to do with..."

"Look. *I* don't see what the President of the United States has to do with my job troubleshooting your security problems...I read all the posters before I left New York." Wilson waited to see how this would affect the man. James seemed frozen. Wilson expected a flash of anger, but he wasn't sure anymore. Maybe this was just too shocking, this insolence. But surely, Wilson thought, James had had an employee take charge before, out here in this land of individualists. Wilson struggled to suppress a grin.

"Fair enough," James finally said and the words seemed to lance his clot of reserve. He swiveled in his chair, his hand ran back over his head. "Fair enough," he repeated.

Wilson could see the man's hand trembling slightly as it moved. It made Wilson say, "Listen, it's basic orientation stuff. I understand why they want you to do it."

"Actually it's more than that," James said. "Perhaps my ineptness at expressing it was the problem."

Wilson disliked this sudden strain of self-deprecation in the man even more intensely than he'd disliked his stiffness.

James said, "What resources are actually there and how to get them impacts everything we do—even in security." His voice had diminished into a tone of cramped humility.

Wilson jumped up from his chair, went to the south window and opened the drapes. He glanced only briefly at the mountains but turned at once to his employer.

James had swiveled his chair to face the window. He seemed braced there, his chin was drawn up just slightly, as if he'd been forced to consider an unpleasant truth. He even said, "Yes."

"Yes?" Wilson returned to the view. Beyond the detritus of Anchorage the flat land ran quickly to the Chugach. The mountains were commanding. Wilson felt them bending him backwards. But now what struck Wilson was the crowded sky. Close in, a seaplane rose, moving right to left over the south edge of the business district. An old Piper Cub moved left to right just beyond the city limits, descending. Out near the mountains were two other small planes, and high in the south, turned orange in the afternoon sun, was the contrail of a jet.

Gordon James was at Wilson's elbow. Wilson started. The man had risen and crossed to stand here with absolutely no sound. He was half a head shorter than Wilson. "Out in Alaska somewhere, inside the earth, is all we need," James said. "The tank's full. We just have to find it."

"I want to get out of this city as fast as possible," Wilson said. "I don't want to even be based out of here."

James's eyes slid toward Wilson but he kept his face on the mountains. "What did Grevey tell you?"

"It was vague...I know *you're* here. And maybe sometimes you'll have a problem in this building. But as a base I don't want anything to do with Anchorage. That's the way it's got to be. I don't like the looks of this place."

James's eyes slid back to the view. "Do you want a drink?"

"No."

James half-turned now to Wilson. "You're a hard-ass, are you, Mr. Hand?" The tone was not hostile. He sounded almost weary.

Wilson hesitated. The epithet didn't fit. No. But he couldn't think what to say. He said nothing.

"Maybe a hard-ass is what I need doing what you'll be doing..." James looked out to the mountains once more. "Fucking Alaska has turned me into a fucking alcoholic," he said.

Wilson began to feel very uneasy around this man. "Grevey said you'd have something special for me right away."

"There's nothing to do up here but to drink," James said, lost in his own thought. "There's no choice. You know, I hate the summers even worse than the winters. Even here in Anchorage there's sunlight all day. The sun just goes down near the horizon and then pivots around back to the east. I feel...clammy all the time...You have to rinse it all away. Wash yourself clean here from the inside out...Drink it away. There's no alternative.''

Wilson watched a light plane circling far out over the basin. He waited for James to stop pitying himself and get back to business. After a long moment of silence Wilson turned and James was gone from beside him. The man had slipped away from the window as silently as he'd come.

James was hovering over a commode in the corner. Then he straightened and came back to his desk, a drink in his hand. Wilson crossed to the chair and sat.

"Something special," James said. "Yes." He set his drink on the desk pad. Wilson noticed a thick pattern of circles on the blotter-surface of the pad, the spoor of past drinks. James pulled a brown envelope from a desk drawer and handed it across to Wilson. "You can look at this later," he said. "Though there's not much in the file to go on, I'm afraid. We don't really understand the problem. That's why I'm glad we've got a hard-ass like you to work on it." James paused and sucked at his drink.

The "hard-ass" had come out more firmly this time. Wilson hoped he'd be out of the office by the time James was drunk.

James said, "On the surface it's simple, I suppose. We're missing documents...Sometimes missing, sometimes just suspicious that they've been...used. Copied.''

"What kind of documents?''

"Seismic and gravimetric records, exploration maps, prospect reports.''

"The documents that tell what you're finding and where.''

"That's right. The information is carefully controlled—'need-to-know' limitations. Our division executive v.p. is very concerned about all this. But frankly it's a bit of a puzzle who'd want these things.''

Wilson inclined his head toward the other bronze building out the window. "The other oil companies?''

James laughed and jiggled the ice in his glass. "We already know what each of us is doing. That's just part of the business. We each have pieces of the same pie."

"Of course...How about the Arabs?"

"That's the possibility we all think the most likely. They want to keep an eye on what we've got here. Their own resources are being drawn down. Deeply. They know just what they've got and where it is and the needle's heading toward empty. Sure they'd like to find out what's up here. If they find out soon enough, they'd know how to screw us in price till we got the operation going to pull our own oil out of the ground."

"So I look for the guy in the burnoose."

James's glass was empty and he glared at it. "If it was that easy we wouldn't need a hard-ass like you."

Now the "hard-ass" came out clenched.

"Where is it disappearing from, this information?" Wilson asked.

"Moonbase up on the North Slope. Most of it. The thefts are subtle. There may be other...interceptions...If it's the Arabs, it could be widespread. They've got the money to buy people off. I think first you should trace the information from its origin. Check the security along the whole chain....Then I want you to go in undercover up at Moonbase."

Wilson tried not to show the leaping in his chest. He didn't want to show this man anything. But the North Slope—the Prudhoe oil fields—the Arctic desert with the long night of winter coming on—his fists clenched to hold back the desire he felt—the physical desire for the place.

"The name and number of the man who'll fly you around is in the file. Clyde Mazer. See him by noon tomorrow and get started. There's a voucher in the file that will let you draw expense money. Do it first thing in the morning." James seemed to be growing increasingly agitated. The glass was in his hand; he was standing.

Wilson rose.

"Come back here when you think you're ready to go north,"

James said.

"All right."

Wilson turned and moved toward the door. He was suddenly aware he'd said no word of good-by to the man. Hard-ass. He wheeled around and found James pouring another drink.

James looked up and said, "We did."

"What's that?"

"We put our bronze building up first, goddamit."

A shock: twenty minutes later, as Wilson stood before the window of his hotel room watching the sky squeeze shut, he felt a sudden, queasy pity for Gordon James. Wilson tried to understand the feeling but couldn't—perhaps it was just his standing at the window like this, as he'd done with the compressed little man in his office. But why pity? Why did James seem so vulnerable suddenly—vulnerable in a way that made Wilson regret his own aloofness, his own impatience. And it had nothing to do with the man's drinking; that seemed clear. Wilson simply wanted to strip away the complications, the conflicts—from himself, from the little man, from the whole situation. Wilson looked at the brown envelope on the bed. Details about missing documents. Complications. He turned back to the window and replayed a fragment of his scene with James and he was saying, Yessir, yessir, smiling at the man, feeling warm, feeling comfortable without any pressure to assert himself. And now there was a vague restlessness in him. Outside, low in the sky, the sun was just barely concealed by a layering of clouds. The clouds were striped grey and light blue and orange and the sun was just out of sight, as provocative as a woman's nipple barely covered by a deep-cut dress, showing the faint beginnings of its areola. Restless.

He crossed and sat on the bed. For the second time tears came because of Beth. Her broken body. He thought of a simple time. He sat on a bed just like this in a motel room and tears had come to his eyes, though not so many and they were from joy, from a vigorous joy as he watched Beth cross to the drapes and peek out. She was naked and he followed the indent of her spine down to the line that split her buttocks, and then down the line of her legs pressed together, down between her calves, to her ankles, the heels of her feet. She rose up slightly on her toes. The light that came through the thin, russeted drapes was grey. The two of them were in a six-dollar motel on the drab edge of Ithaca. Outside, on the two-lane highway, cars passed like the clearing of a phlegmy throat; inside, the toilet trickled, the smell of stale tobacco lingered like the late-night ennui of a commission salesman. The room was bare but he liked that; and it was the first time Wilson had made love to Beth, the first time he'd seen her naked; the room was bare and he could not calm this joy that he expected would make him look like a fool. But it didn't matter. There was nothing he would change. Not in this room, not in himself, not in the thin line of Beth's body that pithed him, humbled him.

"Shit," he said aloud now, through his tears. He wondered if he would weep over Beth only when her death linked itself to his sexual desire for her. He thought of her apartment full of unpacked objects. The thought squared his shoulders and shut off his tears.

He picked up the brown envelope and found Clyde Mazer's telephone number. The number was that of the Klondike Hotel—permanent and transient, the reedy woman's voice said as part of her formalized hello. Mazer's room phone rang six times before a man said, with no inflection of inquiry, "What."

"Clyde Mazer?"

"Yes."

"My name's Wilson Hand."

"I expected you tomorrow."

"I'm calling you tonight."

The tone had hardened quickly on both sides and now there was a moment of silence. Hard-ass, Wilson thought. This man probably gives Gordon James fits, too. Wilson smiled at that but still said nothing more.

Apparently some comparable line of thought had been

followed at the other end of the phone as well, for Mazer's voice, gravelled into friendliness, said, "You caught me taking a shit."

"Six rings?" Wilson said. "Either you're awful goddam fast or you've got a dirty ass right now."

Mazer laughed. "I'm pretty goddam fast."

For the first time Wilson noticed a muted Texan drawl in the voice. Wilson said, "So how are you going to get me out of Anchorage?"

"Fly."

"I mean when do we meet. Where."

"Let's decide that with a drink," Mazer said. "I'm gonna hit the Crazy Moose Saloon about eight o'clock. I'll see you there."

"All right. How will I recognize you?"

"I'll know you by your goddam goofy New York face."

The Crazy Moose Saloon was a clapboard structure as narrow as a garage and running deep into its lot from the edge of the sidewalk—what they called a shotgun house in upstate New York because you could shoot a shotgun from the front of the house to the back and the buckshot would pass through every room. The moment Wilson stepped through the door into the crowded, smoky bar, a large hand palmed him by the shoulder.

"I told you I'd recognize you," the voice from the phone said.

Wilson turned to confront Clyde Mazer, who kept his hand on Wilson's shoulder. Mazer had a craggy moon of a face, filled with a cross-hatching of wrinkles but still seeming—perhaps from the vigor of its grin—to be young. The only things that weren't hard and strong about the face were the eyes—too small, too close together—and a wattle of loose skin under his chin, as if he'd lost a great deal of weight very quickly. The face, cracked open by its grin, loomed into Wilson's, the hand on Wilson's shoulder waggled in preparation for the man's next statement, but Wilson spoke first.

"Recognize me?" Wilson said, casting his voice lower than normal "Who are you?"

The grin faded at the edges and two strong vertical creases appeared in the center of Mazer's forehead. "You're Wilson Hand, aren't you?"

"Hand? Nope. My name's Cochran. Philip Cochran." The name came out glibly—Wilson had thought to use the name of a recent client. He could sense Mazer faltering, he could see Mazer's eyes narrowing in doubt.

"Are you sure?" Mazer said, leaning still closer, a spikiness in his voice that momentarily made Wilson uneasy at having started this.

"What the hell do you mean—am I sure?" Wilson thrust his own face toward Mazer. The man paused, then removed his hand from Wilson's shoulder. Only in its lifting away did the hand's great size register in Wilson's mind. Oh shit, he thought, this guy better have a sense of humor. But he carried the ruse forward.

Wilson turned and crossed to the bar and sat on a stool and ordered a drink. It wasn't until the drink had come and he'd taken a sip that he glanced over his shoulder toward the door. Mazer was still standing there. Someone was coming in and Mazer's face was swinging around to see who it was, but it was clear that Mazer had been looking toward the bar, still studying Wilson.

The newcomer was an Eskimo and before Mazer could turn toward Wilson again, Wilson pivoted his back toward the door and looked up at the television hanging at the far end. On the screen a ramp approached a large stone fountain before a hotel. A motorcycle came up the ramp and stopped. The driver stood and looked around, gauging something, studying the empty space before him. Briefly Wilson forgot Clyde Mazer. He looked at the elements on the screen—a ramp, a fountain, the empty air. He felt that he saw them as the man on the motorcycle saw them. A simple track—up, across, the risk of death, things stripped down so that they were clear.

Then he remembered Mazer. This was worth it—wiping the man's smugness away, even for a few minutes. He glanced over his shoulder and Mazer was sitting at a table. The man was staring at Wilson; an even, calm stare, and Wilson looked back at the television. Clyde Mazer fell away instantly and Wilson again saw the ramp's upswoop as the rider saw it, he felt the keen pitch of jeopardy as the rider felt it. The motorcycle was in position and the rider suddenly hunched down and the cycle sprang forward, running smoothly up the ramp. Wilson lifted with it, the rider came up, the cycle was free in the air, soaring— back wheel drooping slightly—over statues and over a plume of water and toward another ramp reaching up. The cycle arced down. The back wheel touched the ramp, the front came down hard and the rider angled sharply, rode for a moment on his side, his back to the camera and then the rider was free of the machine, limbs jerking, the cycle skidding away, the driver tumbling along the ramp and onto the pavement and rolling, crumpling.

Wilson turned away. He put his glass to his lips but did not drink. The hand came suddenly again to his right shoulder, an arm was laid over his back and Mazer's face drew very close on the left side. "You *are* Wilson Hand, aren't you?"

Wilson lowered his drink and without looking at Mazer said, "Of course I am." Wilson tried to judge the man's next move from the tension that briefly trilled through the arm on Wilson's back and caused the hand to squeeze at his shoulder. Wilson knew nothing of the man but instinctively expected violence. He felt Mazer's face move even closer. Wilson jerked his own face around for the confrontation. Then Clyde Mazer laughed. The laugh did not remove Wilson's expectation of violence, but Mazer only jiggled Wilson with his great hand and sat down on a barstool.

"You had me going there for a minute," Mazer said.

"What's the matter? Don't you have the courage of your convictions?"

"How's that?"

"Don't you know a goofy New York face when you see one?"

Mazer laid both hands on the bar before him and laughed again. "So that's what brought all this on, is it?"

Immediately Wilson regretted his words. He'd shown weakness to Mazer. His mind thrashed around. He tried to find something to say about the slackness under Mazer's chin, or the tiny eyes, the Texan twang. But that was weakness too. Instead, he just looked away, sipped his drink.

"Did I hurt your feelings there, Hand?" Mazer said.

"Don't push it," Wilson said, low, and it was only after these words were out that a tone from Mazer's question registered in him. There was smugness there, and bombast, but Wilson clearly had heard a twinge of sincere concern as well. "I'll buy you a drink," Wilson said.

Much later, four bars down the street, when Wilson's train of thought was smooth and sinuous, Clyde Mazer said, "I really don't think your face is especially goofy, you know...Shit. You could pass for a Texan, even. Of a particular sort."

"What sort?"

"Oh...the kind that..." Mazer's hands rose into the air and spread in thought. "Well, the kind that races around in a pickup with a noisy muffler and shoots off his mouth too much about the whores he's fucked...That's your *face* I'm talking about now. Not your personality and all."

"Let me try to understand this, Clyde...I get the feeling you started out trying to...ah..." The only words he could think of had too many syllables for him to negotiate smoothly at this point. He looked out from the dim corner table where they sat. The place was quiet. The backs were rounded at the bar; a nimbus of smoke surrounded the bare bulb over the wall of bottles. Suddenly things sharpened in his mind, as if he'd gotten a second wind. "You seemed to be trying to soften an earlier insult," Wilson said. "But it just got worse, it seems to me."

"Now that's where you stopped paying attention. I was describing a type of *face*. You don't own any pickup truck I bet.

And you haven't once mentioned a whore...See, *any* Texan-type face is okay. Even if the Texan himself ain't worth diddly-shit.''

"I've got a tattoo," Wilson said.

"No."

"Yes I do."

"Well, see . . . Now that's a good Texan-like thing . . ."

"I lied."

"When?"

"Just now. I don't have a tattoo."

"You've got to stop putting me on, boy."

"What's your nickname, Clyde?"

"Don't have any."

"Now *that's* gotta be a lie. How long have you been flying into the bush?"

"Nearly twenty years."

"And nobody gave you a *nickname?* Not even 'Tex'? *Something*. 'King.' Or 'Iceman.' Or 'Hands', maybe. Your fucking hands scare the fucking shit out of me, Clyde...or 'Lug.' Or 'Bunk.' Or..."

"Ain't got no nickname, Wilson...Oh, they tried now and then. But none of them stuck. I wouldn't let 'em. A nickname would turn me into some kind of cartoon character. Makes it all...cheap."

"Trivial."

"You got it. Goddam trivial. And it gets in the way. I want it to be just me and my plane and that motherfucking cold-hearted country out there. If Clyde Mazer goes up there, things are clear. If 'Grizzly-Gut' Mazer goes up, things get...bent out of shape. You know?"

"I know all about it."

"Sure you do."

"What makes you fly?"

"I like to scare the shit out of myself."

One more bar and they were in the back, near the johns and the jukebox. The jukebox was broken and the toilets gurgled without stop and the two men sat with their heads propped on their hands. For a time Wilson felt only half-conscious; his eyes could not focus and the table seemed as if it were set on a slant. But then words began to shape themselves in his head, words he'd said before, several times, though he couldn't remember where. He wanted to say them again, especially to this man with no nickname.

"I spent a week as a prisoner of the Viet Cong," Wilson said.

Mazer's eyes rose but his face remained in the grip of his left hand. "Was that you or Philip Cochran, the dude with the tattoo?"

"I'm not putting you on, Clyde. It's true."

"And you still got your balls?"

Wilson hesitated briefly before Mazer's jauntiness. But Wilson's words had to be vented off. He said, "I was part of an Army intelligence unit in a base called Homestead. We were out Highway 1 about twenty miles northeast of Saigon. There were three of us—a Captain named David Fleming and two enlisted men, myself and a guy named Clifford Wilkes. Near us, in the village of Bien Hoa, was a Catholic orphanage. Every payday the Captain made a collection at Homestead and we took the money out to the orphanage. The priest there kind of kept his ear to the ground for us, but it was mostly just a goodwill gesture we inherited from previous commands. Once I went there and climbed a coconut tree on the grounds and I fell out and broke my arm."

"Shit, boy. What'd you do a thing like that for?"

"It was the next trip when I got snatched. My arm was in a cast and sling and it was hurting like hell...The orphanage had a wall around it—a little compound. There was a big metal entry door into a courtyard. I was out in the courtyard talking to some of the kids while Fleming was in drinking tea with the sisters, and the gates opened up and there were four Vietnamese with AK-47s. Two of them came to me and they lifted my pistol from the holster under my shirttail and they took me away. I heard gunfire behind me but they just took me away and put me in a taxicab outside the gate—one of the little cream and blue Renault taxis you see all over Saigon—and they took me away. I started laughing at the VC taking taxicabs to their operations. I laughed till they rapped me in the broken arm. The taxi driver, of course, was one of their local supporters—that was how they got around so slick with their weapons...They took me to a little shack in Hanoi's shanty area and...there were chickens in the yard..." Wilson hesitated. Though he'd felt compelled to talk about all this, he was not flashing back, he'd still proceeded under some sort of rational control. Now he'd reached a boundary of that control. He felt the pull of the room, he felt a warping begin inside him, he saw a black hole before him, a black hole but he knew what was on the other side. He would not be sucked through before this man. He gripped the edges of the table. He said, "They kept me there a week. Then Captain Fleming found me. He came and he snatched me back and that was that."

"Shit, boy, you been through it." Mazer's Texan accent was thicker now—much thicker—and Wilson focused on that. Mazer said, "What did they do to you when they had you?"

Wilson gripped harder at the edges of the table. The sound of the toilet trickling intensified—Wilson hated the sound—it was like hearing a man talk who needs to clear his throat but won't. Wilson's head jerked toward the half-open john door.

"What did they do?" Mazer pressed.

"They threatened that I'd have to spend two weeks in Anchorage, Alaska."

Mazer laughed once, a sharp bark of a laugh, then he caught himself and he leaned across the table. "Was that the punchline? Was that all just a set up?"

"Everything I told you was true except the part about Anchorage. And that might as well have been true. I want to get out of here."

"Well, I don't blame you a bit."

"When?"

"How about tonight? Now."

"What?" Wilson looked closely at Mazer. The man had been drinking for five hours. Straight bourbon, mostly. His eyes were bloodshot and slightly jaundiced but they were alert. "Can we get out of here tonight?" Wilson said.

"That's what I'm talkin' about. Go on back and get your stuff together and we'll take off in..." Mazer raised his arm to look at his watch.

Wilson leaned forward to study Mazer's hand. It was corded with veins and looked as large as Wilson's head. But it was steady. Wilson himself felt suddenly drunk. The bar pivoted for a moment around the fulcrum of his nose. "You sure you're not too drunk to fly?" Wilson said.

"If I've got enough left to stagger across this bar and out the door I can get an airplane into the air."

"Somehow that answer doesn't quite get at my...ah...basic concern."

Mazer lifted his arm again to look at his watch.

"It shouldn't take this long for you to read your watch," Wilson said.

"You interrupted me the last time."

Wilson waited a long moment. "You're not done *yet*?"

"I'm trying to figure out when to meet...It's quarter past one. I'll meet you...you staying at the Captain Cook?"

"Yes."

"I'll meet you in your lobby at two-thirty."

"Son of a bitch."

"Don't lie down on your bed. Not even for a second. That's the trick."

"Okay. Okay."

The two men rose and walked out of the bar. Wilson didn't think to watch the steadiness of Mazer's walk because he himself had to concentrate hard on putting one foot in front of the other. Just outside the door of the bar an old man with a full beard, a slouch hat and a gnarled, hard-wood cane bumped into Mazer.

"Watch it, Pop," Mazer said and they stumbled apart a bit

before turning to confront each other. The old man said something harsh but unintelligible and he waved his cane in the air over his head.

"You want to hit me, huh old man?" Mazer said. There was a smarmy, amused tone in Mazer's voice, but Wilson watched the hands clench into fists. "You want to hit me with that cane for bumping you? You want to hurt me, old man?"

Mazer took a step forward and the old man brought the cane down very hard and it thudded into the point of Mazer's left shoulder. The blow glanced off Mazer and he did not flinch, did not move, and the old man drew the cane back. His eyes were wide now, his mouth fell open.

Mazer took one quick step forward and the old man recoiled. But Mazer turned lightly so that he was side by side with the man and he put his arm around him. Mazer talked low, directly into the old man's ear, the voice solicitous, smooth, but the words too faint for Wilson to hear. After a moment, still talking, Mazer began to discreetly work a couple of bills off his roll of money with his free hand. Then he raised his voice slightly and he said, "Take care now, hear?" Mazer stuffed the money into the old man's hand and he strode away, pulling Wilson with him.

They did not speak till they got to the Captain Cook Hotel. Wilson said, "Are you sure we should do this? Maybe we should sleep the night off first?"

"Yes we should do this," Mazer said. "I want to do this very much..." Mazer seemed to become suddenly aware of his own serious intensity. He smiled. "It's for times like this that I've resisted all those nicknames. Let's go up *tonight*."

With this, Mazer turned and walked away. He walked firmly, steadily, but just before Mazer became obscured by the dark, Wilson saw the man rub the shoulder that had been caned.

3.

In its darkness the hangar smelled of grease and paint and fabric dope and Clyde said "Stay close," the first words he'd spoken since his brief greeting in the lobby of the hotel.

Wilson followed Clyde's form in the dark. He felt wobbly from the liquor and his weariness. He was aware of large shapes around him; and the smells—now oil, now wax, now cold metal—sharpened and faded as he moved. He wondered how Clyde could see, and a door opened and they were outside. They'd simply passed through. Clyde turned and closed the door with care, making sure it locked, and then he motioned across the tie-down pad to a single-engine plane. "There," he said.

Wilson looked up into the sky. It was clear and clotted with stars and he felt a lift of excitement. Yes. He would escape now into this empty sky. When he lowered his eyes, he found that Clyde was already approaching the plane. Wilson gripped the strap of his shoulder pack and followed.

The plane was a low-wing Piper with its wheel pants stripped off to fit the oversized tundra tires. Clyde crouched and pulled out the wheel blocks and Wilson looked the way the plane was pointed—out to the taxiway edged in blue lights.

"Get on in," Clyde said and Wilson circled the plane and climbed into the cabin as Clyde opened the engine cowling. Wilson put his bag behind the seat and sat down. He grew suddenly aware of the cold, here in the tightness of the cabin. He hunched forward to wait for Clyde. The tiredness began to nibble at him, at his eyes, at his chest; he felt the drag of incipient sleep in his cheeks, in his jaw, and the excitement he'd felt looking at the sky dove inside, out of sight, ready to reappear in a dream. But he heard a grinding, a sputter, he opened his eyes and the sky was full of red lights. Wilson snapped awake and it was the instrument panel, not the sky. Clyde's hand came before him, the hand itself red in the light, as if its skin were translucent, showing the blood. Clyde's hand set the altimeter and withdrew.

"Go on ahead and sleep if you want," Clyde said as they began to move between the rows of blue lights along the taxiway.

"No. No, I'm fine."

"We've got about four hours ahead of us."

"Somebody's gotta be awake to nudge you when you doze off."

Clyde smiled briefly at Wilson and the plane swung around. Wilson looked ahead and the runway was invisible beyond the short reach of the plane's taxi lights—their path was marked only by two thin tracks of white light stretching out into the dark. The plane strained and whined now as Clyde ran the engine up briefly. Then Clyde throttled down and pulled the mike to him. "Anchorage Tower, this is Cherokee three five eight niner ready for takeoff."

The radio crackled then said, "Cherokee three five eight niner, clear on one seven left."

Clyde pushed the throttle and the plane pressed forward, wedging its light into the darkness and it lifted up and Wilson felt suddenly clear-headed and fresh, as if the effects of the past few hours had been a ground fog that was left below now, farther and farther beneath them. Wilson put his face to the window and Clyde—as if sensing his need—turned off the lights on the instrument panel. From the darkened cabin Wilson could see not the earth itself exactly but its clear implication—from a spot of lamplight clinging there, from the flutter of starlight reflected in water—and just as he began to think he saw the texture of sedge and muskeg in the dark, he suddenly saw Beth in the same indirect way. There was a flicker of a fear of death in him, a

41

wordless cadence left from her voice, a vague sense of absence, and then he thought of her body. He thought of the hands of a faceless aide at the city morgue touching her, the hands running over the surface of her cool skin. Then Wilson sat back in his chair, pressed at his temples with his fingertips. Her mother would have burned her by now. The subject of Beth's death had never come up and it was more than five years since he'd seen the woman, but Wilson knew that she would cremate Beth. He could see the mother clearly, more clearly than he could see Beth at the moment. The woman was squat and thick at the ankles and wrists, her body mocking the image she wanted so desperately for herself. Her wrists and her ankles could not be hidden by her furs and her gowns; they were always sticking stoutly out. The mother would burn Beth—had already done so—it fit the woman's fastidiousness, Wilson thought.

The engine thrummed in Wilson's head and he closed his eyes—briefly, he thought—but when he opened them and moved to look outside again he lurched and found the earth with no light in the dark but clear nonetheless—a vast pale grey— snow stretching as far as he could see beyond the wing and the stars were sharper than ever, as sharp as the cold in the cabin. Wilson glanced forward and gasped aloud. The plane was flying into mountains, looming white, above them.

"Clyde," he barked.

"Hang in there, pardner," Clyde said and the plane seemed to skid to the left and they were in a pass, a mountain rearing up on both sides. Wilson could distinguish rock outcrop from snow bank; the mountain was near enough that Wilson sensed it as a pressure on his face.

"Houston Pass," Clyde said. "My very favorite." Clyde looked over at Wilson, kept his gaze there until Wilson stirred in anxiety. Clyde's eyes went to the front again and said, "I could fly it blindfolded, this one. I could even fly it dead drunk at four in the morning."

"Which is what you're doing."

"Which is what I'm doing."

Wilson watched the mountain passing and it was suddenly gone and he felt the same lift he'd felt when they first took off. Then Clyde jerked the bottom out, the plane dove down. Clyde turned the instrument panel lights up to a dull red glow and the Piper dove sharply toward flatland beyond the mountains. Wilson gripped the seat hard, but he said nothing.

The ground rushed up at the plane and Clyde flared out and flew low but level. Wilson saw the altimeter at twenty feet before he looked out the window. Clyde turned on the landing lights and craned his neck.

"Should do okay," Clyde said. "Snow's just a crust here." Clyde cut the power and pulled back slightly on the controls and it was up inside his butt that Wilson felt the touch and release and touch again of the plane to the earth. The Piper taxied only briefly and swung around and the engine cut out and the lights were off. The propeller cycled to a stop and then there was only the ticking of the metal and then even that stopped.

"Shit, Clyde," Wilson said very low. "Do you know what you're doing?"

"What do you think?" Clyde said and he opened his door and stepped out onto the wing-tread and disappeared. Wilson twisted around to find where the man went but he could see nothing and he opened his own door.

Outside, Wilson's legs wobbled and he felt a brief, faint nausea. He stepped down into the shallow snow and on the ground the nausea subsided and he was all right. He knew at once that he should get away from the plane. For the first time since he left New York he felt close to something he wanted. Wilson strode away from the Piper, seeing Clyde behind the tail pissing into the tundra. Wilson stopped. "Is that what we landed for?" he said, regretting the question at once. He didn't want to talk.

In answer Clyde arced his piss higher into the air—a thin silver cord—Wilson realized now that there was a moon low in the east. In his mind Wilson thanked Clyde for his silence. He wondered why he and Clyde had tested each other for so long earlier in the night. They seemed to understand each other instinctively.

Wilson turned and walked further away from the plane. The patter of piss ceased and Wilson stood and looked back to the mountains they'd flown through. For a brief time his feelings were pure, were as simple and monolithic as the mountain that rose up before him. But the purity of feeling was linked to the flight through the pass and the dive to earth. In retrospect now Wilson was exhilarated—not just by the danger of it, he knew—indeed, he sensed that had very little to do with this feeling. But it didn't last. Standing clear-minded in the dark, in a barren plain before these mountains, he felt the clutter beginning to tumble into his head. He could not focus on the mountain. He felt only his right boot pinching too tightly on his instep, he realized that he had to piss, he wondered if Clyde was watching him and he wondered where the brown envelope was that Gordon James had given him—in his bag or back on the bed in the hotel. He thought of James's charge of hard-ass and thought he should simply have answered no. Wilson grew angry at himself. He yearned to quiet his mind. But he did not know how—the struggle itself drove him deeper inside, where the chaos was even worse.

He turned abruptly and Clyde was just beyond arm's length away, watching him. They looked at each other for a long moment and Wilson felt his thoughts settling.

"What are you doing in Alaska?" Clyde said and his voice had no trace of its drawling wryness.

Wilson's reaction was complicated. He felt oddly close to Clyde—the man's casual intensity about this whole night flight reverberated in Wilson. But he didn't have a clear answer to this question—not yet, he didn't—and he felt a twist of resentment at Clyde for asking. He said, "Do most people have an answer for that?"

"Oh sure. They have answers. But they're never the truth."

"I have to piss."

"That's as good a reason as any."

Wilson laughed. "I was changing the subject, Clyde. Pay attention."

"One thing I know," Clyde said.

"What?"

"You don't give a shit about whatever it is you're investigating."

Wilson did not hesitate. "You got that right, Clyde."

They flew into Trumiak on Norton Sound and the sun was up and Wilson turned away from the glare off the snow. Clyde flew straight to the tiny airport and landed so smoothly on the hard-packed snow of the runway that Wilson wasn't sure when the touchdown had actually occurred. Now that the sun was up, he felt even more keenly the exhaustion of the night. Inside the terminal—a one-room, clapboard shack with hard-wood benches and a wood-burning stove—Clyde phoned the Royal operations center for a car while Wilson sat on a bench and stretched his legs out straight.

Clyde approached. 'They'll be here to get you."

"Aren't you going out to the center?"

"Nah. Man out there ain't one of my favorites. But mostly I've got to get skis on the Cherokee for our next hop...When do you think that'll be?"

"What?" Wilson had missed the sense of the question—he'd snagged on Clyde's not going. "When...?"

"I said when do you expect to be wanting to leave this place?"

"I don't know. Soon, I'm sure. But we need some sleep. Tomorrow, maybe."

Clyde smiled. "Hey. You gotta at least make a show of this, don't you?"

"Even James doesn't expect me to find much here. I'm learning the system."

"Okay. Okay. Just looking out for you."

"I know how to do these things, Clyde. Even if I don't give a shit about them anymore."

"When you're ready, call me here." Clyde was scratching with a nub of a pencil in a shirt-pocket notebook. He ripped off the page and handed it to Wilson. The small piece of graph paper had a phone number and smelled of grease.

Clyde said, "If a woman answers, I'm on top of her."

"Will you be able to talk?"

"I can always talk."

"I'll give you a call."

Clyde winked and turned and walked out of the terminal. Wilson watched him go, even as Clyde's shadow leaped in and out of the room as he passed the windows. Wilson regretted the man's going. He had no clear, rational answer, even for himself, about why he was in Alaska. But he knew that with Clyde he was moving closer to an answer than he would be pursuing those missing documents. He put his hand into the outside pouch of his bag and felt James's brown envelope there. He cared so little about this work that he had to be careful.

The operations center was just outside Trumiak, out beyond the log cabins and battered frame houses and idle garden patches and Quonset bars and yards full of cannibalized, unidentifiable equipment. The building was rather small and shiny-skinned and slick—an abstract reflection of Thomas Givens, the man who met Wilson in an office off the entrance foyer. Wilson knew at once that this was the man Clyde didn't like. Givens was a small man and his grey hair was oiled down flat, his skin was pale and smooth. Givens was as slick as a newborn mouse but without a mouse's animation.

"You're early," he said to Wilson behind the desk.

"I wanted to get started on this."

"The document thing."

"That's right."

"I must tell you that I'm not as concerned about this as Anchorage seems to be," Givens said and Wilson had an immediate and strong impression that the man was lying. Givens began to elaborate and Wilson did not listen to him but tried to decide what the man had done to belie his words. His voice had been perhaps a little swallowed-back, he'd shifted his eyes away, something; Wilson could not identify it.

"Do you have access to everything that goes out of here?" Wilson asked, cutting Givens off.

"Of course," Givens said with an off-handedness that surprised Wilson. He'd expected to goad Givens with the implied suspicion, but the little man was placid, unaffected.

"Who else has full access?"

"Oh, several others. Several. I'll give you a list of their names, if you like. But nothing has been missed from here. It's up at Moonbase where the problem has mostly been. And it's been just bits and pieces. Amateurish. Some hardcopy stuff yanked out of files, I'm told."

"Some of it was like that," Wilson said, drawing on James's brown envelope. "Yes."

"Amateurs. They don't even know what they're looking for."

"If you haven't missed anything, how do you know the same sort of thefts haven't taken place more professionally down here?"

"Because if it's all one plot," Givens said, leaning across his desk with a schoolmarmish taunt in his voice, "why should they be professional about it in one place and amateurish in another?"

"So you think I'm wasting my time here?" Wilson said, happy to have an excuse to leave at once.

"Look, I'm sorry, Mr. Hand. I'm not telling you how to do your job. We just collect the numbers here, massage them, send them on. Numbers are our business. We know how to handle numbers. We aren't sloppy with our numbers, Mr. Hand."

Wilson thought he'd probably found the reason for Givens' earlier lie. The man's professed lack of concern about the thefts was meant to signal his absolute control of his own operation. But if Wilson's hunch was right, and Givens was in fact concerned about the thefts, then he wondered why. The thieves seemed to be amateurs. The information had not surfaced anywhere. The other oil companies knew all this anyway. The slick-cheeked immobile little man before him was a stranger. This had always interested Wilson most about his work—having to extemporaneously probe the minds and hearts of people he didn't know—having to make guesses about what was inside them. Like drilling for oil. "Tell me, Mr. Givens, why do you think Anchorage is worried about this thing?"

"Ask *them*."

"Well, they won't really make that clear. Some vague threat of the Arabs is all I can gather."

Givens did not react. He made no motion at all. His eyes held steadily on Wilson. Wilson waited and Givens seemed to be waiting, so Wilson said, "You're not worried about the Arabs stealing your numbers, are you, Mr. Givens?"

"I was just thinking about that."

They both waited a moment more. Wilson tried another approach. "If you were to *imagine* something to fear about your numbers, what would it be?"

Givens leaned back in his chair. "You ask very unusual questions, Mr. Hand."

"Tell me what you'd fear."

"That they'd be used in the wrong way. People don't understand. They get panicky. Or they get suspicious. Or they get angry. Sometimes they want to drive the prices down—take away our ability to...search...to find the numbers, the oil. Sometimes they want to...want to..." Though Givens seemed agitated, his face, his body, did not show it. Outwardly he remained impassive. "Sometimes they want to find other ways. They want to run away from oil...But you can't do that. There are thousands of things we make from it. Thousands. From false eyelashes to aspirin to..."

"Food processors," Wilson said, Beth suddenly intruding. He felt his mouth twist into a smile.

"What? Yes. There's a lot of plastic in that. Certainly. And all the vehicles. It's the only portable fuel, really...Our society would fly apart. We must have oil. And people use numbers to try to obscure that fact, to stop us from finding it."

"Is that what you're afraid of?"

"*If*, you said. *If* I were to be afraid."

"So whoever's taking these numbers, they could misuse them, couldn't they? In the way you're saying?"

"Not from here. Not from here, they can't take them."

Givens seemed short of breath. His hands rose slowly from out of sight and came to rest on the desktop.

Wilson woke before dawn and he knew he'd been thrashing about, his head clogged with dreams. But already the dreams had faded beyond recall and he switched on the crane-necked lamp by his bed. He expected to be hung over but only had a muted headache. The room—an empty operations center crew room—was tiny and stuffed full of plastic furniture and wardrobes in the primary colors of a child's room. Wilson dressed quickly and went down the hall toward the foyer. He nodded at the guard in his station at the middle of the foyer and stopped at a payphone by a water cooler. He took out the scrap of graph paper and dialed the phone number. A woman answered after the first ring and her voice was clear. "What?" she said.

"Is Clyde Mazer there?" Wilson held back from saying, "...on top of you."

There was a ruffling sound and then, with exactly the same inflection as the woman, Clyde said, "What?"

"Are you up already?"

Clyde laughed. "Boy, I'm up *again*."

"I've got to get out of here."

"You're always in a rush."

"Just get me out of here."

"They give you the location of the mobile rig?"

"I've got it written down."

"I'll meet you back at the airstrip in an hour."

"Good. Yes."

Wilson heard Clyde's voice recede and say, "Hang this up,

honey.'' Then there was the ruffling sound again and a click and silence. The sound—he had an image of a naked woman moving beneath a sheet—could have evoked a skin-surface memory of several women for Wilson but Beth came again. Beth who had grown more persistent in him in death than she'd been since the divorce. Her death had remarried her to him and he saw her shoulder rise up as she turned away, the ruffling sound, and then the wide bare plain of her naked back. He kissed her shoulder blade and Wilson found the phone still in his hand, the foyer guard staring at him. He hung up and figured that in two hours at the most he'd be in the air again.

4.

Clyde squinted off to the northeast and Wilson put his bag down on the step-tread of the wing and looked off in the same direction. The intermittent clouds thickened out where they were flying, thickened but remained white.

"There's going to be some weather, I understand," Clyde said. "Up the Koyukuk River." Clyde turned to Wilson and looked at him with a faint tilt of inquiry to his head.

Wilson did not answer but he sensed his own eyes widen; he felt like a beseeching child.

Clyde smiled and said, "I'm just saying it may be a little touchy. I don't mind for myself. Been in a lot of crazy weather."

Wilson did not answer but picked up his bag, mounted the wing, and entered the cabin. He watched Clyde do his pre-flight checks along the flap hinges and in the fuel tank holes and under the engine cowling.

The take-off, in daylight, felt slower but smoother than the one from Anchorage yesterday morning. Wilson thought the skis were probably responsible for the smoothness.

After Norton Sound had disappeared and they were out over the wide, white plain of the tundra, Clyde said, "Now *this* guy I kinda like."

"Who's that?"

"Artie Phillips."

"He's the guy at this mobile rig."

"Right. I fly mud chemicals into him whenever they set up a wildcat out there. Always have liked him."

Wilson saw Clyde's eyes slide away and fix on something ahead. Wilson looked and saw a vast cliff-face of white clouds. The clouds were still a few minutes ahead and Clyde was studying them carefully, looking up to their heights and down to their wispy bottoms at ground level.

"You don't want to tangle with that," Wilson said.

"I see some cracks...If you and I were sensible critters we'd turn back around right now. But I do see some cracks and they told me this weather disappears not too far along."

"But still, if we were sensible..."

"We'd wait it out."

Wilson wondered why he didn't simply say to Clyde, turn back. But he looked at the tidal wave of cloud ahead, stretching up beyond his vision and he wanted to go in there.

"Who's going to make this decision?" Wilson asked.

"You already have, haven't you, pardner?"

Wilson could feel Clyde's smile on him but he didn't turn to it. "Find the cracks," Wilson said.

The plane swooped down and Wilson watched below. The snow-covered tundra was split by a river and Clyde angled down toward it. Wilson could see the movement of the water—murky and grey from glacial powder—the rock ground fine by the glaciers and swept away in the current. Now Wilson saw the shelf-ice along the banks of the river and Clyde leveled off and the air suddenly had texture. They were beneath the cloud and flying a hundred feet above the river. Wilson saw the water parting for a rock, carrying a tree limb, a floe of ice. For a time, dark willows ran along the river line and then stopped abruptly. The river disappeared in an ox-bow and reappeared. Clyde held the plane steady at this altitude and the air thinned and thickened and thinned again.

"We're going to wriggle on under," Wilson said.

Clyde didn't answer. Wilson looked at him. The man was watching the river below, keying on it. The cloud suddenly rushed up to the windows, held them close, and Clyde nudged the plane down until they could see the river again. Wilson looked at the altimeter and it read eighty feet. Without turning, Clyde seemed to know Wilson's thoughts. He said, "I can land almost anywhere along here if it gets bad enough."

Wilson felt his energy drain away. He leaned back. His hands unclenched.

"No danger, pardner," Clyde said and Wilson knew the man read him wrong for once. Clyde thought Wilson was relieved, but Wilson knew—though it was something of a surprise—that what he felt was vaguely disappointed. The edge was off.

The cloud began to lift and Clyde drew them back up—a hundred feet, two hundred. The cloud had great, white rifts above, the air was lightening, the world was growing white, the snow below was white and from the brightness around them the sun seemed very close, the cloud that surrounded them seemed to be giving off light of its own, a diffuse, white light.

"Oh shit," Clyde said.

"What?" Wilson said. He was focused once more. But he knew, even before Clyde answered, he knew the problem, for he couldn't see a thing now.

"Whiteout," Clyde said.

There seemed to be no cloud nearby but Wilson could see nothing, nothing at all, not the ground below, not the sky, not even the film of cloud. Nothing. Wilson knew that Clyde couldn't tell which way was up, there was nothing to hold on to, no bearings, nothing at all but the whiteness, and if he flew for even a few minutes like this he could fly them into a mountain or into the ground.

"Watch for anything dark," Clyde said. "Caribou maybe. The willows along the river, if we're lucky."

Wilson pressed his face to the glass and felt the nose of the plane dip and heard Clyde throttle back the engine. He could see nothing in the whiteout. His eyes narrowed and throbbed. Stripped down now, stripped of sight and with the droning in his head of the engine, the sound getting slower and slower, he could see out the window of the shack to an utterly empty sky, chickens muttering as they rutted out of sight, the sky blue and empty and Wilson closed his eyes briefly and wondered if he'd die in this room, if the VC would kill him. But he was aloof from the question. He opened his eyes again and the hot blue Vietnamese sky drew him toward it in his motionlessness, he felt himself rise even as he held very still, even as his arm throbbed, even as he heard the sudden bark of one of his captors, a hard, clear, foreign word.

"There."

Was he to die then? Was the word an order to kill? From his suspension before the sky he could ask this with great calmness.

"Look. There."

The words were English. That was clear to Wilson and the whiteness hissed back around him and he turned to find Clyde straining upward in his seat, his face at the window. The man laughed once, a pop of nervous laughter, and he pressed slightly at his control wheel and throttled back again.

Wilson looked down on his side and could see nothing but the seamless whiteness. Then he leaned forward like Clyde and before the wing he could see, almost straight down, a blur of black—thin slips of black rushing past. Trees.

"Willows," Clyde said. "Along the river."

Suddenly the engine sounded as if it were racing madly, though the plane seemed to be going more slowly. Wilson realized that the outside rush of air—the faint wind-sound—had ceased. Wilson turned and saw the stall light before Clyde, blinking red, on and off, on and off. The engine labored and Clyde dipped the nose just slightly and the engine settled.

Suddenly Clyde looped the plane hard to the left, then back to the right and left again. "We have to follow the meanders," he said. "We don't dare let go of our little river."

Wilson looked down and the trees were farther apart, an erratic flash now and then—but he saw they were very close. The altimeter read forty feet. But even when Wilson saw the trees, he had no sense of ground beyond—the snow did not show its texture, it was blurred still in the whiteout. They had to continue to fly, to follow their willow trees.

"You haven't been very talkative over there, boy," Clyde said. "You okay?"

"I'm fine, Clyde."

"This is just…"

"I'm fine, I said."

"I was going to say this is just a matter of life and death."

"I'm sorry for cutting you off…I'll let you say that."

The engine was beginning to race again, the stall light flashed. Clyde dipped the nose once more and this time added a bit of throttle. Then he pulled back on the controls and added more throttle. Wilson turned and they cleared a tall, maverick spruce, felt the scrape on their underbelly. Wilson gasped, late, very late, instinctively. Then they saw the break. Ahead they could see a line—at first two gradations of white coming together, but with a clear, horizontal separation. Then the whiteness dimmed and took on a wispy form—cloud—and then even that broke and the clouds suddenly lifted up, like the nave of a church and the tundra, cracked by its river, knobbed by its rock outcrops, was firmly, clearly below.

"Just in time," Clyde said.

Wilson saw the ground rising up, felt the plane rise. These were benchlands now, and ahead were mountains.

"Just in time," Clyde repeated and Wilson knew the man felt the same excitement he did.

Beyond the mountains the tundra took up again, and out in the center of the snow-covered flatland was Artie Phillips' camp, the only vertical shapes for a hundred miles. Clyde flew in and circled the place once. There were a wildcat drilling rig, a clustering of tracked vans and, fifty yards away, a dark piece of machinery that looked like a combination of the other two—a small derrick rig on mobile tracks. By now there were two figures in parkas walking stiffly out of the vans, waving their arms. Clyde leveled and dropped the plane abruptly, straight toward them, buzzed past, waggling his wings, circled and landed the plane, taxiing to a stop between the wildcat rig and the mobile unit.

The two figures thumped at Clyde as he stepped down from the wing and they all laughed. Clyde introduced them—they were two oval faces fringed in fur now—one face craggy, large-featured, like Clyde, and the other dark and flat, an Eskimo. Wilson caught the Eskimo's first name—John—but missed the last. The other man was Artie Phillips.

They all shed their parkas in a cramped entrance area of one of the vans and then went into Artie's office, which was not much larger than the entrance. The room smelled of kerosene—from a heater in the corner—and its walls were covered with large-scale U.S. Geological Survey maps, all in pale topographic pastels, each subtly different in its arrangement of shapes, like the works of a cybernetic Monet.

Artie perched on the edge of his desk while Wilson and Clyde sat before him on wooden chairs. John—who wore a dark blue necktie with his flannel shirt—stood just behind Artie.

"You two look a little drawn, a little haggard," Clyde said, obviously needling them, for the two men looked ruddy and robust. But Wilson thought he saw a flicker in Artie first of surprise and then of something else—a nanosecond of something complicated and serious in the man. Then Artie's eyes bulged in the suppression of a grin and his foot jumped out and kicked the sole of the shoe on Clyde's crossed leg.

"It's just cancer," Artie said, keeping his face straight.

"Both of you?" Clyde said, with exaggerated seriousness.

"He gave it to me," the Eskimo said.

"No, John, you gave it to me," Artie said.

"No, Artie, you gave it to me. Like Columbus brought syphilis to the New World."

Clyde said, "Like Columbus? You two been screwing?"

"You see?" Artie said to John. "You gave the man the wrong impression just so you could look smart by working in some damn historical thing..."

As the men bantered on, Wilson waited for all this to stop. He felt himself grinning but he was uneasy. He thought of Clyde's not wanting a nickname—of his resisting his life being turned into a cartoon. The feeling Wilson now had was similar. He expected these men to start scuffling soon, to run outside and have a snowball fight on the tundra. Damn fools, he thought. Damn them.

Artie began to glance occasionally at Wilson as he talked, as if he were aware of Wilson's disapproval. He looked less like Clyde outside of his parka. Unlike Clyde's craggy solidness, Artie's face was in almost constant motion, responding to the words being spoken to him, the thoughts in his head. His brow furrowed and smoothed, his lips drew in and relaxed, a cheek clenched, an eyelid drooped. Then, abruptly, Artie turned to Wilson and leaned forward, very near, looming above him. "So, Mr. Hand," he said, "you're on the trail of our thieves, are you?"

"Do you think this is part of the trail here?"

"Here? No. I doubt it. We just go out on the tundra and take our readings and send them on back into the hands of the people you're chasing."

Wilson said, "When Gordon James...You know him?"

"Oh sure."

"When James suggested I do a little peripheral work on this matter—find out how the information flows from start to finish—this was the sort of place I was most interested in."

"Yes? Why is that?"

Wilson had started this tack in the absence of any clearer approach with Artie Phillips. Wilson always found it useful to make people talk to him about their work, making them think he was deeply sympathetic and respectful. But now he found that what he said was true. This was the place, short of Moonbase itself, that Wilson was most interested in. The Alaskan wilderness. Because this was true, he couldn't fake an answer so easily when asked why. He could not express the truth—he hadn't even fully comprehended it—and yet the presence of that truth cut him off from lies. He simply stammered. "Well...I..."

Clyde glanced over to him, puzzled, and Wilson wanted to

say to him, You damn fool, you're so surprised at me not having a glib answer but you've been acting like a cartoon idiot. Then Artie took the burden off Wilson in a surprising way.

"I don't blame you, Mr. Hand. I like it out here myself." Artie's smooth mouth drew straight back, briefly, in a flat, blissful smile. "We're going out with the mobile rig in a few weeks and frankly I can't wait."

"Yes?" Wilson said, aware he was about to throw back at Artie the question that had made Wilson stammer just moments earlier. "Why is that?" Once the question was out, he knew he hadn't asked it because he was a hard-ass, but because he wanted to hear Artie's answer. Wilson felt the man had some awareness that Wilson wanted to share. This made it painful for Wilson when the man seemed caught off guard, just as he himself had been.

Artie's mouth drew down, his face pinched in as he shrugged. He glanced toward Clyde and then back to Wilson. "Maybe it's…Well, I've got this damn Eskimo here to take care of." Artie tossed a nod over his shoulder toward John, who grinned, as if on cue. "He's a goddam stratigraphic expert, see, a fucking genius but he's used to ice houses. This van life is just too fancy for him to adjust to."

Clyde and John laughed, but as they did, Artie's eyes settled quietly on Wilson and Wilson wondered if it was his imagination but he thought Artie had more to say to him that he couldn't say in front of anyone else.

In the van holding the team's laboratory, Clyde excused himself and left to get something to eat and John hunched over the shoulder of a man looking into a microscope on the far side of the room. Artie was talking about drill cuttings—the bits of rock taken deep from the hole by the wildcat rig outside. "We sniff it, chew it, feel it, look at it under a microscope, this Alaskan earth. You can't get any closer to it than we do." Artie paused and looked around. Wilson did, too, noting that they were separated now, private. He watched to see if the man's manner would change. Artie's thought continued then, seemingly unbroken, but his pliable face grew still, his voice grew slightly softer. "But the earth holds back. Its big secrets—they're tough to crack. All the chaos down there in the layers. All the damn salt plugs and faults, the bad porosities and the lousy migration timing. When we don't get solid rock, we just get carbon residue."

Artie had slipped into a mood Wilson wanted to understand, but the man grew more and more technical. Wilson said, "Can we sit down somewhere? I'm still a little tired from all the flying of the past few days."

"Clyde'll wear you out." Artie smiled. "Sure. Want some coffee?" Artie led Wilson through a doorway into a tiny room off the lab, next to the cab of the van. There was a bench with a thin mattress and a hot-plate on a shelf. Wilson sat down and looked out the door into the lab while Artie poured the coffee. John was sitting now beside the man at the microscope. Artie sat down next to Wilson.

Wilson felt suddenly awkward. He didn't know what to ask. "You and Clyde seem to go way back."

"Way back," Artie said. "Back when everything up on the North Slope was just wishful thinking. Clyde flew whiskey, which was supposed to be banned, into us thirsty wildcatters freezing our asses off in a goddam Arctic desert."

"You've been here a long time, looking for..." Wilson wanted to finish this question in something other than geologic terms, but he didn't know how.

Artie gave Wilson a half smile, as if he knew what Wilson was after. "Looking," Artie said. "Just looking."

Wilson became conscious of the wind, a soft, alto scream; he felt the van quivering slightly. He closed both hands around his coffee cup and lifted it to his face, feeling its warmth before sipping, using the heat to draw into himself. He didn't know what to say to Artie. Me of all people, he thought; my only investigative talent is pumping strangers, goading them into saying useful things and I can't think what to say to this man. But

Artie was as inaccessible to Wilson as parts of his own mind. He looked at Artie; the man's eyes were on his own coffee cup, his mouth moving subtly, the lower lip faintly pushing up and relaxing and pushing up again.

"You haven't been in the country long?" Artie said.

"In Alaska?"

"Yes."

"Not long."

Artie nodded toward the lab and said, "The boys out there would cut my balls off for saying it, but it's good to get somebody in from outside now and then."

Wilson didn't know how to answer this. He waited. Artie said no more and Wilson began to feel panicky, felt he had to speak to keep the frail bond from breaking. "The boys out there all...think alike?"

Artie smiled and turned his face to Wilson, his brow furrowed. "There's a little town up a hundred miles north of here. Kachuk. Little town full of old-timers, mostly, trappers and prospectors. First time I was there, things seemed a little odd. The people were very friendly, quick to smile, but I had a crazy feeling something was peculiar. Later on I found out why. It was those smiles. The town had gotten a mail order catalog and one of the items had been a kind of do-it-yourself false teeth kit. Not bad teeth, I'm told. You heat up the wax, bite into it to fit it to your gums, the wax cools and you've got a dandy set of teeth. Those old-timers needed it and damn near the whole town sent away for the kit. Only problem was—all the teeth were alike. Every damn smile in the town was exactly the same. Damndest thing I've ever seen."

"So they're all alike in this country?" Wilson said, trying to make the connection.

"I don't feel like the others," Artie said. "They act so cocksure. This place is a mystery and they spend half their energy trying to deny it. Sometimes I want to leap down that hole myself. See what's down there." Artie took a swallow from his coffee cup. Wilson noticed there was no steam. His own cup was still steaming and he knew Artie was drinking whiskey. Wilson thought of Gordon James saying there was nothing else to do in Alaska except drink.

"But it's good to see somebody from outside," Artie said. "I have some questions. Can you answer them?"

"As somebody from outside?"

"Yes."

"I don't feel that way, though."

"But you're recently come from there. It's okay. It's the same."

"What do you want to know?"

"Do they think we're all crazy in Alaska? Criminal or crazy?"

"No. They don't think about you at all."

Artie nodded at this as if it had been expected. "Do they think the oil people up here are lying to them?"

"Some do. Most, I guess."

"They think we're hiding the oil?"

"They don't know—anytime you seem to benefit, they don't believe you...For a long time, when there seemed to be shortages, they didn't believe it."

"Yes."

"They thought you just wanted to jack the prices up. Now the President and others say there's all we need. Stay with oil. But you have to jack the prices up to *find* what's there...So now they're starting to doubt that."

"It's always this way," Artie said very quietly. The tone surprised Wilson. Artie said, "Man is the doubting animal... One more question."

"Yes?"

"Does anybody down there still believe in God?"

Wilson opened his mind to the question but only Beth came in, Beth sitting in her apartment surrounded by all the things she'd bought.

Artie said, "Not the people who wave their arms and jump around and not even the quiet ones rolling the same words off their tongues every damn week. They all just believe in believing. I want to know if anybody outside of Alaska actually believes in *God.*"

This time Artie's question seemed to carry its own answer. He did not need Wilson to speak.

Wilson lay in the dark and felt the van shaking around him. Clyde was snoring across the van—the sound cutting through the wind—but it was the wind, the sound of the wind, that filled Wilson's head. It blew and blew until he was numb and then he knew—just moments before, a premonition—he knew that he would flash back. He had time to think that it had been a while since the last one and then he was curled in the dark in the room, the guard a dark shape against the open doorway, the shape tight and rounded as the man sat in the flat-footed Vietnamese crouch and Wilson had no sense of humanity about that shape, he felt alone in the room and it was then that he felt afraid. He was aware of the irony—it was the illusion of solitude that scared him far more than the presence of these two men who held him captive, who perhaps would soon torture him. The fear had come only this once. Wilson knew that, even as he relived it; he had that much distance, at least, in this flashback. He knew the five nights that had followed this one and they had been different. He lay curled on the hard wood-plank floor in the tropical night and he tried to think of his own past.

This had been the Army's training. Alone, isolated, a prisoner, focus on your own past. Walk around the childhood home, room by room, talk to your mother, your father, greet them warmly. Do not weep. But he could not concentrate. He was afraid but he could not remember anything. He heard the guard spit out the door, heard the bombs falling on the horizon, but Wilson could not focus on anything in his past. His mind had been wiped clean. There was nothing. Nothing but the night beyond this shack. He could sense its vastness. He could see through the window to a scattering of bright stars. There was no pattern there, an alien sky. The room fell away, he curled tighter, the distant, hollow flutter of bombs faded and he watched the patch of night sky and now certain of the stars seemed to move his eyes always in the same direction, linking themselves to other stars, shaping in him, a clear shape there, a new constellation, his own constellation, six, seven, eight stars forming a mountain peak: barren, dark, thinly etched with the stars rising to a peak, falling briefly, to a second, lower peak— Mons Major, the mountain. He felt a breeze against his face, coming through the window, sweeping down from the dark mountain, and he was no longer afraid, the breeze quickened and he closed his eyes to it and the wind pressed him, shook the walls.

Wilson sat up. The van was quaking before the cold wind and he lay back down. He pulled the blankets around him and covered his head and he felt his isolation now, felt alone and vaguely fearful. This was the link back, he decided. He'd been afraid of the dark, of being alone, and that was what made him flash back. If he could just stop his mind at the right moment— he knew the cues, the handful of cues that always led him back. But his fear now, here in Alaska, nagged at him. He imagined how cold that wind was—a killing cold—and he tried his Army trick. He thought of his father, vest covered with dandruff from the forelock of his hair, pulling Wilson to him, hugging him. Good boy. Good boy. The finest little friend. His mother from across the room: Yes. Yes, he is. How fine, Wilson thought. How consistently fine they were. How fine they *are*, he corrected. They were still alive, still fine, loving him unstintingly. He was their only child. And he hardly ever thought of them anymore. Hardly ever. He knew why. Because they were so good. Because their love shaped him so perfectly, made him so secure in that way, made him so independent, so self-sufficient that he could leave them without a thought except how good they were. He knew this must hurt them. Parents were never weaned from their children quite as well as their children were from them. They'd set him free. Free to seek something else. Other people were trapped in their lives seeking their parents—human parents. Wilson yearned now on some other scale. The wind blew hard in the Arctic night. Wilson quaked. He was ready to go to Moonbase.

5.

After conferring with Gordon James, he had one more afternoon and night to spend in Anchorage before flying to the North
Slope. Soon after he entered his room at the Captain Cook
Hotel, he found himself touching the phone, thinking of his
parents again. He looked at his watch. It was shortly after one.
That meant it was very early evening on the East Coast. He
picked up the phone and dialed.

His mother answered. "Yes?" she said, drawing the word
out, sounding, as she always did, vaguely fearful, as if bad news
were expected.

"Mother."

She brightened at once. "Wilson," she said. "Wilson."
Then her voice briefly withdrew from the phone. "Honey, it's
Wilson." Her voice returned. "Your father is home. He's
coming to the phone."

"Good. Yes."

"Where are you calling from?"

"Anchorage."

"Are you there now?"

"Yes."

"Hi son. Hi," his father said, a little out of breath on the
extension.

"Hi, dad."

"He's in Anchorage," his mother said.

"Are you there now?" his father said, using the same inflection as well as the same words that his wife had, though he
clearly had not heard her.

"We weren't sure when you were going," his mother said.

"I know. I meant to tell you. I meant to come down...But they wanted me on short notice." Wilson hadn't even thought to put a day aside and get on the train and go ninety minutes down to Philadelphia to see them before he went. "How are you both doing?"

"We miss you," his father said but there was no hint of recrimination in his voice; there had been none in his mother's voice either.

"I miss you," Wilson said and his eyes filled quickly with tears because he knew that in any compelling sense it was a lie and because he wished he had remembered to go see them before he'd left.

"Anchorage," his father said and his wistfulness carried even over the faint telephone connection. They'd never traveled much, never had much money, had always devoted their resources to him, to educating him, to staking his little business, to helping him through tight spots and not asking for anything back. "Tell me about it," his father said.

"It's...not very impressive. A lot of...bars and pickup trucks and pawnshops. You know. Barracks buildings. It's like an Army base. I don't know." Wilson was struggling to keep his voice from cracking. Their just being on the end of the phone raked him with images of their love: their arms always around him, always; their quietness about these past years of separation; never an accusation, only unsullied delight at the rare moments of their contact. What's the matter with me? Wilson demanded of himself.

"Is it very cold?" his mother asked.

Wilson could see a bank building time and temperature display through his hotel window. "It's 39 degrees right now," he said.

His father whistled. "That's not bad."

"Anchorage is in the south and on the water," Wilson said. "I've already been farther north. Just briefly. It's a lot colder there."

"And I'm sure Anchorage will soon be a lot colder too," his mother said.

"Yes...I'm sure," Wilson said.

"Yes," his father said.

And they all fell silent for a long moment. Wilson tried to think back—when were they closer, when could they talk? Before Vietnam. Before that, certainly. Again Wilson felt his eyes fill. For four of the seven days he was in captivity, they knew he was missing. It had devastated them. Even after it was over. Even when he'd come back home and their arms were around him, he saw it in their eyes, the ravages there. Could Lazarus' mother ever feel the same way again for him? And once Lazarus had died, could he feel the same for his mother? The human balance between them had been destroyed.

"This call must be costing you a lot of money," his mother said.

"It's all right," Wilson said. "Really. I wanted to call and tell you I'm thinking about you and tell you I love you."

"We love you too," his mother said, his father overlapping the same words, one beat later.

In the moment after the jumble of voices, Wilson knew his mother was beginning to cry. He said, "I like being here very much. I'm going up to Prudhoe Bay, the North Slope, tomorrow and there's...something here, I think. Something I want...I'm glad I'm here."

"Good," his father said. "Good. You know that's what we want for you."

"Yes..." Wilson felt drained. He felt suddenly very weary, felt nothing else. He forced life into his voice. "Well...I've got to go now. I've got to get going."

"Okay," his father said.

"Yes," his mother said, her voice husky.

"Good-bye," Wilson said.

"We love you," his father said.

"We do," his mother said.

"Yes," Wilson said. "I love you too."

The phone was down and he pushed at his forehead with the heel of his hand. He wondered if the connection he'd made a few moments earlier had been true: had that week of captivity—the week that dogged him still—been the reason for this distance from the parents who loved him? He tried to remember the time just before he'd gone to Vietnam, but he could not. He had no concentration, no energy, his hand fell from his forehead to the bed, propped him there.

From a trail of associations he was only half conscious of, he thought to make another call. He found himself thinking of Beth. He felt closer to her now that she was dead than ever before. There was only one person he could talk to who would reflect something of Beth into his mind. He picked up the phone and dialed New York City information and the number was familiar as soon as it was spoken. He dialed Beth's mother.

The woman answered after eight rings. Her voice was weak. "Hello?"

"Esther, it's Wilson."

"Wilson?" The voice recognized the name but seemed in some other way confused. "Oh, Wilson. I have terrible news for you. Terrible."

"I know. I heard."

"Wilson, I..." Esther's voice was stripped of the pretense, the hyper-precision, the pinched aloofness that he remembered. It was a nakedly emotional voice, though Esther seemed to be composed. "I...can't understand why...She was sick, of course. I knew that. You knew it too...But you were sick as well. You were a very sick boy. Don't forget that, Wilson. Maybe you're still sick." The composure was crumbling. "Maybe you're still sick. Maybe I'm sick, too."

"Did she leave a note?" Wilson asked, hoping she'd hold herself together long enough to at least answer a few questions. He himself felt suddenly quite calm, as if she were a stranger he had to question on an interrogation.

"A note?"

"A suicide note."

"Sort of a note. Sort of. She left a note on her dresser. Nothing very much."

"What did it say, Esther?"

"Well...I..." The woman's habits of attitude began to return, even though her voice still had none of her affectation. She was too fastidious now, too refined, to reveal what the note said—that was what was beginning to draw her words back, he knew.

"She's dead, Esther," Wilson said, forcing her away from the refinement, forcing her back toward her own feelings. "She killed herself, Esther...What did she say about that?"

"Oh, Wilson. She's dead..."

"What did she write in the note?"

"She wrote, 'There's too much.'"

"Is that all she said?"

"That's all."

"'There's too much.'"

"It means she's taken too much," Esther said. "She took too much from shits like you, Wilson. Shits like you. She had plenty of shits like you. Before and after. She had too many shits like you." Esther was beginning to shout.

Wilson spoke her name gently over and over, trying to calm her. But she wouldn't stop. The words clattered over the line and he had no anger for her. No anger at all. She was chanting over and over now, "Shits. Shits. Shits like you..." Wilson felt a sadness come over him, a sadness that prickled his skin, and he said, "Good-bye, Esther," and gently hung up the phone.

After the phone calls, he left the hotel. He and Clyde were meeting for a farewell drink later in the afternoon, but he had to get out of his room. Nearby, on the edge of the Cook Inlet, was a large wooden structure built into a steep bank and topped by a statue of Captain Cook. From the sidewalk level Wilson entered the top of the structure and he followed a winding ramp down to a lower deck. He leaned on the railing and looked down another level, across a grassy patch of ground to a railroad track, and then, beyond, to the grey mud flat of low tide and the still, bronze drumskin of the inlet spreading on to a distant mountain. Off to the right was a tank farm and a tangle of derricks on the water's edge. A seaplane skipped away from the shore and lifted into the sky. Wilson's eyes rose with it and he saw a small plane flying past, low and level, trailing a long sign with the words "Energy Independence" and the President's broken chain symbol.

Wilson pulled back and followed the ramp to the lowest level. He hoisted himself over the railing and dropped down to the ground. Across the track before him was the water's edge. But the mud flats cut him off and he didn't want to go out to the water anyway. He turned and ducked under the bottom deck and, farther in, under the structure, he stood up among trees stunted from the permafrost. He leaned against one of the trees but his mind would not untangle itself, would not focus and he stayed only a few minutes.

When he crouched to crawl up from beneath the deck, he heard, above him, the ricochet sound of a camera shutter. He stood up and looked and a young man was dipping and leaning with his camera on the lower deck level, photographing a young woman in a black fur coat. "Sorry," a voice said, "closed for a few minutes," and Wilson saw a man up at street level deflecting two women away from the deck.

"Chickie," the woman said softly to the camera. The camera pinged and she pouted her lips and then she said "Chickie" again. She was pretty, though in too vivid a way, her lips too large and too red, her eyes too sharply outlined. She twisted her torso in a different direction after each shot, clutching the coat closely around her. The coat had a large collar that curved up around her head and the coat was very straight and very long, its dark fur falling nearly to the woman's ankles. She was a face; a wide, dark column; the point of a foot.

The photographer leaned back and said, "Okay" and the woman suddenly opened her coat. Her arms spread and the coat opened wide and she was naked beneath. The pinkness of her in the cold air, the disks of her nipples, the dark triangle of her pubic hair, all suddenly revealed beneath the coat took Wilson's breath away, filled him with wonder.

"Chickie," she said.

In a bar with a caribou head over the beer spigots, a loud argument was raging over whether Jimmy Hoffa had been buried somewhere in the earth or dropped somewhere into the water. Two men, each husky and bearded, seemed to be the main contenders. Clyde got up from where he sat and led Wilson to a table farther back. When they were sitting again, Clyde smiled. "Half this town's Teamsters," he said.

Wilson nodded and watched the two bearded jaws jut closer to each other. "I wish you were flying me, Clyde. I could get you to take off right now."

"You're up to my speed, pardner."

Wilson looked at Clyde and wondered how much genuine feeling was behind his remark. Clyde's large hands suddenly rose and spread and he shrugged and Wilson knew the man had tried to make some clear expression of friendship. Wilson said, "I'm gonna miss you, too, Clyde."

"Hey. I fly into Moonbase every so often. I'll find you."

Before Wilson could answer, there was a crash and a thump and shouts from up front. Wilson could see the bearded men grappling, yanking each other around, knocking over barstools. Clyde did not turn to look. "You let me know if they're flying this way," Clyde said.

"Shit. I've got to get out of this town," Wilson said.

"When do you take off?"

"Tomorrow morning."

"You going up on one of the worker flights?"

"That's right," Wilson said and he watched the bartender lean over the bar and angle a shotgun at the two men who were on the floor now with the half dozen other patrons gaggling around them.

"That'll not even be like flying," Clyde said. "You go up in a 737 with a plane full of roughnecks from Moonbase. Everybody up there works one week on, one week off."

"At least they'll all be sucked out and hung over, going back up."

Clyde laughed. "Guess so...You want to go ahead and get drunk now?"

"What?" Wilson heard the question but it had surprised him and he needed a beat to adjust his thinking to fit it.

"Drunk," Clyde said. "Should we go on drinking all afternoon now and get drunk?"

"I don't know why it should strike me this way, but that seems the damndest peculiar question to hear from you, Clyde. Getting drunk together isn't that . . . ah . . . premeditated, is it?"

"Just think about the question," Clyde said.

Wilson paused and it struck him that no, he didn't want to be either drunk or hungover for his flight to Moonbase. Not at all. Clyde knew this already. That was why he'd asked the question. Wilson simply said, "You're right, Clyde."

Clyde rose up as the bartender began shouting curses and the two bearded men scrambled to their feet. Clyde looked down at Wilson and said, "Well, *I* sure as hell want to get drunk, so why don't you run on now, pardner."

Wilson opened his mouth as if to speak, though he didn't have anything in mind to say. Clyde cut him off anyway. "I'll see you at Moonbase. Go on now, pardner. Good luck on whatever you're after."

Wilson rose and Clyde's hand came forward and he shook it; he found the shake from this large hand gentler than he'd expected. Again, Wilson had no words. He and Clyde nodded once and Wilson followed the two Teamsters out of the bar, a shotgun waving at his back.

The waiting area at the Anchorage airport was full of bearded young men in quilted vests, half of them clomping about, half of them immobile in their chairs. Wilson decided that the difference between the two groups was in what they'd done with their week off—the clompers had whored, the sitters had drunk. A woman's voice on the public address announced the wind chill at Moonbase—minus eighteen. Not all that severe, Wilson thought; it was still early in the season.

He edged past the men who were leaning into each other and pounding shoulders and laughing and he waited near the gate. When they boarded, he was first onto the plane, nodding at the stewardess' greeting and heading for a window seat far forward. There was no galley in the plane, with seats all the way up to the cabin. The plane filled with the other men and Wilson pressed his face to the window at takeoff. They entered a cloud almost instantly and he thought of Clyde's remarks at the bar. He was right. After a few hours in the Piper, this didn't seem like flying at all.

The plane lifted from the cloud into the glare of sun and the sky was a very pale blue. Against the cloud he could see the shadow of the jet and its contrail. The sun glinted on the skin of the jet and the plane's shadow below was circled by a metallic rainbow. Wilson soon tired of watching his own shadow, resented the clouds from this height, wanted very badly to see the earth below.

He turned away from the window and the weariness came upon him again, in spite of where he was headed. He was in suspension for a time and his thoughts dissolved until he abruptly sat up straight. He'd dozed. For only a few minutes, he was sure. The other men were quiet, the plane was level, Wilson looked out the window and the clouds still covered the earth. To the east they stretched away to the horizon and to the north—Wilson angled his head to see—the clouds rose and peaked.

He looked for a moment seeing clouds and then—with a little twist of surprise and fear—he realized they were mountains. It was the same feeling he'd had with Beth beside him—driving fast along the road from Marrakesh. In the fields camels grazed with cows, boys in kaftans herded sheep with a stick and a handful of pebbles, and the fields themselves were strewn with rocks, they were as cluttered as a beach after a storm, full of rocks. He was driving and ahead he saw a line of clouds at the horizon and then—just as now—there was a moment when he realized they were too rigid—his sense of this came in a stroke and it chilled him. Look, he said to Beth, turning his face to her, look at the mountains, they seemed like clouds. Beth glanced only briefly there. She did not speak but immediately turned back to the fields filled with rocks. His face pressed to the window of the plane. Wilson waited for more of Beth to fill him. But the memory stopped. That was all of it. He dipped his head and tried to understand what he'd found so notable in that moment. But there was only the mountain range ahead and Beth was quiet and focused elsewhere. Wilson let it go and he looked out to the mountains that were passing now below the plane.

Beyond the mountains the plane began a rapid descent, entering the clutch of the clouds, quickening Wilson with the clear promise of the North Slope. Those mountains had been the Brooks Range, the last barrier before Prudhoe Bay and the Arctic desert of the north.

The clouds became wispy and then below the plane was a dim, flat land. Its cover of snow and ice held shapes in its whiteness—the faint spoor of lakes, all elongated on the same axis—the barest imprints in the snow—and the dim arterial tracks of iced rivers—all this the landscape of the brief northern summer fallen now into its winter silence, slowly disappearing beneath the ice. The land grew dimmer and blanker and suddenly a thin dark shape cut across the blankness—the pipeline—its stanchions lifting it, carrying it in a square cornered wave-form from one hazy horizon to the other. The plane crossed the pipeline and it was gone and the earth was blank again until it was suddenly filled with a faint mosaic of shapes, interlocking polygons—the tesselated permafrost terrain showing its ice bodies deeper down.

Then Wilson saw a light on the white desert—a spot of flame—the plane drew nearer and he could see the flame undulating—a gas flare. The plane was very low now and it banked and turned and he saw the pipeline again, but not isolated this time. The pipeline was attended; other pipes came and went, splicing in and splicing out and they led sometimes to square pads, rigs, low buildings. The polygons returned—a vast garden for computer chips—and there was a grinding sound—the landing gear—and the plane sank and touched and Wilson saw a low red building spank past with a radio tower rising from it, flags stretched straight in the wind, huts on pilings and the plane swung around. This was Deadhorse Airfield, serving the Prudhoe Bay area.

In the terminal the vending machines were all kicked in and the air was thick from cigarette smoke. Men jostled and shouted and Wilson edged to the side of the disembarking group and looked around for the driver who was supposed to meet him. He saw his own name lettered crudely on a piece of cardboard and held up chest-high by a man who at first glance was the same as all the others coursing through the terminal—he was young, certainly under thirty, and he had a ruddy, square face, a hacked beard.

"I'm Wilson Hand."

"Welcome to Prudhoe Bay," the young man said, though he didn't offer to shake hands. "Come with me."

Outside, Wilson followed the young man to a van and they drove off through Deadhorse, a street-wide settlement of support companies for the oil fields—heavy machinery repair, tire supply, building materials, the "Deadhorse Regal" hotel—a trailer on blocks with rooms for a hundred and fifty dollars a night.

The young man said nothing and drove out of Deadhorse to a juncture of the gravel road. One branch went west to British Petroleum's base camp, one went north to Arco's camp, and one turned east to Royal. Wilson was struck by the man's silence and in this he was thankful for the man's difference from the other sober Moonbase workers he'd seen. Wilson did not want to talk now and he looked out to the southwest, away from the oil fields. Snow stretched in an unbroken plain and the clouds came down, blurring the horizon, and to the south the earth seemed simply to dissipate in the mid-afternoon dimness.

He quickly became accustomed to the barren landscape before him and so, when the van turned and he looked ahead to see the Royal base camp, he was awed in the way he might be awed to suddenly see, from a raft in the middle of the ocean, the Titanic bearing down on him. A red, slick-skinned central facade faced him three stories high with a wide, metal-canopied entrance glowing yellow in the dusk. Off the central unit, two-storied wings stretched out to each side filled with vertically narrow windows, like a battlement. The buildings gave a sense of massiveness far out of proportion to what Wilson knew to be their size—and they all sat high off the ground, elevated by dark stanchions, the wind howling through, the loose snow swirling there, whipping under the buildings and on through, out into the open again.

They entered the wide doorway and the reception area felt confined, with a low acoustical ceiling and a great triangular wedge of a desk with two rather heavy young women behind it. Polished metal lamps threw columns of light in careful, peopled directions, leaving dim areas filled with man-tall potted plants and rya tapestries. Wilson felt a pressure in his ears as if he'd just entered an underground tunnel.

The driver led Wilson to the left, past a security station behind a large glass window, this space the opposite of the reception area with every corner brilliantly lit in fluorescence and the room full of the hard edges of gun lockers, a control panel of lights, a computer terminal. Ahead was a hallway—pinspotted and carpeted like a new convention hotel—but the young man turned Wilson in at a doorway and then he himself backed out and disappeared.

"Come in. Come on in," a voice said from an inner office. Wilson entered and a man rose from behind a desk. "I'm Brian Finn," the man said.

He was the chief administrator of the camp, the name Wilson had been given as the one contact at Moonbase who would know who Wilson was and what he was there for. Wilson masked his surprise and shook Finn's hand. Unlike the other Royal men-in-charge, Finn was young, barely thirty. He had a thick, pale blond beard and wore a flannel shirt and an open down vest. He looked very much like the oilfield roughnecks from the plane except for something that Wilson couldn't place for a moment.

"I'm Wilson Hand."

"Yes, I know. Of course...Close the door, won't you?"

Wilson turned and closed the door and again he felt a pressure in his ears. He worked his jaw to release it.

"Please have a seat," Finn said, and as he moved his arm, gesturing toward a chair, Wilson realized in what way the man was different. Beneath the beard, beneath the vest, Finn was slender. His shirt was not taut at the biceps and chest, his eyes were sunken and his neck was too long—he had the surface trappings of the field workers but he was a different animal underneath—not frail, that wasn't the sense of him, but reliant on defenses that had nothing to do with physical strength.

"Mr. James briefed me on your purpose here," Finn said.

"Good."

"We're going to portray you as a corporate communications man, doing a number of projects on Moonbase, some for the public, some internal. That should give you an unquestionable excuse to go anywhere and ask anything."

"That's fine. And I don't have to fake any expertise."

"In fact, if you seemed to know anything, you'd blow your cover." Finn laughed at his own joke on public relations people, though the laughter was subdued, as if reluctant. Wilson joined the laughter as a matter of courtesy, but he felt the impulse to stretch the man a bit, just to see what he could learn about him.

Wilson said, "How'd you end up here? Is your MBA from the wrong school?"

Finn laughed again—it seemed a genuine laugh—and in that moment Wilson imagined the way it might go from here: Finn says, Does my MBA show? Wilson says, It takes more than a down vest to make you one of the boys. Finn says, That's true—I hate all these sons of bitches here. But Finn's laugh simply dwindled and stopped and he said, "There are certainly some compensations in Alaska."

Wilson nodded and decided that in spite of Finn's little joke he sounded like Gordon James, had the same abstractness in his speech, the same vague aloofness. This made Wilson want to prod Finn some more, break through his crust. But Wilson was conscious of where he was—he had an even stronger desire to get to his room, to sit by his window and watch the Arctic night begin. He could probe Finn another time.

Finn said, "Please forgive me for saying this, but I'm required—at Moonbase we allow no drugs, guns, gambling, alcohol. No alcohol at all. Not even beer or wine. There. That's done. Oh...except the guns. Your status in internal security gives you the right..."

"I don't carry one."

"All right. But suit yourself on that."

"Do you know what it is they're concerned about in Anchorage?" Wilson asked.

"Oh yes. This is the one place they know they've missed something."

"But I suppose you're not worried about it either."

"Is that what you've been finding? Nobody's concerned about the stolen documents?"

"Outside of Anchorage, they're not. On the surface, at least."

"Well, I'm personally more concerned about drugs, Mr. Hand. I hope Mr. James puts you on that one some day."

"Perhaps he will," Wilson said.

"These documents have been missed at our records center. I'll show you the center myself tomorrow morning...For the rest of your background—for the future work I'm sure you'll be doing for us—we'll give you a look around the whole oil field, all the operations."

"Good," Wilson said, his irritation at Finn's manner brushed away by the prospect of getting out into the field.

"And it will help solidify your cover identity," Finn said.

"For the rest of the tour I'll put you back in the care of Ronnie."

"That was the man who drove me here from Deadhorse?"

"Yes."

"Good." Wilson almost asked Finn to instruct Ronnie to keep up his silence on their tour, but he decided it would sound too strange.

"You *have* been briefed about the weather, haven't you? Right now it's balmy out—minus twenty or so. But we're heading into our long night, Mr. Hand. Around Thanksgiving the sun will stop rising here until the middle of January. We often see the wind chill at minus seventy five or worse and exposed flesh can freeze in thirty seconds at that temperature. Don't get caught off guard."

"Thanks," Wilson said. "I've been briefed...I'm a little tired now."

"Surely." Finn came around the desk, moving stiffly, as if brittle in his thinness. He passed Wilson, touched the doorknob, then turned back. "One more thing," he said.

"Yes?"

"It's a very tight-knit little world here. People are observant and word travels fast. Be very careful about how you portray yourself. And I'd suggest you confide in no one but me."

"Thanks. I'll remember that."

"Ronnie will show you to your room," Finn said as he opened the door. Ronnie was revealed sitting in the outer office, his arms folded across his chest. Finn didn't even glance out the door; he knew Ronnie was there.

Wilson nodded a good-bye and wondered again what was under Finn's crust.

Ronnie led Wilson back to the reception area and then to the left and past it. They came to a railing and Wilson found himself on a balcony that looked over a recreation floor below. There were pool tables, lounges, card tables. "This way," Ronnie said and they circled to the right along a wide walkway with overstuffed chairs and rubber plants. They turned into one of the convention-hotel halls just as Wilson smelled chlorine. ''A pool?'' he asked.

''Farther down,'' the young man said, his voice flat, not quite unfriendly.

Wilson was beginning to feel a little uneasy over all these amenities but then they were at the end of the hall and a door was open and he stepped into his room. It was very small and pinspotted like the lobby. A bunk and a desk, linked with a clean, smooth curve of plastic from desktop down to bed frame, filled one wall. The opposite wall was closet, dresser with a TV on top, and a doorway into a tiny bathroom. The far wall, opposite the entrance, had a chair beneath one of the thin, vertical windows. Outside, the light was nearly gone. Wilson's eyes returned to the TV, the only part of the room that troubled him. ''They get TV signals up here?'' he said.

''No, they get tapes in by plane and they're transmitted internally.''

''I see.''

''Any other questions?''

''No.''

''There's one rule you should know—don't try to fuck the maids.''

Given the young man's reticence so far, this remark made Wilson laugh—a single, sharp bark of a laugh. ''They leave them to you, huh Ronnie?''

Ronnie did not reply but turned to go. At the door he paused. ''Any other questions, dial two on your phone...I suspect you were joking, but you're wrong about me and the maids. Dead wrong.''

Before Wilson could say anything, Ronnie was gone. He put out of his mind the clutter of all the cryptic feelings of all the men he'd encountered in Alaska. At last he was where he wanted to be. The room fit him tightly, bound him in. For now that was all right. He went to the closet and put his bags inside without opening them. He shut the closet doors and switched the lights off in the room and moved to the window, approaching it with his chest pinching tight, his breath snagging there.

The window was doubled, like a jet's, and Wilson could see, off to the left, the jut of another wing; off to the right, a double-circuit electrical tower. But directly before him was a view into oblivion: the empty, white tundra grasped out to the horizon. Something moved. A change of texture in the snow, moving, stopping, close in. Wilson strained his eyes as the light faded and he saw a white fox, its head cocked. Then the fox began to dig at the snow, its paw moving and Wilson could feel it on the surface of his own skin. Deeper. Then he felt the movement of the fox's paw in his fingertips, his own hand moved there with it. The fox stopped. Wilson's hand closed, the fist tightened, and the fox disappeared into the darkness.

6.

Wilson woke and the room was bright and then there were shards of shadow falling softly through the room—something torn apart outside in the sky—he jumped up, crossed to the window and he saw, settling on the roof of the next wing, a score of great, black birds. Ravens. They settled after their flight, their necks stretching, their wings jutting and folding then growing still. Ravens in a row against the blue sky and he looked out onto the tundra and there were two more birds against the snow, their blackness a deep scorch against the white earth and then they too spread their wings and rose up and wheeled away first to the right and then swooped high and back to the left and down beside the others.

"Ravens," Wilson said to Finn in his office that morning.

The man looked at him with a faint exasperation. "Yes. Ravens."

"Here."

"They're always here."

"Always?"

"All year round...That...flock..."

"Murder," Wilson said.

"What's that?"

"The collective noun for ravens. That murder of ravens..."

"They're here year round," Finn said. "Living off our garbage. And carrion. The foxes' garbage."

"About the record center..." Wilson said. He didn't want Finn elaborating on the ravens.

"Yes?" Finn said, sounding slightly shaken.

Wilson realized he'd used one of his preferred interrogation techniques—shifting the subject abruptly—though it was prompted by his own discomfort and not by an interest in probing Finn. "I want to see it now," Wilson said. "We should get on with this."

"Yes...All right...Since, for the sake of your cover, we'll be able to do little talking about the...problem...while we're there, I should tell you this much first. We have a computer in the record center. All the people in records know how to access it. And anyone else who found out a couple of simple software code words could access it, too. The computer does keep a record of its output, however. And we know that five weeks ago someone output a hard copy of some production reports. No such data had been officially requested by anyone. There was no record left by the requestor of its use, no authorization. Also some hard copy files were found to be incomplete...Things had been removed."

"What exactly was missing?"

"I'll give you a detailed list. But mostly field exploration reports from...well, from up here on the slope, out on the shelf in the Beaufort Sea, down in the Yukon River basin, some other spots. A little bit from all over. But the thefts were not terribly systematic. Someone seemed to be fishing. But rather clumsily."

Wilson grew impatient with Finn's words. The more Finn spoke, the more lugubrious his voice became. Wilson knew he should be concentrating hard on all this for the sake of the investigation but he'd never liked the puzzle-solving part of his job and he suddenly realized that Finn's office had no window and he felt irritated at the man for this. "Let's see the record center now," he said.

"Very well. I'll take you down there myself." Finn's voice was bloated and Wilson realized that the man was in some kind of distress. Finn stood up and his hands jerked off the desk and his face rose too high, his eyes went briefly to the ceiling.

Wilson knew how to play the moment. He'd been far too preoccupied with himself to see what was happening, but here was a gift and he knew what to do. He remained seated and fixed a knowing half-smile on Finn and waited for the man to lower his eyes.

Finn looked down at Wilson and when he saw him still seated, his shoulders sagged just a bit. Wilson thought he might speak but Finn seemed to be waiting, as if he expected Wilson to ask a devastating question.

But Wilson didn't know what the hell was going on. Behind the fixed half smile, his mind thrashed around trying to think what to say. Then he decided that he probably had a wide range of choices. Finn had worked himself into this state on his own; he'd open up on his own as well. He thought of background information he still needed and then he faked a low, knowing tone and said, "I want a list of the names of all the people who were working in the record center in the weeks surrounding the thefts."

Finn moved stiffly to the desk, without a word, opened his desk drawer, and pulled out a piece of paper from the top of the pile, as if he'd been waiting for this request.

"Here," Finn said, passing the paper to Wilson.

Again Wilson expected the words that Finn obviously wanted to say but again Finn said nothing. Wilson looked down at the paper, as if to read the names—a meaningless act, strangers' names; he wondered if Finn realized how meaningless this was. There was still silence and Wilson began to read names: John Bowman, Steven Westfall, Gabe Nethers, Mario Laval, Tom Gold...Wilson's eyes went on down the list—there were a dozen names altogether—and then Finn spoke.

"I want to tell you one thing," Finn said.

Wilson raised his head slowly, held his body still, said very gently, "Of course."

"I can't stand what this is doing to me. It's filling me with hate and I have to fight that...I've been hating you." Finn's fists trembled before him.

The control Wilson felt he had in the situation—even though he'd not consciously brought it about and really didn't know where it was leading—began to disappear. He braced himself. His own fists clenched.

Then Finn said, "God doesn't want me to hate."

"God?" Wilson said reflexively—he'd not meant to speak—certainly didn't want to divert Finn's thoughts—but he had been startled by this. Finn had unwittingly used Wilson's own trick on him.

"I can't hate you," Finn said. "And it's just to cover up my own shortcomings. You'd find this out anyway...I was...remiss...in the security...The record center should have had a guard there...all the time. But there was no one. Anybody could walk in. Every maintenance and service person has a key. No one was there to protect the place and that was my fault. The list you have there is...worthless...I might as well give you a list of everyone at Moonbase. Anyone could have gotten access to the information." Finn sat back down, his arms fell along the arms of the chair, the palms of his hands turned up in the release.

Wilson felt uncomfortable in a way he could not bring into focus. He felt teased, teased by something he sensed was important but that kept itself hidden.

"It's gone," Finn said. "I don't hate you anymore. Praise God."

Wilson's confusion tightened in his chest, threatened to propel him across the desk to grab Finn by the throat. He much preferred the man's hatred.

Wilson walked down the hallway from his room, his parka over his arm, and he thought of the record center. His impression of it was vague, even though he'd been there only a few minutes earlier. There'd been the smell of ozone, like the air after a thunderstorm; there'd been a wall of files, a floor of desks, a computer terminal. He'd seen nothing, though, that suggested a line of inquiry in his investigation. He'd not known how to concentrate. Physical evidence meant nothing to him.

Perhaps he'd interview each of the dozen people on the list; but it was an idle thought, for he had no clear plan of action at all from this point on. And for the moment he didn't really care.

He was passing into the reception area and he was aware that a woman was sitting at the front desk. He saw her from behind as he approached. It registered on him that she was not heavy, as the two women the day before had been, and then he was distracted, looking for Ronnie. The man was nowhere in sight. Wilson turned to the desk.

He recoiled slightly. The woman's face chilled him. It was looking at him, motionless, and in the splash of fluorescence from the desktop below, and the column of incandescence from above, the face was simplified in a way that made him uneasy, frightened him even, in spite of the face being oddly beautiful. Her eyes were large and very dark—the eyes did not flicker, did not move—and her face had no subtlety in its parts, just the large wide-set eyes and the high moon-arch of forehead and the broad curve of her jaw—her face was a nineteenth century American primitive painter's rendering of a beautiful woman, as if she should have a daughter in a baby's cap on her arm with an exact miniature of her face.

Wilson moved nearer, though he remained hesitant, a little fearful. "Do you know a man named Ronnie?" he asked.

The face didn't stir.

"He works for Brian Finn."

The face still did not move, did not acknowledge his existence, even though her eyes were on him.

"Is there someone there?" Wilson asked. "Are you alive or painted?"

The chin rose slightly and she said, "I'm thinking about it, smartass...I assume you want to know where Ronnie is, not just if you and I happen to have a common acquaintance."

"I'm no smartass. I just like people to make some acknowledgement when I speak to them. Common courtesy." This close now—Wilson could reach out and touch her if he chose—her face kept its exaggerated beauty. But it was delicate at the same time; her skin was pale and smooth and made her seem fragile behind her air of self-possession. At her temples the blue tracings of her veins showed faintly through and Wilson wanted to touch her there softly, with his fingertips, wanted to touch the long, slow curl of her hair that fell along her face.

The woman said, "He's about fifty feet behind you and moving this way."

Wilson had not noticed her eyes look past him to see anyone approach. He leaned forward, until he felt the heat on his face from the lamplight overhead. He was beginning to think that everyone in Alaska was slightly mad. His desire to touch her face grew very strong. He was bent forward now, prepared to speak, and he found that he had nothing to say. He felt a flush of panic.

"Mr. Hand," a man's voice said behind him.

Wilson knew he should use the voice as an excuse to turn, to cover his speechlessness, but the woman's eyes held him. Her eyes were so dark they seemed totally dilated, opened up as wide as possible, asking him to enter. She said, "Mr. Hand, please don't say anything. I hate cute banter with strangers." He did not withdraw at once and she said, "Really I do. I loathe it."

Wilson straightened up and the woman's head cocked slightly to the right and her eyes would not let go of him. He expected her to smile—just faintly—but she did not. He turned and there was Ronnie.

"All right, Ronnie," Wilson said.

"I'm sorry. I've only got about an hour this afternoon," Ronnie said.

"That's all right. We'll do the tour over a few days. I don't want to rush anyway." He watched Ronnie's attention shift past him, to the woman. Wilson started to turn to her, to see her again—he would just say thank you for her help. But in fact she hadn't helped him and it would only seem like the banter she despised. He put his parka on and followed Ronnie out the door without a glance back.

Wilson was high up on the safety platform of a drilling rig. A man with a hard-hat under the hood of his parka—the drill chief—was talking on about his operation. Wilson looked out toward the horizon to the south, and beyond the flat, snow-covered tundra he could see the jagged line of the Brooks Range. He looked down at the gravel pad surrounding the rig, the skids stretching to the west, straddling a row of drill holes topped by the "Christmas trees"—the red metal plugs, covered with valves and gauges, that sat on the casings of each flowing well-hole. The crane engine ground away and down below, by the rotary table, bodies lunged about as they changed the bit on the drill.

"The bit goes dull every few hours," the chief was saying. "Takes two twelve-hour shifts to change the fucker."

Wilson nodded in feigned interest, wanting to look back out over the tundra. But as he saw a length of pipe coming up out of the ground, he felt a contraction in his groin as if he were watching a hypodermic needle piercing and drawing out of an arm—a woman's arm, smooth and soft. The image pulled him two ways at once. He sensed the earth beneath him—an opening in the earth—and he thought briefly of Artie Phillips wanting to jump down the hole. But Wilson also thought—unexpectedly—of the woman in the reception area, the translucence of her skin. It was that unsettling, the penetration of the earth down there where men were drawing out another section of pipe—as unsettling as a needle in the skin of that woman, that pale skin.

"I know in my hands what's happening," the chief was saying. "It's a feel, an instinct. I know two miles down when that drill head is wearing out."

"And you know what's there in the earth?" Wilson said. "You know that in your hands?"

"Sure."

No, Wilson wanted to say. I don't believe that. "You know where the oil is?"

"Once we've found it..."

"But you don't know just from touch..."

"I meant my rig. I know my rig." The man laughed. "If I knew where to find oil from my hands, I'd be a millionaire. They couldn't pay me enough..."

Wilson turned away from the man. He didn't think about being rude; he just moved to the platform railing and looked out, away from the drill pad, out to where the earth was untouched. He felt a sudden restlessness.

The twilight sky was still cloudless when they came back to the operations center and as Wilson got out of the van he felt movement above him. He looked and the ravens arced overhead. He shut his eyes to them and they stayed motionless there in the image in his mind: black holes in the sky, well holes.

He lowered his face before opening his eyes. He knew they'd disappeared now and he climbed the steps and it wasn't until he was through the front doors that he thought of the woman at the reception desk. For the brief moment before he could see the desk he felt himself quicken. Then he saw that she was gone. Two rather plump women were there—the two who had been behind the desk yesterday, when he'd come in.

He said thank you to Ronnie—warmly—he felt a regret at having agitated the man over the maids. Then Wilson passed the reception desk and walked along the balcony toward his corridor.

Sitting in a chair in a pinspot was the woman. Her eyes were already on him and he was aware of his own hands waiting to move; he forced them to be still. He stopped before her. There was a chair empty next to her. "May I sit?" he said.

"Yes," she said.

Wilson sat down. "I had no banter anyway, this morning," he said. "I leaned near to you and I drew a blank."

"It's not just between strangers that I hate banter," she said.

"Was I doing it just now? I thought I was being straightforward."

The woman cocked her head again and this time she did smile—exactly the smile, the faint smile with only the corner of one side of her wide mouth turned up—that he'd expected this morning. The smile filled him with her smell—it opened him to the scent of her—the faint fruit-smell of her cologne—he fancied he could even smell the soap she'd rubbed on her skin—Wilson was ravaged by his closeness to this woman. Beth, he thought. Beth. He'd not made love to Beth for five years—not since before their divorce—but he seemed so recently parted from her, felt her now, felt her near him. He was not conscious of her for her personality, her companionship, but for something else—first for her madness and then for her death. For the knowledge she had now. But this woman's faint smile made his hands want to move to her. He held himself back, seemed instead to sink deeper into the chair, to recede.

"You were fine just now," she said. "I knew at once this morning that you were different from the men here and you'd think you could...reach me...by prancing your wit around. I didn't come here for that."

"I didn't either," Wilson said. "Believe me."

"The night's coming," she said.

Wilson knew instinctively that she was not talking about the evening of this day, was not making a sexual advance. She paused and Wilson said, "The Arctic night."

"Yes," she said and her brow furrowed, her eyes narrowed briefly at him in acknowledgement of his perception. "Yes," she said again. "The long night...I fear it like death. All joy drains away, all of the intensity in my body..."

She stopped speaking as if there were more to say and Wilson waited. He thought to ask her why she was here, why she stayed, but he did not.

"I'll meet you here again tomorrow," the woman said and she stood up.

Wilson began to rise and the woman stopped him with a brief lift of her hand. "Tomorrow," she said.

The next afternoon there were sun dogs. Wilson saw them for just a moment as Ronnie led him into a great corrugated metal building at a far edge of the oil field. The two mock suns flared low in the sky. He did not look at the true sun—he could not look at it directly—but these two held him. He wanted to stay, to watch them. Would they vanish or would they verge beyond the horizon? But he had to turn away.

Inside was the flow station, where the oil from wells scattered over the tundra was collected. Wilson entered a large control room with a wide triptych desk with computer cathode ray tubes and a bank of TV screens, each showing a bleeder valve flaring gas. Wilson tightened. He followed Ronnie through a doorway and down a concrete hall and then into an enormous shed holding house-high tanks, its ceiling a tangle of pipes, and filled with the hum of oil passing around them. Wilson wanted to back out of here into the cold sunlight and escape. The catwalk and motors and tanks and pipes stuffed his head full and he felt the same desperation he'd felt at Beth's apartment. He sensed her near, heard her sigh in the hum of oil in the pipes, saw her padding before him on bare feet through her apartment and he felt a twist of desire. He let the desire move his mind to the woman back at the operations center. He concentrated on her eyes, held her face before him as he followed Ronnie down the corridor.

She stayed with him until he was walking again past the reception desk and his step grew quicker as he entered the balcony and she was there, as she'd said she'd be. Wilson approached and sat down in the chair next to her without a word. She looked at him and smiled. He assumed he'd won the smile for his silence and he maintained it; he waited for her to speak.

Finally she said, "Why are you here?"

Again, he felt he knew what she meant, in spite of the ambiguity. He preferred to fake a misunderstanding and answer, Because you're beautiful and I want to touch your face with my fingertips. But that would be bantering and she'd turn him away. She meant why was he in Alaska, and he silently cursed his job for forcing him to lie from the outset with this woman. "I'm from the corporate office. I'm a writer..."

He was ready to say more but she said, "A p.r. man?" There

was a faint sneer in her voice.

Wilson's anger at his position sharpened, but it drove him deeper into the cover. "You a former reporter or something?" he said. "You said 'p.r. man' with a hot-shot reporter's contempt."

"I'm sorry," she said, though there was no warmth to it. "No, I've never been a journalist, but..." she hesitated briefly. "Well, press secretaries, press agents, flacks, aren't exactly a mystery to the world at large."

"Hey, look," Wilson said. "It's a job. My identity isn't staked in it...Anymore than your being a receptionist..."

"You're right," she said with finality.

The two sat in silence for a time, the woman's eyes fixed on Wilson. He did not feel uneasy, though. He was excited by her gaze, as if she were watching his penis. Then he said, "May I ask your name?"

"Marta."

He waited a moment for her last name, but she was done.

"I'm Wilson..."

"Hand."

"Yes." He remembered Ronnie saying his name yesterday morning in her presence. He was pleased she'd noticed, and his pleasure instantly struck him: he desired this woman very much. He waited some more, holding back from his urge to talk, to probe.

Then Marta said, "Yesterday morning, when you went out with Ronnie...why didn't you look back at me?" She said this with the same steadiness, the same self-possession that she'd shown from the first, but Wilson suddenly felt her vulnerability.

"I wanted to," he said.

"Yes?"

"I didn't know what to say, if I turned."

"Why would you have to say anything?" she said, irritation rushing her words.

"I didn't think of that. I was still smarting from your remark about banter and the only things that would come out of my mouth if I turned would be..."

"You didn't need *any* words..."

"I understand."

Marta sat back in her chair, puffed her cheeks briefly in exasperation. Wilson wanted to press her, probe her exasperation. But he knew to wait. Then at last she said, "If I ask you to come with me now. To my room. Can you keep quiet? No words?"

For a moment he could not answer. He could not fill himself with enough air to make a sound. The skin on his chest felt as if it were exposed to the air. His ardor, he knew, led him to the ideal response anyway—he simply nodded.

Marta smiled again. Her eyes were still wide but they seemed to soften. Her hands rose up and they were slender; Wilson looked at her fingers and the thought that they would soon touch him made the fingers on his own hands stretch and spread like an infant's.

He followed her. They turned into his hallway and he almost said, I live down this way too. But he caught himself. No words. No words. And he felt his mind let go to this—the simplicity of it, stripped down—and he sensed its rightness for him. This woman knew. She was in touch with what he'd come to Alaska for.

They stopped before a door. She opened it and they were in her room. It was, in shape and content, exactly the same as Wilson's. And it was bare. No photos, no prints, no desktop clutter. Only a hair brush by the TV, a sweater on the bed, a stack of *New York Times* on the desk. An article was outlined in marker pen on the top front page—an article on oil imports. And that was all. No other signs of her in the room.

She was standing in the center of the floor and the light from the window held her in a hazy penumbra and for the moment Wilson's eyes could not see her very well, she was dark in the shadow. But he saw her arms lift and the sweater she wore was gone and then she began to unbutton her blouse and by the time she was naked before him he could see her clearly, his eyes had dilated like hers, had opened wide to her. The skin of her body was as white and fragile as her face: she seemed more naked than any woman he'd ever seen. Her nipples were large and dark and he stepped to her, bent to her, kissed each nipple and she touched the back of his head with both her hands, gently pressed him down to his knees, drew his face into her softest flesh.

As he kissed her there he heard the wind blowing, out in the Arctic dusk. He kissed her there, stroked her with his tongue, stroking in long curls, modulating with the wind, following the barren wind, his eyes pressing shut and he grasped her now tight against his face, his hands spread on the back of her thighs. He felt he was the culmination of the wind, he was its final reach as it swept cold and dry down from the pole and suddenly, in this final touch and swirl, grew warm, grew wet, linking him to this woman, this soft woman, this wordless woman.

She kneeled now, removed his clothes, quickly, her hands adept at button, sleeve, pant leg, he was naked before her and she laid him out on the floor and she made a sound, low in her throat, as she grasped his penis in her hand and bent to him. She had a thin gold chain—as thin as the thinnest necklace—around her waist and another thin gold chain at her ankle. He spread his arms out and closed his eyes and she made no more sounds as she sucked at him, not a sound, and the wind fell and he could hear only his own breath. He wondered if he would slip back; there was no image yet of the room in Vietnam but he expected it, imagined it shaping somewhere inside him. But the wind quickened, it filled Marta's room now and he felt himself being compressed, all the nerves of his body being drawn in, tighter, like the mass of a collapsing star, into the head of his penis, held deep inside Marta's mouth. Then she drew back, stood up and crouched down on him, fitting him to her and he pulled her torso down and she was breathing very fast, he felt her chest heave against his, and as he came he felt her begin to quake as if in the wind, and at that moment their mouths touched for the first time.

They lay together on the floor and Wilson wanted to keep the stillness in his mind, the stillness Marta wanted, but he was full of questions about her—he knew nothing, nothing at all, not even her last name—and as much as he wanted only to listen to the wind and hold her against him, he could not stop his mind. He knew he would soon speak, so he rose and dressed and as he did she curled tight on the floor, as if she were sleeping. When he was dressed he knelt beside her. The gold chain around her waist accentuated her nakedness, began to nibble at his desire again, but he simply bent and kissed her on the point of the hip and stood up.

"My week off starts tomorrow," Marta said without moving, without opening her eyes. "I won't go. I'll stay here. Come back to me tomorrow."

Wilson did not speak. He knelt again and pushed the hair back off her face and he touched her lightly on the temple, the faint blue veins, he kissed her there and rose and left the room, closing the door so that it made no noise at all.

The next day the fog came in and there was little light, even at midday. Wilson looked out the van window as they crossed the tundra, moving away from a cluster of drill sites, on out the gravel road lined with hand-sized reflectors. They passed a snow-blowing truck going the opposite way and then there was nothing to see at all, just a segment of road preceding them into the fog. Wilson had a memory of Marta on the surface of his skin—along his chest, his arms—but he did not consciously think of her. Moving through the fog, out on the tundra, the world empty, he felt a pleasure now, a keen pleasure that held him in suspension, made him think he might even know what he was doing in coming to Alaska. He felt the way he'd briefly felt with Clyde, flying through the pass at night, flying in the whiteout. The edge of physical danger was gone, but moving through an empty landscape—this was what touched him, cleared him, clutched into him, finding a correspondence there. In this emptiness he didn't feel empty. He sensed something shaping in him and he tried to speak it, speak it in his mind, simply shape a clear thought around it, find words to touch it, probe it like a quiet suspect. This was a mistake. The feeling vanished. He groped harder after it and he became suddenly aware of Ronnie beside him tapping a finger on the steering wheel, became aware of the smell of stale cigarette smoke in the van, felt the flow of hot air from the dashboard vent, heard the heater motor grinding above the engine. Marta was right, he thought. No words. But still he wanted to understand, clearly.

He tried to focus on the fog. He pressed his face to the window. But he thought instead that this trip would soon end; they'd soon be inside another great shed full of pipes and sounds. Pump station number one was their destination, deep in the center of the field, where the oil was sucked on out of the system and into the pipeline.

Ahead was a cycloptic eye emerging from a hazy dream: a light spot emerging, quivering: a napalm-yellow flare quivering in the fog: a flare stack, its flame burning in the center of a cluster of buildings. Two red and white crude tanks passed and the van turned and stopped by a large metal building.

Ronnie began to talk, his voice moving by rote over the procedure of oil to metering building to holding tanks to booster pump. Wilson blocked out Ronnie's voice. He was prepared to feel the same uneasiness that he had at the flow station, the same sense of clutter that he knew was part of what he'd left in New York. But then he heard Ronnie say, "That's the beginning of it."

"What?"

"The pipeline. There." Ronnie pointed before them to a small, gray, corrugated metal shack. Out of one side of the shack a forty-eight inch pipe emerged, jogged left, and disappeared into the fog.

Ronnie opened the door of the van and began to get out. Wilson moved slowly, opened his own door, put the hood of his parka over his head, and he was caught by the modest grey shack. All the oil from all over the North Slope was drawn out here, purged, cast off. This vision fit him, fit his state of mind, blotted out the scattering of buildings and stacks and tanks nearby, brought him back to the fog and the tundra. Ronnie said,

"This way," and he tried to lead Wilson to the main pump building. Wilson grew conscious of a sound from there, a whine filling the air—the modified jet engines running the main pumps —they whined without modulation, crying for some climactic sound but never achieving it—they cried to him of the tangle of machinery inside, the confusion, unresolved.

"No," Wilson said. "I want to go there instead." He pointed to the grey shack. Ronnie shrugged his shoulders and Wilson followed him.

Inside the shack, things were simple. The pipe rose from the ground with a brief flurry of gauges and then moved through the wall. Wilson took a step away from Ronnie, stood alone in the center of the place and he felt a faint vibration in his feet, heard a deep, liquid sighing repeated over and over, a sound that drew Wilson even nearer to the pipe. The curve of metal, darkness, the tundra beyond and the fog, and Wilson removed his glove and laid his hand there on the pipe. It was warm. The sighs from inside it gripped him. He felt as if he were being stripped—his clothes, his skin, the layers of his mind—and it was pleasant— the removing of heavy garments in a warm place. But the sighs sharpened, the sounds from the pipe, from the earth, grew insistent, the sounds turned from sighs to a sibilant keening. And Wilson was aware of the oil being pulled from the earth—he was aware of a source of sustenance being drawn down—draining away—he felt the process physically, in his own body—he felt weak, his legs grew weak, he sensed the oil flowing, lost forever, he felt it beneath his hand. He stepped back. He was suddenly afraid. He'd sought this. Alaska called him for this. He wanted to strip away the clutter of things. But this scared him. He was afraid the earth would begin to crumble under his feet, the great, deep wells emptied, unable in their emptiness to support the earth above. He was afraid that there was nothing in this land, nothing in himself. Beth knew. Beth knew to put down layers of things—possibilities—Beth was right—but the thought of her scared him too—the thought of what she was, what she'd become before her death—and all the things, all the clutter, did not block the path to the balcony—the railing—that leap. Wilson backed off. He backed off and turned and pushed past Ronnie and out into the cold wind, his eyes burned, his hand burned in the cold, the hand he'd placed on the pipe; he raised it to his face and found it was still bare.

He met Marta's ardor aggressively with his own that afternoon, with the panic of his vision in the pump station driving his limbs, his hands, his mouth. Afterwards, Marta lay motionless and naked beside him on the floor of her room. She was on her back, her arms straight at her sides, one knee drawn up, her eyes closed. The darkness had come already outside but Marta had turned two lamps on before they'd begun and in the lapping circles of light from desk and chair her nakedness filled him up at last. Wilson crouched beside her and his hands went gently out, one touched a breast, its nipple poking up at once, one touched the tuft of her pubic hair. Then he lifted his hands just slightly so that he could only barely feel her skin on his palms— not quite knowing if he only remembered the touch, or if it was just her warmth that he felt, or if he actually touched her lightly. He moved his hands, passed them over her skin like this, he closed his eyes, moving his hands, and he thought of Beth, of how, when they began to fondle their way toward making love, she always grew impatient if his hands were still, how she always wanted his two hands in different places, both active, each touching a different part of her. Her very skin desired clutter, he thought now. And she was gone. Suddenly he felt her absence in his hands. The body he'd touched had vanished. He felt the vacancy in himself. He had to fill that space. He opened his eyes to look at Marta's body. Marta. Her nipples were large, they could fit his palms, and they were the color of Chelsea brick. He leaned near her breasts and her nipples held all of this woman: they did not prompt memories of her words, her gestures, her walk, but rather they subsumed all of that, they fixed him with their own vivid particularity and his arm ached for a moment, his broken arm, one of his captors had hit it with his rifle butt that morning, hit it with just the right force to hurt Wilson but not unset the bone. Wilson thought of his own reaction—the pain had contracted his mind and in the contraction all the fear, all the hatred had been squeezed out; he'd felt cleansed. He turned his head and through the window beside him a sharp-edged shaft of sunlight came through. There was silence in the room. A scrape of wood as one of his captors stretched a leg, then silence again. Wilson thought he could hear the movement of the palm fronds outside in the breeze but then his eyes fixed on the motes of dust moving in the sunlight. Hunched tight on the floor of this shack, yanked out of the flow of his life, placed on the edge of torture and death, he watched the motes of dust floating in the sunlight and they flared in reflected light for a moment and turned and vanished with their thin edge and turned further to catch the sun again. The dust floated up the shaft, the motes of dust dazzled Wilson, took his breath away and there was a hand on him. The dust twirled faster, flashing in the sunlight and the hand pressed through to his bare skin.

"Wilson."

He turned his face and for a moment he saw nothing. The room was empty. Dark.

"Wilson."

Marta was sitting beside him, her face very close, her dark eyes open to him. "Are you all right?" she said, her voice finally as soft as her skin. She leaned forward and kissed him on the forehead and put her arms around his shoulders as if he were a child awakened from a bad dream.

He let her hold him for a moment, did not move; he was afraid to frighten off this sudden tenderness in her. His flashbacks, Beth, the fear now of Alaska—he wanted to wipe them all away. His hand came up slowly and he laid it gently on Marta's bare back. He wanted to clutch her to him but he waited. "Marta," he said.

"Yes?"

"Sometime I want us to talk. Not banter. But I want to know you."

"Yes," she said, her voice still gentle. "Yes...Tomorrow, my love."

Marta slowly pulled away. She rose and turned off the lights and drew him into the bed. He entered her and they moved only enough to keep him firmly there; they stayed linked for as long as they could and listened to the Arctic wind outside speaking of the ceaseless night to come.

7.

Wilson woke and Marta was gone. He turned and the room was full of light. She was standing naked in the center of the floor and she was watching him. They looked at each other in silence, but this time the silence did not seem tense or tyrannical. They were silent from the ease between them, the connection. Then the shadows of the ravens fell across her—a dark pox passing through her skin—and the shadows were gone. Wilson wanted to hear her voice.

"Do you feel the difference in this silence now?" he said.

"Difference?"

"This moment now. How it's different from the silences between us before."

Marta smiled and crossed to the bed. She lay down beside him and said, "Don't worry. I remember what I said last night. We'll talk about each other, if you want."

"That's not why I said..."

"I know."

"Besides, don't you want to know something about me? Who I am? Is this just a concession you're making for my benefit?"

Marta pursed her lips in thought. Wilson wanted to kiss them, but he held back; he was more interested in her answer.

She said, "There are things I want to know about you...Yes ...But every man I've ever known who tried to explain himself to me just talked crap. Trivial crap...And they made me talk the same way about myself."

Wilson felt the look of incomprehension on his own face, though in fact he understood clearly what she was saying.

Marta flipped her hair back with a little toss of her head. "Don't you know how easy this is for me?" From her gesture, Wilson was surprised that her voice wasn't brittle again; instead it was weary, almost sad.

"How easy what is?" he said.

Now her voice hardened a bit. "Going to bed with a stranger."

Wilson winced at this—the reaction surprised him—but he kept it inside.

She softened again; her eyes that could fix on him so intently shifted away. "I've made love with an awful lot of men in the past few years."

In his limbs Wilson felt the flush of a vague jealousy. He said, "And none of them talked much."

"Most of them weren't the talking type."

Wilson's face grew warm. He puffed out air as if his lungs were filled with smoke.

"I bet you regret making me speak now," Marta said.

"No," Wilson said at once. "No."

"Listen," Marta said, her voice hard—an act of the will, Wilson knew—"Listen," she said again. "Only two reasons a woman would come to a place like this—men or money...I've always had all the money I need."

"I'm sure you've always had the men you need, too," Wilson said, though he did not mean it to bite in the obvious way. He was not lashing out at her professed promiscuity; instead, he knew she was lying about Alaska—he knew her presence here wasn't as simple as she implied.

"I've always had men," Marta said, angry now. "But outside, they all want to talk. I can't stand their goddam prattle." Marta sat up abruptly, turned as if she were about to rise from the bed, but she paused. She stayed where she was.

Wilson lay back, watched the ceiling, wondered if he should try to say any more.

"Listen," Marta said. "I don't think you're like that. I wouldn't have said this much if I did."

Wilson looked at her. Her back was still to him. He felt her bare back drawing Beth near and he touched Marta's shoulder. He didn't want Beth in this room.

Marta turned at his touch and said, "You know, I feel two ways at once. I could love any man I'm with or I could love no one. It's such a tiny shift in me."

"Why are you here?"

"You're right," she said, answering the unspoken premise of his question. "I didn't come here for men. If anything it was a resolve to shift the other way. I got tired of life down there."

"Where, exactly?"

"California."

"Yes?"

"I liked the...what?...rigors of Alaska. I thought I'd just get away from all the crap. I'd already tried to fuck my way to some kind of resolution in my life. This seemed to be the other path...I don't know."

"Did it work that way?"

"No. No, it didn't."

"You went back to..." he regretted starting the question but instead of breaking it off, he just finished it elliptically. "...the other way?"

"I started fucking around again?" Her voice was very hard.

"I don't mean to..."

"Don't back out of the question," she said. "From the way I've acted so far with you, I should admire it. It's a logical, no-bullshit question."

"But I don't want to know."

"Why?"

"I just don't..."

Marta closed her eyes and shook her head, a gesture of faint exasperation.

"Don't be alarmed," Wilson said. "It's not that I'm getting serious about you. At least not in the way you've no doubt learned to fear."

"What is it you want me to say to you?" Marta asked, the hardness gone.

Wilson didn't know. There was no clear objective for his questions. He'd felt suddenly empty in Alaska and then Marta filled him up. He wanted more of her and he knew he'd be cut off by their silences. But now it seemed that they had to force things. He could not remember what it was he'd wanted to know the night before. What did he care about? He thought of Beth and he said, "Death...Somebody has died in my life...Let's start with death...What do you know of it?"

Marta stretched out beside him again on the bed. She touched his mouth with her fingertips, watching her own fingers move or watching his lips—he wasn't sure what was in her mind. Just as he thought she wouldn't speak, she said, "My father died when I was twelve. That's the only real experience I've had."

"Tell me about him."

"Not much to tell. There...wasn't much time to know him."

"You had twelve years with him."

"We existed concurrently for twelve years. That's not the same thing."

"He was distant?"

"We were very rich," she said. "He was a very big man in Wall Street. A broker. He had six children by another wife who'd died and I was my mother's only child. Not that he was very close to the others either. We'd flock about him on Sunday afternoons like he was a politician on an election stop. Oh, there were gifts, too, of course, and I guess those were supposed to make it all up. When I was nine he bought me a doll house as tall as I was and furnished it down to the poker at the fireplace. That year his love was a doll house. When I was ten he bought me a horse. Equestrian-love. Eleven it was a movie camera. Filmic-love. Then he died. So I missed out on debutante-party-love, trip-to-Europe-love, Maserati-convertible-love."

Marta stopped speaking. Wilson thought of her room here. Only a hair brush, a stack of newspapers, her clothes scattered on the floor. Did she answer the same call that he did to come to this place?

"But death," she said. "You asked me about death...You know the worst part?"

"What?"

"When he was dying—it took him three weeks—he wanted me with him. He had me sit beside his hospital bed and hold his hand and he wept and he told me he loved me and he had this terrible regret—the worst regret of his life, he said—that he hadn't spent more time with me. He clasped me in his dying hand for three weeks and he said all the right things. All the things I'd lived twelve years craving and doing without. And instead of weeping too and accepting what he was finally giving, I grew harder and harder. I hated him." Her voice was very low, almost obscured by the wind. "I hated him for it," she said.

Wilson touched her hand but she drew it away. He understood the feelings that moved her and he wanted to make love now, wanted to enter her quickly, while this feeling was still strong, to join his orgasm with his understanding. He tried to take her hand again but she propped herself up and turned on her side to face him.

"Who died in your life?" she said.

Wilson didn't want to talk. He was aware of the irony of this, but he could not bring himself either to express the irony or talk about Beth. He remained silent.

"Are you going to start cheating at this game?" she said.

"No."

"Then talk to me. You're the one who began this shit."

"My ex-wife died. She jumped off her balcony a few weeks ago." His voice was flat. He was detached from Beth's death. He suddenly felt detached from Marta as well. He still felt he understood her in some fundamental way. But it was from a distance now and when he realized this, he said, "Damn."

"Damn what?"

"Nothing. I'm sorry. This isn't working out like I planned."

They were silent a moment. Wilson expected Marta to chide him for initiating this talk and then trying to drop out. But she said, "Was she in your mind last night when you were passing your hands over me?"

"My hands?" He repeated the words reflexively, surprised by her insight.

"Last night after we'd made love, you closed your eyes and you touched me very lightly all over with your hands. Was she in your mind?"

"Yes," he said and the feeling that he understood Marta sharpened, made him feel close to her again. "We seem to know each other pretty well."

"Have you thought of her a lot since we've been together?"

"No. No, I haven't. I've thought of you."

"You don't have to say that," she said, her voice brittle. "I'm just curious."

"It's true. But you can consider it unimportant, if you wish."

"I'm not jealous of her, is all I mean. I'm not jealous of anyone...I hope you're not."

"You don't have to worry," Wilson said.

"I'm not very loyal. Not to people. Not to places..."

"You don't have to worry, Marta," he said sharply. Speaking her name felt very odd—she flinched and he pulled back, a little ashamed, as if he'd just hit her.

"I'm sorry," she said.

"I don't know your last name."

"Walsh...Did you hear me?"

"What?"

"I'm sorry. I didn't mean to...create friction around your ex-wife. This thing about jealousy...I just want us to relax with each other, enjoy each other without all the..." She paused to find a word.

"Clutter," he said.

"Yes."

"It was my fault for making us talk."

"That was all right. We talked about things that mattered."

Wilson pushed back her hair and put his fingertips on her temple, on the faint blue veins there. He and Marta were finished with words for the morning but he wanted to keep just enough of them in his head—about her father's death—so that he would feel close to her in the way he had moments ago. But when they began to kiss, all the words were gone and all the closeness he felt danced in his prick.

In a windowless room with an acoustical ceiling Wilson watched a man with a face constellated with warts—one of the names on his list—as he panted smoke rings into the air. "Never," the man said in answer to a question by Wilson. "I never work beyond six. It's a one-shift department at the record center but we get it all done...You gonna take photos for this brochure?"

"Ah...yes," Wilson said, wondering why a man with this face would be wanting to know about photos.

"If you do, I'd like to get some prints of my buddies," the man said.

"I'll see what I can arrange."

"Good."

"How much of the exploration information do you work with?" Wilson asked.

"Exploration reports? Oh, just pieces of that."

"Pieces only?"

"That's right."

"Who works with it all?"

"Exploration. Not current production?"

"That's right."

"None of us, really. The big picture on potential reserves shapes up in the computer. The analysis...most of that—all, really—goes on back in Anchorage."

"But all the pieces are here, between the computer and the files."

"I guess so...Sure."

Wildon nodded; the tape recorder stopped. He flipped the tape and started the machine again, thinking this p.r. cover was a mistake. He could ask questions but he couldn't really dig at anything without arousing suspicion. He wanted to surprise this man now, make him uncomfortable, see where his flash points were, but Wilson felt constrained by his own pose.

Later, he stopped at Finn's office and said, "This cover is too tight. I can't ask the tough questions."

Finn shrugged. "We thought it would be all right—the best for you, this way...No one really knows about the thefts, even around the information center. The man who discovered that something had been taken out of the computer..."

"Fred Parini."

"Yes," Finn said.

"I saw him today."

"We said thank you very much to Parini and played it very casually...I found out about the hard copy thefts myself after that...No alarms or commotion...This way, if you wanted to sit in at the center, you could do it as some vapid p.r. guy on assignment and there'd be no suspicion that..."

Wilson grew weary of all this. "Forget it. It's okay."

"If you prefer to come in as an investigator, that's your decision. But people get uptight...They stop talking, don't they? I don't mean to tell you your business..."

Wilson's teeth hurt, his shoulders hunched, as if he were listening to the screak of chalk on a blackboard. He grunted at Finn and turned and strode from the office. Stake out the information center, spend time there. A logical way to proceed. But Wilson wanted no part of that. He'd talk to the people on his list—and take his time at that—and hang on to Alaska for as long as he could. He had several months of grace, even if he made no progress at all.

He stopped at the balcony railing behind the receptionist's desk. Alaska still shortened his breath; he still sensed the life of it being pumped out. The pipe came up from the ground and broke through the wall of the pump station and keened its oil away. A foolish fear, he knew, and it was fading. But he realized it wasn't Alaska he was hanging onto now. It was Marta. He walked off briskly toward her room; he wanted to run. And he was determined to keep his silence now, to do it her way.

Soon the days shrank to a brief rise and fall of the sun and then a bright dusk and then, the day before Thanksgiving, darkness. Wilson recognized the beginning of the Arctic night without anyone pointing it out—his body knew it clearly, felt the brief crack of midday light seal up. On that day he and Marta touched each other softly; he entered her gingerly, as if a stern parent were sleeping beyond a thin wall. When they'd come, Wilson stayed inside her; they did not move.

"You know what today is?" Marta said, almost whispering.

"Yes."

"It frightens me."

Wilson tightened his arms around her; she kissed him on the throat, a reflex. He liked her fear. But it reverberated in him and he said, "It's odd."

"What?"

"I know a sensible thing for me to say right now is let's get away from here. We're neither of us doing work we like, we've found each other, and if the place frightens us, let's get the hell out."

"That's the sensible thing."

"But I'm not ready to leave," he said. "It's out of the question and I'm not sure why."

"I know why."

"Yes?"

"When I get scared, it just sharpens my enjoyment of this." She drew the cover up over their heads and cupped his penis in her hand.

"Is that why we're here?" he said.

"Yes."

They kissed and began again to make love. Just as he was about to enter her, Marta said, "I've got a little surprise for you."

"What is it?"

"You like words so much...A little surprise."

He smiled at her telling him this at a moment when he would be least inclined to ask more questions.

The next morning Marta took Wilson down to the first level, past the darkened glass doors where he smelled chlorine and deep into the central building to a double doorway.

"Here's your surprise," she said, and they pushed through the doors. They were at the back of a small chapel. There were wooden pews full of men in flannel shirts—Wilson saw no other women—a wooden lectern on a six-inch high platform, and a large black metal cross against the back wall.

"This?" Wilson whispered.

"Him," Marta said and she nodded toward the lectern.

A man was speaking. Someone shouted "Amen" and the man talked on. He was thin and silver—his hair was silver and there was a flash of silver on the lapel of his navy blazer. But his face seemed young—smooth and pink and molded with prominent ridges and hollows like a cheap hand puppet; his eyes were the only thing animated in his face and they were large—as large as Marta's and as dark—and they widened and narrowed with every nuance of his words. He raised a Bible for a point.

It finally struck Wilson that this was what Marta brought him here for; she'd even made a special event of it, a surprise. He looked at her and she was watching the preacher at the lectern. He felt a low-grade awe before Marta—the same sort of feeling he'd had for Beth just before the end of her life—a feeling that there was a cold, alien fire in her—a madness of great purity.

"Do you believe in this?" he whispered to her.

"Listen to him," she said.

Wilson turned back to the preacher. The Bible was still lifted high. His voice was loud and full but with the suggestion of more to come—he was in the middle of a build. "You know what I'm saying is right."

There was a ripple of affirmation in the crowd. Amen. Tell it, brother.

"These other pansy-assed churches want us to get close to the ritual instead of getting close to God."

Amen, voices said from the crowd.

The preacher said, "They ask me to cling to the raft when

God wants me to swim in the sea.''

Amen. Amen.

The preacher boomed, ''And that's chickenshit.''

The congregation brayed its approval. Amen. Chickenshit. Amen.

The preacher stepped back and his hands spread at his sides. His voice pitched low and he said, ''And they don't really want me to believe that Jesus existed as a man like you and me. Let me tell you something about the way he died. When they hung a man on a cross they stripped him down to that part of him that would die and rot. Do you think they gave a damn about his modesty or ours? When Jesus was put on that cross he was stripped naked. Totally naked. His tribulation in this trap of human flesh was fuller than any of your pansy-assed churches have ever let you know. Every crucifix in the world is a sacrilege, a spit in Christ's face, a denial of the shame he suffered for us. Jesus had a cock. And it was exposed on the cross. If you can't think of that, if you can't say it, if you can't look at it, then you're not understanding what the hell happened back then. They hung Jesus naked there...'' The preacher's voice cracked, he stopped for a moment. Wilson could see the tears in the man's eyes even from where he stood. ''...and it was worse than the churches have ever let you imagine...They sanitize it, abstract it, print it in careful little numbered lines on paper...'' The preacher was howling now, his arms had risen above him. ''Tell us in Alaska that's the way it was. Tell these men in this room that's the way it was—a modest drape, a bent knee, a graceful pose . . . It's a lie.''

Amen, the congregation cried. Amen.

''It's a lie!'' the preacher bellowed.

Men jumped up in the congregation and raised their arms and their affirmation grew unintelligible, the shouts skidded and bumped and lurched through the room.

Wilson looked at Marta. She was quiet and she seemed to sense his gaze and she turned to him. She smiled her faint, half-smile and then transferred the smile to the silver-haired man. Wilson understood why the man interested her, why she thought that bringing Wilson here was a special event. The preacher certainly did strip away the trivia that Marta hated. Wilson wanted to touch her now, pull her to him, take her to their room. The shouts and sweat and movement in the chapel were beginning to make him uneasy. But he turned his own attention back to the preacher.

The man was calm again, beginning another build.

"And who would the world expect?" the preacher said. "Who would *you* expect if you'd never seen what you felt to be the true God? He's going to walk into the room tonight in human form. Who would you expect? Who could command this long night, these enormous mountains, this great Arctic land? A carpenter? A man with no possessions but a simple cloak, a staff, a pair of sandals? A man who tells us to love those who hate us? A man who had only a handful of fishermen and working men as his inner circle of followers? Could you see God as a nobody, a man with no wealth, no possessions, nothing?" The preacher stopped abruptly again and in the silence Wilson became aware of the graveled richness of his voice. Wilson found himself leaning toward him, waiting for the next words. He thought of Marta telling him she had this surprise for him because he liked words. Yes, he thought. This man was full of arresting words.

And the preacher said, drawing back, his hands spreading, his voice soaring in mock-surprise, "What an amazing thing. What an astonishing vision of God. This nobody. This humble man, quietly trekking a few dozen miles here and there two thousand years ago and he ravaged the world with his love...I know some truly evil bunglers—multitudes of them—got hold of his word and they screwed it all up...They're doing it still. But God can still talk to us. Powerfully. Through that nobody who owned nothing and went nowhere and who even himself despaired at the last minute...That's what you have to be thankful for today. Be thankful, workers of Alaska. He's here right now. Closer to you than to anyone else."

Then the preacher led the congregation in a song from their hymnal—a loping, commercial-jingle of a tune with doggerel verse and Wilson stepped out of the double doors to escape. Marta followed.

"He's a real show, isn't he?" Marta said.

"Do you believe in his God?"

"I think only *he* believes in *his* God."

"The others seemed to be with him."

"He talks their language..."

"I was a little surprised at your interest in all this," Wilson said.

"I've seen him a few times as he's passed through. He does a circuit, preaching up here. I thought you'd find him amusing. That's all."

"Do you know him well enough to introduce us?"

"Sure," she said. "Maybe he'd be interesting in this brochure or whatever, that you're doing."

This reference to his cover identity as if it were real, particularly from Marta, shocked him. He realized how completely he'd let his job at Moonbase slip. He hadn't even thought of his cover in several days. "Perhaps," he said, and the preacher's words bled into his thoughts: I feel like I'm swimming in the sea.

The double doors burst open and the men began to flow out, talking volubly in twos and threes, laughing, peace brother, God bless you. Marta and Wilson pressed past the departing men and back into the chapel. Two familiar faces went by—Brian Finn and Ronnie, moving together; Finn saw Wilson and nodded with a quizzical expression.

The preacher was at the lectern talking to two men who pulled away with God-bless-you's as Marta and Wilson approached. The preacher turned his face to Wilson first and then to Marta, and up close he still seemed an odd combination of youth and age, his face pink and rubber-smooth, his hair silver. The flash of silver at his lapel was not an Energy Independence pin, which Wilson had expected, but a stylized silver fish, the secret sign of early Christians.

"Hello," the preacher said, his voice full and resonant, as if he'd just said amen to a long prayer.

Marta said, "I'm...Marta Walsh."

The preacher's brow furrowed, as if he were vaguely surprised at this.

She went on, "I want you to meet Wilson Hand. He's a communications man from the corporate office. He's doing some projects up here at Moonbase and I thought he should meet you." Marta turned to Wilson and said, "This is Eli...Is it *Pastor* Eli?"

"Eli is sufficient."

"Eli..." Marta hesitated.

"Marcus," the preacher said. The man's eyes moved to Wilson and his face became fixed, summoning again the image of a puppet's head to Wilson—a benign face but lifeless behind its animated pose.

"I was interested in your message," Wilson said. "But in view of it I was surprised at the vapid song you had them sing afterwards."

Eli's eyebrows arched high and he seemed to be considering his next gesture. Then he smiled. "You're right, of course."

"You challenge your believers and then you give them doggerel to sing."

"I surrender," Eli said, raising his hands. "Go easy on me, Mr. Hand. You had me with your first salvo...The song was crap. Nearly all the songs in that hymnal are crap. But these are good bedrock fundamentalists and they need their little tunes as well. They need their little bits of poster-slogan verse. I can't remake them all overnight, now can I?"

Wilson had nothing to say to this. Eli had shut him up, blocked him off from the kind of probing he prided himself in. And he felt no resentment at this; he respected the man for it, admired him even.

Eli stretched out his hand and laid it on Wilson's shoulder. His voice grew soft. "Really, the point you made is very well taken. It makes me happy that you have such a sensitive understanding of my most important message.''

Wilson did not know how to interpret Eli's attitude. Was the man sincerely and gently anxious that Wilson not feel he'd been put down? Or was he smugly patronizing? Wilson suddenly knew he could probe the preacher, could open him up. But he said nothing. He was tired of all this. The mood of Eli's sermon had not yet faded from the air of this place—its aggressive seriousness—and Wilson preferred to keep a sense of that than to talk any further to the man himself. He wanted to take Marta to bed now: more strokes of the swimmer in the sea.

''Do you know how important we've all become?'' the young man said and his hands reached out over the table. Wilson tried to place this bland, round, small-featured face from the chapel yesterday. This fervor reminded him of Eli's congregation.

''I bet that's what your articles are going to be about,'' the young man said.

Wilson had questions to ask to bring this man back to the point, but he didn't ask them. He stared sightlessly at the list of names in front of him. He'd started at the bottom of the list and the last five were scratched off. The young man babbled on and Wilson shifted about in his chair. He wanted to return to Marta who was probably napping now, naked in their bed. He wanted to sit at their window and watch the spill of light outside and wait for the ravens to fly through—shards of the long night, tumbling in the wind.

''All this oil here,'' the young man said, ''all these wonderful reservoirs underneath us...we just have to tap in.''

Wilson raised his eyes. The round face floated there, serene, confident. A broken-chain pin glinted on his collar. ''It's all here,'' the man said.

And in spite of Wilson's boredom at this job, in spite of his irritation at the young man's mannerisms, in spite of his desire to be somewhere else, Wilson saw the oil below them, vast oceans of oil roiling beneath the earth, and the last traces of the fear he'd felt at the pump station vanished.

"It's in our best interests now," the young man said with a smile, a confidential tone. "I mean *Royal's* best interests—to start tapping in to all the oil that's here...The time's right. But we've known about it all along. I guess you won't get into *that*, right, Mr. Hand?"

"No. No I won't."

"I wanted to go into p.r. once," the young man said.

"That's all I'll need from you. Thanks," Wilson said, trying to cut him off.

The man prattled on about public relations as Wilson rose and guided him to the door. He let the man go out and closed the door and leaned against the wall; his head lolled back, he looked at the even rows of holes in the acoustical ceiling. He was tired of the game he was playing. He had no interest at all in finding the documents. He wanted to make love with Marta and sit at the window. All these other demands on him made him feel frantic. He wanted to touch Marta—yes—but even that was distant at the moment—he felt crowded—he closed his eyes—he hated the investigation and that pressed his eyes open again. He felt suddenly reckless.

He stepped out into the hall. He would go to Marta now. She would touch him and he'd be able to focus his mind again. He took two steps and stopped. Up ahead, the young man he'd just interviewed was standing by the reception desk with the man with the wart-filled face. Wilson wanted to shake them up, wanted to grab them and throw them aside, like toppling the boxes in Beth's apartment. He moved forward and had difficulty drawing a breath. He passed by them, clenching his fists, holding any words inside. But the young man turned as Wilson passed. "Hi, Mr. Hand," the man said. "Are we going to get copies of the thing you write?"

"Don't forget the pictures," the other man said.

Wilson stopped and turned and said, "Don't you know who I am by now?" The two faces went blank at once and Wilson felt a rush of pleasure, his hands jumped up in front of him. Wilson said, "Things are getting close enough to resolution now—all this chickenshit posing isn't going to be necessary much longer." The faces were beginning to gape. Wilson fought back a laugh. He said, "Just don't depend on your brochures and photos, boys. Things aren't quite what they seem. Just wait for the shit to hit the...pump station."

Wilson heard himself panting, he saw his hand cutting at the air in an insistent but vague gesture. The two men glanced briefly at each other. Wilson felt a sudden, intensely rational calm. He'd pissed away his cover. Okay. To these two men. He turned his face to the desk. The two plump women. He turned his face toward the corridor. Two men were standing there as well, watching. Fuck them all, Wilson said very calmly in his mind. Fuck them all.

He turned and walked briskly away. He went to Marta's room and knocked. There was no answer. He knocked again. "Marta," he said. "Marta."

He laid his head against the door. "Marta?" he said very softly, knowing now that she was out.

He sat down on the floor and leaned against the door to her room. Half a dozen people had heard his dark hints, had watched him fumble off his mask. Half a dozen people. By this time tomorrow anyone at Moonbase could know. "Fuck them all," he said as softly as he'd said Marta's name.

A few minutes later Marta was standing over him. She was a little out of breath and she smiled her half-smile. "What the hell are you doing down there?" she said.

"Waiting for you."

"I would have come to get you."

"It's all right. I didn't mind waiting." He stood up as she unlocked the door and then they were in the room and the door was closed and they were holding each other.

Marta's body touched his in familiar places; he pressed her close and at crotch, at upper thigh, at chest he felt her pressure; her smell—faintly citrus—was familiar, too, and her kiss on his jugular, the wet inside of her upper lip, the dry ridge of her lower lip. All this was intensely familiar to him; and the room, the brush on the desk today instead of the dresser, the stack of *New York Times* slightly taller, the top paper with an energy story circled—"Gas Production..."—and he closed his eyes. Holding her like this, knowing her now, knowing the little ridges and hollows, the sighs and gestures: he should have felt closer to her than ever. But he felt detached from her, as if she were a beautiful painting that had been on the same wall for years. His focus wavered.

"What do you think of all this up here?" he said.

"All what?"

"The oil. Taking the oil out. All the work up here...Maybe I sound crazy. I'm feeling restless today. I don't know."

Marta pulled back, looked him in the face; her brow furrowed, her eyes narrowed slightly. "The oil? What do you mean?"

"That preacher, I guess."

Marta cocked her head.

Wilson said, "I don't feel I'm swimming far enough out. I feel...bound up."

"Cabin fever."

"No. No, I don't think so...Do the wells affect you?"

Marta smiled. "That's an odd question."

"Is it too trivial for you?"

"No...I think about the oil sometimes...the operations up here...It's like sucking at God's tit."

He held her closer. He liked the leaps of her mind. He realized that his last few forays outside this room—yesterday with Eli, today's interview—had each ended in his wanting to do nothing but touch Marta. But with her in his arms now, her seriousness crackling between them like static electricity, he felt no clear prompting to begin. They held each other—the clinging of agitated electrons—for a long while, his erection a thin wisp of hair pulled up by the static, his feelings lumpy and immovable. Her hands were motionless on his back, her head lay motionless against his neck.

"I want to tell you something about myself," he said.

"Yes?" She did not move her head.

"I'm not a p.r. man." Even though she was very still against him, he sensed some further cessation in her.

Wilson was briefly reluctant to go on with this, but he knew that the truth would likely get around anyway and he wanted her to hear it from him. "I'm here on an investigation. There've been some...thefts at Moonbase and they sent me in here with a cover i.d. to let me nose around."

Marta had not moved.

He said, "You know, of course, this has nothing to do with us...I'm sorry I couldn't tell you this before. I..."

"No more words," she said.

Wilson kissed her and the tip of her tongue met his with a kind of languor and when the tongues touched they did not move but the hard tips lay against each other until it was time to undress. Wilson and Marta separated and began slowly to remove their clothes. His limbs felt heavy. He looked at Marta and she was folding her clothes neatly and placing them on the chair. He stopped and watched her. She held her skirt up and aligned the waistband and shook the wrinkles out and folded it very neatly. He looked at himself. Only his shirt was off, though it seemed as if he'd been undressing for a long while. He felt the impress of the buttons lingering on the tips of his fingers. His back itched in the center and he stopped and reached and scratched the spot; he scratched it for a few moments for the low-grade pleasure of it even after the itch was gone.

In bed they touched only corresponding parts—mouth only to mouth, thigh only to thigh, chest only to chest; they clung briefly and he entered her and he heard the buzz of the fluorescent light in the bathroom, the squeaking of the bedframe.

The coming was quiet—his while his mind was elsewhere—hers perhaps not at all. They lay beside each other without a word and he wondered at this encounter. He imagined it had been crouching in a doorway waiting all this time, like a mugger. He and Marta had been mugged by a banal fuck. Now he lay on an antiseptic table with minor wounds and a fear of it happening again.

Marta was sleeping. He rose quietly with a sudden urge to go out. He dressed and went down the hall to his room. He opened the door and switched on the light and it was as if he were in the same room and he'd just made Marta vanish. The same light was on, the chair was angled in the same way, the dresser top was clear. He went to the closet and opened his bag. He pulled out his cold-weather clothes and he began to dress for the wind he could hear sharply now, seventy-five below and even more severe in the gusts.

Wilson put on long underwear, cotton socks, thick wool socks. He put on a flannel shirt and a wool shirt, then a pair of wool trousers. He put on down pants, insulated rubber boots and he picked up his parka and woolen face mask and mittens and he left the room and went down the hall, his heart beginning to race. He knew now where he wanted to go—back to pump station number one.

He stopped at Marta's door and listened; there was no sound. He moved on down the hall, his rubber boots sucking and smacking in the stillness and when he turned the corner at the end, Eli Marcus was sitting on a chair on the wide balcony. Wilson passed him and wanted to say nothing but Eli stopped him. "Why, hello, Mr. Hand."

"I thought you'd gone on your way on the circuit," Wilson said.

"No. I'll be here through Sunday. Why don't you come on back and attend a full service?"

Wilson's feelings at this were complicated. He did not have a chance to analyze it—his impulse to test the man, to challenge his hold on him, gained quick ascendancy. "I'm afraid I don't like what you say or the way you say it, Pastor Eli."

Eli didn't show any surprise at this. He smiled and steepled his fingers before him. "Well, I'm afraid I can't help you much in *what* I say. But how I say it is, by and large, conscious rhetorical strategy. For example, in response to what you've just said, I might reply, 'I'm sorry you feel that way but bless you, Mr. Hand. I hope you find peace.' But instead I'll just say—and I want you to understand it *means* the same thing..." Eli leaned forward and smiled gently at Wilson. "...Mr. Hand, go fuck yourself."

Wilson thought he heard a tremor in Eli's voice and he kept his own voice very calm and said, "God bless you, Pastor Eli," and he turned and walked off, past the reception desk and into Finn's outer office. From a desk drawer he got the keys to a van that had been assigned to him and he put on his parka and his mask and his mittens and he went to the front door. He paused there briefly and watched the sprays of snow dashing past in the light. Two figures in parkas and masks came up the steps and through the doors and Wilson took a breath as if he were diving from a high board and he went through the two sets of doors and into the wind.

The force of the wind made him lift his shoulders and for a moment he was not aware of the cold. But as soon as he moved down the steps and out of the spill of light from the front doors his skin knew—even through all the layers, his skin sensed what the wind carried here. And he felt the thin, biting slip of air into his lungs. He knew he should walk slowly but the vehicle shed was not far and he moved as fast as his boots and down pants and parka would let him. At the door of the shed he turned back and looked at the center, high on its stanchions, the wind, its form visible in the snow dust, rushing beneath. And then, above the center, just outside the reach of its lights, he thought he saw a movement—but dark, not light—at first he fancied he could see the wind in the movement of the darkness—but then he knew it was ravens. One swooped briefly into the light and rejoined the others and Wilson's eyes rose as the murder of ravens swept up against the sky—his eyes moved with assurance, following them though in fact he did not really see them, black birds against midday black.

Wilson turned and entered the shed and passed along a row of vans glowing faintly in the halide lamps, a baby nursery of vans, each with an umbilical cord linking its battery to an electrical socket. He unhooked his van and checked the field map. He started the engine and pulled out of the shed and at last he was in the night, rushing past the center and onto the gravel road. He turned and sped off, pushing the darkness only a van's length ahead of him with his lights. He felt the van wanting to buck and twist in the wind; snow swirled in his headlights; the reflectors at the edges of the road flashed and receded. He looked in his rearview mirror and the van's reach of light was less than arm's length there. He felt wedged into the darkness as if it were a tight space and he felt the heaviness drain out of his limbs. He leaned forward over the wheel, glad to be out here; his sense of purpose—vague though it was—was renewed.

The two-way radio crackled and a faint voice said, "Five twenty-two, what is your location?"

"Just leaving JFK with a full boat," another voice said.

The "JFK" turned Wilson's head to the radio, but he thought that it was an ironic name for an airstrip nearby.

"Gimme your count," the first voice said.

"Okay," the second voice said. "I've got a Great Neck, two Roslyn, two Greenvale, an East Norwich, and a Huntington Post Office."

Halfway through the list of towns, Wilson knew that he was listening to a New York airport limousine service. The towns were all on Long Island. He'd heard of the phenomenon—radio bounce, where radio signals bounced on a level of ionization in the atmosphere and ended up somewhere else, far away, ready to be heard by any radio tuned to that frequency.

"Shuttle at Little Neck," the first voice said.

"10-4."

Wilson looked ahead at the maw of dark, and the New York voices, the place names, made him squirm. "Shit," he said.

"Control, this is two eighty."

"Go ahead two eighty."

"The Cross Island's backed up northbound. Accident on the Whitestone exit..."

122

New York began to lurch around in Wilson's head and he said "Shit" again and turned the radio off, wishing he'd turned it off as soon as he'd heard the first voice.

Wilson looked in his rearview mirror and saw nothing and he slowed the van, stopped it, and turned the engine off. To clear his head, to place him again in the Alaskan tundra, he sat in silence. The car stopped ticking and he listened to the wind, he sensed the darkness as a pressure on his eyes. With the heater off, the air in the cabin of the van began to turn cold at once, like a time-lapse film of a crystal growing. Fucking New York limousine, Wilson thought; a last fret, for the wind shook the van and he felt the cold in his lungs and there was only dark around him and he was calm once more.

He glanced at the rearview mirror and saw two distant spots of light, another vehicle. He started the van and drove on, soon reaching a junction. He turned left, off the Spine Road and onto a road that was slightly narrower, leading to the pump station. For a time he was surrounded by darkness again but then he saw the two headlights in the rearview mirror, somewhat nearer. Wilson cursed softly at the intrusion; he looked ahead and concentrated on keeping the van on the road.

Far ahead was a cluster of lights and he saw the flame of the flare stack undulating in the dark sky—the stack itself invisible still, the flame an unstable sun. Then he was driving past the crude tank, the great sheds, and he parked where Ronnie had parked weeks ago.

The shack that held the pipeline's first rise from the earth was dimly lit, a fan of sodium-orange light at its base, a mesh-enclosed bulb over the door. Wilson approached slowly, letting the cold press at his eyes, taking the cold air slowly into his lungs, holding it there like smoke from a joint, letting it out, his breath as profuse before him as manhole steam.

Wilson entered the shack and again he saw the four-foot pipe rise from the earth, again he heard the soft woman's-grief of a sound filling the space, again he sensed the faint trembling beneath his feet. And again he felt a twist of fear—he felt the oil being pulled out of the earth—sucking at God's tit—Marta's image came to him and turned the sound into God's voice, God's grief—Wilson felt the draining in his own body. But he cast off the feeling. "No," he said aloud, sharply. "No."

He strode to the pipe. He knew all that was needed was somewhere in the earth. The fear was sucked away, along the pipe and out into the night, but Wilson's head filled with catch-phrases—all we need, tap into it, just produce it, exploration reports...Wilson broke away, he turned and left the shack.

Outside he found he was breathing hard. He held his breath, tried to calm himself. It was dangerous to breathe too quickly in this cold—the air going in did not warm sufficiently in its passage and could frost the inside of the lungs. By the time he reached the van he had cleared his mind and the buildings nearby annoyed him but he knew it would be all right as soon as he was out on the road.

He climbed into the van and turned on the engine and he backed out of the space and drove off. The crude tank passed by and then he was in the darkness again. He looked at his gas gauge and he thought about driving around, out on these roads, before he went back; he had a quarter of a tank. He looked into the darkness ahead of him and, to place himself clearly, he glanced into the rearview mirror to see the darkness there as well.

He saw headlights, following very near. He held his anger in; he thought to pull calmly to the side of the road and let the vehicle pass. But the road was only wide enough for two lanes and he did not trust the terrain off the edge, out beneath the crust of snow. He slowed down drastically, inviting the vehicle to go around, but the lights slowed as well, held their place.

Now his irritation at the intrusion began to be tainted by another feeling, inchoate still, but insistent. He sped up again and the lights did too; the lights drew suddenly nearer, came up almost to the back bumper of Wilson's van. He could see nothing of the cab of the vehicle but it was a van, somewhat larger than his own. The cab was outside the reach of his tail light; no human being seemed attached to its movement and Wilson's irritation was gone, for a moment he was blank—just a flicker of a transition—and then he was afraid.

He floored the accelerator and the lights dropped behind. But immediately they rushed back up and still Wilson saw only the headlights and the metal grin of the grill. His hands tightened on the wheel, his head felt pumped full, he imagined he would soon rise, lifted from the seat by his own buoyancy—an odd way to feel fear, he thought—he raced on into the dark and he did not look back. He raced on and the dark ahead was shifting and swirling like a black aurora, full of texture and shape. He heard a clicking in his throat and then he laughed—a short pop of a laugh, like Clyde's in the whiteout—he plunged into the darkness and he glanced just once into the mirror—the lights were there, the brights were up, they burned his eyes and he looked ahead, to the dark, undulating there, sweeping around him, palpable, and he knew the junction was coming soon.

He began to slow—just enough to take the turn—he'd turn and then it was a straight rush to the camp. Ahead were lights—a yellow light, two headlights below—he saw the junction and, parked blocking the Spine Road back to camp, was a snowblower. It was parked diagonally just beyond the turn—there was no passage—Wilson knew at once that this had all been planned—and he raced past the junction and on into the dark, straight on this road. His mind thrashed about, trying to remember the map, trying to remember where this road led, but he could not recall. He looked in the mirror and the lights were still there.

The accelerator was on the floor, the van strained at Wilson's arms, strained to fly off the road, strained to take him out onto the tundra—Wilson felt the tundra waiting—the van pulled the way part of his mind pulled, but he held to the road, rushed on, his own bright lights groping ahead, feeling for turns.

He looked in the mirror and the headlights had dropped back—a van length, another, and when Wilson turned his eyes to the road once more he saw the low wooden barrier and he

125

cracked through and he felt the van lift, felt weightless and then fall—brief but the van hit hard, his hands flew up, his head compressed and there was only darkness.

8.

Wilson woke. All of his body ached. He was folded sideways against the dashboard and he knew at once what had happened. He moved his arms, his legs, and what he'd thought was pain in them was coldness. But the pain high on his head was different—he'd taken a blow there.

Wilson sat up and the cold in his limbs seemed to drain into his chest. The headlights of his van squinted on into the night but there was no road before him—only a stretch of snow, its levelness broken by fist-sized knots—rocks beneath a thin crust. Wilson remembered the barricade, the leap—this was a gravel pit.

He fumbled at the ignition with his mitten, turned the key. The engine was dead. The axles were probably broken anyway, he thought. With the van inoperable his first thought was that he'd wait till morning. This held him for a moment, soothed him, but then he knew there'd be no light—morning or night was irrelevant—and this pit could be idle. Wilson leaned sideways to find the flashlight under the seat. The cab spun, blackness pinched Wilson's sight; his hand grasped the flashlight, he drew himself erect and he did not lose consciousness. The spot on his head throbbed, the cab rotated slowly about him; he leaned forward gently against the steering wheel and waited for his head to settle.

He thought of the radio. His vertigo suppressed any lift of hope at this thought and then he remembered that the engine had to be running to operate the radio. He knew he had to go out onto the tundra and it was now that he felt the lift. The spinning had stopped, the weakness was gone. He thought of the crash through the barrier, the fall of the van. The wind spoke of the uselessness of the casing of steel around him, the handles and wheels and dials and panes of glass. He opened the door and stepped out. The wind gusted, pushed him, Wilson turned and grasped the door to close it. He realized the absurdity of the gesture and he smiled and nodded his head and left the door open.

He switched on his flashlight and shone it into the dark along a wide, grey gash that led from the rear of the van—its skid mark. He knew he was lucky the van had not pitched or rolled. He stepped into the center of the gash and he began to follow it. He passed a wheel and the gash grew lopsided as he played his skid backwards. The gash stopped—impact point—and Wilson raised his flashlight and saw nothing ahead. He put the light on the rocky ground and noticed some of the stones were bare. Perhaps the pit was active after all. He walked on another fifty yards and then raised his light again and before him was a chest-high escarpment. He moved to it and tried to lift himself up. His parka and pants dragged at him as if he were trying to swim in them. He laid the flashlight down and backed up and tried to run—he waddled instead but his momentum allowed a leg to catch at the top of the escarpment and he pivoted on his chest and rolled once and sat up, his breath coming fast, hurting, biting deep into his lungs. His head wobbled, the land tilted, and he leaned forward slightly, tried to stop the heave of his chest. The dizziness darkened his mood, took the rush out of his fear, slowed him down too much, trickled a taste of brass into his mouth, throbbed in the spot on his head.

When Wilson's head felt steady again he picked up his flashlight and shone it away from the pit. Twenty yards off was the wooden barricade—a frame standing on both sides—hinged on the right—the wood fragments scattered on the ground. Wilson stood up and held the light on the stubs of cracked wood still jutting from the frame. He tracked the light along the ground—his wheels had bitten in here—he must have hit the brakes instinctively—and then the marks cut off at the edge. Wilson moved the light on out into the air—the path he'd followed—and he could not quite see the impact point out in the darkness.

He was starting to feel cold again. But he moved his flashlight one more time to the barricade and traced his path—across the narrow shelf and out into the gasp of space and down into the pit. He played the leap again in his mind, and again; he was drawn to it, quickened by it, he played it over like an adolescent going over his first kiss.

His arms and legs were aching, his hands and feet felt prickly—the cold was cutting into him. He was perhaps eight miles from the operations center. He was dressed properly and if he didn't push it and if his head stayed clear he could be back at the center in two hours. He was reconciled to frostbite somewhere on his body—but he would survive this. It was my own damn fault, he thought, as he began to walk back up the road he'd been forced down. Who'd tried to kill him? "Anybody," he said aloud. "Anyfuckingbody." As the curse was vented into the air, the issue vanished from his mind. He walked swinging his arms, flashing the light only every minute or two to verify his way and save the batteries.

During one of the periods when the flashlight was off, before he reached the junction, he saw headlights up ahead, approaching. He had only a few moments to make a decision. He could slip out into the tundra and let the vehicle pass, if he feared that this driver was one of them. He reasoned no further. As soon as he thought of the attempt on his life, he stepped to the side of the road and turned on his flashlight.

He watched the headlights rushing nearer. He braced himself, prepared to leap out of the way. But the vehicle slowed—it was a truck, he could see—a dump truck with a stubby, flat-faced cab. The truck stopped and the driver's window rolled down and a face appeared. "What the hell are you doing out here?"

Wilson felt a vague sense of disappointment. He wanted to say, Don't you keep your fucking ears open around camp? But he circled the truck, crossing through the beams of the headlights and when he was in the cab with the man he said, "I ran off the edge."

Wilson lay very still in his bed and he had no idea how long it had been since he awoke. He would lie here—as he'd done each day for two weeks—and wait for Marta's knock. His body had been right for ten days, but he told Finn he was still dizzy and that was the story that went back to Anchorage. He insisted on silence about the attempt on his life and so he looked like a hero—waiting for the next attempt to help the investigation along. He had told Marta only that he'd had an accident.

Wilson drew the covers around him in the dark and listened to the wind and he stepped consciously into the flow of his mind like stepping into the current of a river. The van crashed through the barrier and he heard the splintering of the wood, the very separation of fibers and then he was free falling and he did not know how far down he would plunge, he waited for the van to flip to roll to crack open and fling him far on into the night out across the frozen empty land, flying between two sheer peaks, death holding back, an arm's length away, less, easing even nearer, letting his shoulders glide along the slick surface of it.

Wilson heard his own breath filling the room. He was breathing fast, his mind focused, his mind simplified: the dark, an empty surface—cliff-face or tundra—the wind, himself. And then he could listen, then he could wait for something more—or for nothing—he had no clear expectation, only that he could strip down to what mattered, a hot sky, a palm frond moving, the motes of dust, and a voice, alien, a whining swoop of sound and the face thrust close to Wilson's—the VC with the oval blue mark on his face. He shouted at Wilson, words came that seemed to be English but Wilson could not understand them, blocked them out. Wilson did not see the hand coming at him—never did see it—but his face jerked to the right, he felt the open-palm slap. He straightened his head again and the man wanted him dead and Wilson could only see the long column of sunlight falling from window to floor. He knew the man wanted

Wilson's hatred, yearned to have his own feeling requited like a schoolyard lover, but Wilson looked at the dark, twisted face and he felt nothing at first, then he felt concerned for that bluish mark. He was certain it was cancer. He wished he were a healer. The man's hand moved again, slapped Wilson's cheek, and Wilson wanted to reach out with his own hand and wipe that mark away. The face disappeared and there was only the window before him, its buttress of sunlight, its panel of empty blue sky. Wilson closed his eyes. But he knew that there was an irony to this gesture—he felt open at that moment, as his eyes closed he felt, in a wide swath down the center of him from forehead to groin, a sensation of opening up: he heard a chicken stretch in the yard—the bird was out of sight, vocalized no sound—but Wilson heard the lift of its wings, the movement of its sinews, its hollow bones, the rise and cock of its head, the hinge-pop of its beak.

Wilson opened his eyes and it was dark. He knew at once where he was. He linked to his flashback by listening for the movement of the ravens out in the wind—and he saw Beth laying her head on his bare chest, the two of them held, as he now was, within the covers of a bed. In the six-dollar motel room on the edge of Ithaca, she talked of her childhood—an affliction—and he wished he could have known her then, healed her. She'd been subject to recurring petit mal—the "little death"—the doctors searched unsuccessfully for five years for the lesion they knew was in her brain—she'd begun at age eight to die—over and over—seized unexpectedly and thrown down in a mummery of death. Then at age thirteen the attacks stopped. But Beth remembered her childhood from blank spot to blank spot; there was never a recollection of the little deaths. Wilson put his hand on her head and felt the warmth of her cheek on his chest. And he envied her, her knowledge, even if it was beyond her recall. And he saw the sudden rush of the barrier, the cracking wood, the leap.

Footsteps. The coincidence of thought and sound yanked him from the bed, his breath gone, his hands in fists before him and his senses open, open to the crush of carpet pile, the swish of cloth, the stopping. The knock. He moved to the door but he knew now that it was Marta, the hard, thin-knuckled triple-rap. He was naked and he simply unlocked the door and she opened it just far enough to slip in.

They said nothing. She was a form in the dark that moved past him, without a touch, to the chair. He stood waiting and listening to the zip and ruffle and flap of clothes. They met then at the bed and embraced and moved quickly over the paths of their bodies that had been defined clearly now—her preferences, his preferences—his tongue along her armpit, her nipple on the tip of his penis—they sweated and rolled in their choreography and did not make a sound from their throats.

After they'd done and arranged their legs and arms in the way they'd long ago found to be best in the narrow bed, Marta spoke. "I'm going on vacation for two weeks."

Wilson waited for more, but the silence persisted. "When?" he said.

"Next week."

He was conscious of his indifference. She was not asking him to go with her, and he knew he didn't care, he didn't want to leave Moonbase, even with this woman whose body and mind he thought he understood. But from curiosity he asked, "Where are you going?"

"California."

"Your mother?"

"Yes."

"Your step brothers and sisters?"

"One or two. Most of them are shits." With this she shifted her body, drew her knee up along his thigh; her voice had been pitched low, and he felt the ripple of feeling in her—the anger, the longing.

"I want to tell you something about me," he said, the impulse speaking itself before he realized what it was. He wanted to tell her about his time in captivity.

"Another revelation?" she said. Wilson heard the edge in her voice.

132

"I'm sorry I kept my cover story so long," he said. This was the first time she'd hinted at her irritation at the lies about his work. But he didn't want to deal with this now; he had a stronger concern at this moment. She said no more and he began to tell her about his capture. He realized as he spoke that he was using almost exactly the same words as he had before—with Beth, with Clyde—he talked of the orphanage, the gates, the blue and cream taxicab, the shack.

Marta was turned sideways, her head propped on her hand. When Wilson stopped, she said, "How did you get out of that?"

The question didn't register in him immediately. The words simply held back their meaning for a moment and then when he understood, he had to concentrate hard to find an answer. He knew it was a natural question; he even knew that logically the answer should be part of the tale; but his rescue was an event that seemed out of place.

"My commanding officer found me," Wilson said. "He figured it out somehow. The afternoon of the seventh day the door suddenly crashed open and he was there. I didn't know who it was. I couldn't see him. He was just a shape at the door. I thought he was after me. I thought I was dead. But I was very calm. Then the VC were flying around the room. I still thought the figure was one of them but I thought he was just the worst fucking shot in the whole fucking world."

Marta remained propped on her hand, and Wilson felt her eyes cutting through the dark, though he could not clearly see them. He turned his face away, turned it toward the wall. He felt faintly embarrassed.

"You're full of surprises, aren't you," she said, the words a stroke of his cheek in spite of what he saw as their potential bite.

He turned his face to her. "Two weeks?" he said, low.

"I'll be back," she said.

On the first day that Marta was gone, Wilson extended his reverie, and scenes returned that were as familiar as Marta's

133

body—Beth's face disappearing in the steam, the VC captor putting his rifle back together, Wilson's own constellation in the Vietnamese night—he followed the sequence of these memories as he'd followed the sequence of touching with Marta.

On the second day, at the time when Marta would come to him, Wilson rose up and dressed and stepped out of his room. He walked down the hallway. Each step closer to the hallway's end was lighter. He looked at the opening there, the crossing of the balcony; he watched it coming nearer and he thought of the motorcycle daredevil on the TV at the Anchorage bar, his approach to the edge of the platform, the leap, and he thought of his own leap into the pit and he imagined the men who'd tried to kill him waiting now beyond the end of this hallway.

He stepped out onto the balcony and the padded chairs were empty, the rubber plants drooped in the shadows, he heard the clatter of billiard balls beyond the railing. He walked to the staircase leading down to the recreation floor. Voices, another clack of ball against ball. He went down the steps.

The floor was nearly deserted. Two men stood by the billiard table. One, bent over his cue, looked up at Wilson and then back to his shot; the other man did not raise his eyes from the ball. Wilson tried to find some knowledge in that glance, tried to see some tightening now in the man's body, a clenching in his jaw. But Wilson could not be sure and as he acknowledged his uncertainty he realized the foolishness of this paranoia. There were over six hundred people at Moonbase. How many would want him dead?

He walked past the billiard table, a ball dropped into a pocket, and the shooter straightened up and flashed a smile at Wilson— an eager, open, warm smile, and the man said, "Got it."

Wilson nodded and walked on and he felt vacant. This feeling persisted until he entered the TV lounge. There were two dozen men in the room and on the TV screen was a film clip of a top administration official. The lounging men filled the vacancy in Wilson. The government official on the screen was saying, "This planet is all we need. This planet can keep us."

There was a scattering of hoots at this. One of the men shouted across the room. "See, Cooney, you Californians are all fucking moonbeams."

The official ran his hand back over his dark, slicked hair and his home-state tan was turned almost green by the TV and he said, "The efforts in Alaska, for instance, will show what the President has been saying all along..." The men hurrahed at the mention of Alaska. The official went on, "And I think it's refreshing to hear a President speak the straight truth on energy to the American people. We've got all that we need."

From the back of the room, Wilson watched the men straining their heads toward the set. The percentages were much better in this room—there could very easily be someone here who'd tried to kill him three weeks ago—or at least someone who knew the truth about it—knew the men who'd made the attempt.

The official was saying, "That's why it is vital to keep the price of energy up at the level that will support the exploration. The energy's all there but we have to pay for it. It's that simple."

Wilson went to the side aisle and he began to move down it, toward the front of the room. It was clear in his own mind now, what he wanted to do. He was even conscious of the first level of his motivation.

"It would likewise be foolish," the official was saying, "to put too much emphasis on chancy new technologies, alternatives that have been untried. Let the free market find the place for them."

Wilson reached the front of the room. He leaned against the wall there, facing all the men in the lounge, his arms folded. He stood there consciously scanning their faces. He knew he looked like a damn fool—but he wanted to remind them all that he was still at Moonbase; he wanted to provoke someone to action again; he wanted—and this motive was clear even to himself—to make his presence at Moonbase a matter of life-and-death again, to quicken his own senses.

He saw eyes slide his way and then return to the TV. A face

turned to him and then turned away, and another face and another. Wilson stood there and made sure that every man in the room noticed him and when that was done he moved back up the aisle and out the door.

Wilson spent the following week appearing at midday in the lounge, shooting pool by himself, sitting prominently on the balcony, motionless beneath a rubber plant, watching the workers come and go. He did not go out in the van again but he walked the empty halls slowly, sat in the lounges or at the far ends of the balcony when no one was around; he made himself as open and vulnerable as he could inside the operation center and eventually the exhilaration of his defiance, his challenge faded. Sitting late in the afternoon in a pin-spot on the balcony, a man three chairs down the way snapping his newspaper, one of the plump receptionists passing with a coy smile, Wilson thought of going back out in the van, inviting another attempt out there. But now this all seemed artificial to him. The meaning that he was giving to Moonbase, to Alaska, was forced, unearned, the life-and-death of jumping a casino-hotel fountain before a gaggle of tourists. He rose up and went to his room and dead-bolted the door and stripped off his clothes and climbed into the bed.

He thought of Marta, wanted her here. But as soon as he wanted her he was pressed into the bed, as if from the g-force in the fall of a plane, but pressed by the thought of their recent weeks together, the silence, the familiar movements. He focused on her pain, her father, he wondered if she was with one of her step brothers or sisters now. And he saw Beth. He was sitting beside her in her mother's apartment, their feet side by side on a Chinese rug, their legs touching, her family scrapbook opened on their knees. And Beth pointed to a picture of a young man smiling, the face echoing Beth's around the eyes, the nose. That's my brother Charles, Beth said. He was the only person in our family who was happy. I hated him for it. I always wanted to crack open his skull to see how this thing could be.

Wilson clenched his fists. He wanted to touch Beth's head, hold it tight in his palms, press her sadness away, hold the life in, make her live, make her want to live. He began to weep. He was glad for the tears. He let them flow, though he made no sound and he held Beth's head in his hands and he knew it was no use. He felt the cold track down his face and it did not surprise him as he began to slip back—Beth and the captivity, the captivity and Beth, they followed him together, twinned now, and he saw his constellation in the tropical dark—Mons Major, the mountain—and he heard the bombs on the horizon and on that night of captivity he thought of the horizon sounds of his boyhood, he lay in an open field, a camping trip, his parents sleeping nearby and he listened to a hum at the horizon, even out there on a mountain slope in Pennsylvania on a hot summer night he could hear the horizon humming with life—life that did not break itself down into individual people, places, objects, but just hummed itself without speech, without form, and Wilson wept briefly, wept on the mountainside with a kind of joy, wept in that shack in Vietnam—from what? from fear? a moment of sentimentality for his own life? Wilson's mind now filled with questions, his head was stuffed full, cluttered with questions and he pulled the covers around him and concentrated on the Arctic wind and he squeezed himself into sleep.

He woke and it was the day before Christmas. Late in the afternoon he thought of Eli Marcus and wondered if the man would be preaching at Moonbase during the holiday. Wilson dressed and went out of his room. He slowed as he approached Marta's door and he stopped there. He touched the door with his fingertips, listened to the silence from within, and it struck him that it always sounded this way—whether she was in the room or gone, the silence surrounded her. He felt a hard little knot in his chest even as the thought of Marta aroused him, as the silence beyond the door created the illusion that she was there, naked, waiting for his knock.

Wilson broke away from the door, hurried down the hall. He

turned right and moved on along the balcony, down stairs, past the doors to the pool, into the back corridor that led to the chapel. He stopped at the chapel doors and eased them open.

The chapel was dim. He stepped inside and the door closed behind him. The metal cross was pin-spotted on the back wall, the only light. As his eyes dilated, a man grew visible in the front row and, as if in response to Wilson's notice, the face turned. He could not see the face in the dimness; he only knew the man was looking at him.

"Sorry to disturb you," Wilson said. "I wanted to find out if...Eli Marcus was going to be preaching on Christmas."

"He's not," the man said and the face turned to the front again.

Wilson stood for a moment watching the lectern. He imagined Eli there talking about the deepest darkness of the Arctic night, the closing down of the soul, the separation from God, linking them all with a profane defiance—but then Wilson was not so sure. Eli might like the darkness. Wilson backed through the chapel doors.

And his head jerked back, a clamp came around his chest, his mouth was pressed shut. He yanked with his chest but he could not move, his arms were pinned, powerful arms were around him and he was being dragged along a corridor. He dug in with his heels, but they would not hold, his feet skipped and kicked up. A face in a ski mask appeared and vanished and Wilson's legs were lifted, clamped together in an arm. He could see the ski mask again for a moment and then he was twisted back and he saw the ceiling moving, he heard a metal door slam open and he felt a flash of cold. For a moment he stopped, held suspended, a corrugated ceiling above and the cold biting at his chest, his hands. His legs began to tremble and then there was a pop, like a vacuum broken, the creak of metal hinges and a rush of wind. The cold bit deeper and he was being carried out and he was lifted and his limbs were free he was flying again, briefly, the cold raking him and he hit the ground with his shoulder, his hip.

He heard the fire door slam shut. Outside here in the cold without coat or gloves or mask, Wilson knew he had perhaps thirty seconds before his flesh would begin to freeze, a minute before he would be immobilized. He scrambled up and the pain in his shoulder and hip blended into a wider pain, a pain that flowed across his skin like a river. He turned and the light from the windows striped the snow and he began to run along them, pumping hard, sprinting with his legs high, and ahead was the thrust of a residence wing. These wings had only fire doors, locked from the inside. He would have to circle wide around the wings and then back again to get to the front door of the main building, the only door he could be sure of entering. He looked to the right, toward the place where he knew the main door was, and he judged the height of the stanchions, their spacing, and he ducked under the building's central section.

He ran hunched over, weaving through the stanchions, the wind screaming around him, harder here, compressed under the vast bulk of the center, the bulk that weighed on Wilson's back, his neck. Wilson feared losing his way. He angled to the left, around a stanchion and then back to the right to keep his course. Another black metal leg and he went to the right, then back to the left. He felt his hands fading, his face, the feeling was going, his body prickled with pain, all feeling was being squeezed out, and he strained his eyes ahead and he saw a wide splash of light. The front door. Close now and he had a light to key on. He pushed harder and he fell—straight out, he could not feel the impact on his hands, he went down flat and it was then that he felt that the building was about to collapse on him, the tons of concrete and steel above him stretched as vast as the sky and were bending the frail stanchions, cracking them, the building was falling, crushing him into the frozen earth. He cried out and scrambled to his feet, he could not straighten up, the rockmass above him was easing down, about to drop, he was running again, each step a breath a cry, the light drew closer and he lunged and he was out from under the building.

He straightened and pushed himself up the steps, stumbling

once, twice, his feet were numb, his hands, he clawed up the last few steps and got to his feet and pulled open the outer door and stumbled inside, the warmth plucking at his eyes; he opened the inner door and staggered into the reception area.

The two women behind the desk stood in unison, their eyes wide. Wilson drew himself stiffly erect and walked past them, the pain in his body patchy now, feeling beginning to return in little fan-arcs at his knees, trickles in his chest. Wilson walked on, toward the railing of the balcony. There were loud noises from below. Men shouting in laughter, singing. Jingle bells, jingle balls...Balls...A shout of laughter...Jingle balls...Wilson stood at the railing, holding very still and below him were ropes of silver paper strung from balcony to balcony, a Christmas tree, a long table of food, and a hundred men, two dozen women, scattered around, leaning into each other, clapping arms, laughing.

"Son of a bitch, boy. Where you been?"

Wilson turned and it was Clyde. Wilson's body began to tremble now, his jaw clenched, he felt a spasm of cold rush through him, he could not stand and as he fell, Clyde Mazer's large hands moved toward him.

9.

As the doctor at the infirmary worked on Wilson's hands and feet and face, dressing two spots finally with phenol and camphor, he said nothing about Wilson's obvious sojourn outdoors without proper dress. Wilson took the doctor's silence to mean that he knew his true identity and was being discreet. The rumors about him, Wilson suspected, were being widely circulated. Then the doctor did say, "You came very close to serious frostbite. I don't know where you were or why but if you'd been there twenty seconds longer you'd be in big trouble."

In the receiving room Clyde rose as Wilson appeared. He said, "That was the worst case of whiskey-shakes I've ever seen."

Wilson said, "You get those from too much or too little?"

"Too little, boy." They were out in the hall now. "But I've got the cure in my bag."

Back in Wilson's room, Clyde sat on the bed, Wilson sat in the chair by the window.

"Season's greetings, boy." Clyde raised his water glass without ruffling the three fingers of whiskey.

"Same to you, Clyde." Wilson drank and the faint quiver of cold in him finally ceased. "What are you doing here?"

"Thought I'd drop in and wish you Merry Christmas."

"Truth, Clyde."

"That is the truth." Clyde's drawl was muted and Wilson took this to mean he was serious.

"I'm glad you're here," Wilson said.

"I bet you are...What the hell's going on?"

"Somebody's been trying to kill me."

"You must be making real progress on your investigation."

Wilson laughed. "None whatsoever. I've all but given the damn thing up. I just blurted out my purpose here in a public way and somebody—a group of somebodies—has been after me ever since. They ran me off the road a couple of weeks ago and they tossed me out a fire door tonight."

"Sounds like they only half-intended to get the job done."

"You're right...They haven't tried in any decisive way...But I'm sure they're running out of patience with me. I keep hanging around."

"So you just hang around, fuck the investigation, and you wait till they stop playing and kill you for real?" Clyde's accent faded again.

Wilson did not know how to answer this. His interests in Moonbase were still too obscure to speak. He watched Clyde lift his drink, the tumbler itself invisible in the large hand. Wilson thought of that hand working gently at the throttle of the little plane, easing the Piper down to find the run of willows.

"I want to get out of here for awhile," Wilson said. "A day or two maybe."

"Anchorage?"

"No. Not Anchorage. Definitely not Anchorage."

"Artie Phillips was telling me there's a little settlement of hippies between the Koyukuk and Yukon."

"Hippies?"

"That's right. Longhairs. Castoffs from some other decade."

"Artie said...?"

"Artie Phillips. The guy at..."

"I remember him," Wilson said.

"He says howdy."

"Tell him howdy back."

"So hippies are always suspicious," Clyde said with a slow wink. "Let's fly down and see 'em. Maybe they've got your documents."

Wilson laughed. Then he thought of flying in the Piper again,

this time across the North Slope and through the Brooks Range.
"Sure. Let's go down there. When?"
"How about tomorrow?"
"Christmas morning?"
In answer, Clyde raised his glass high.
"Tomorrow morning," Wilson said.

Early on Christmas morning the Piper skimmed along the runway at Deadhorse and the lights fell away and Wilson's eyes filled with tears. He was glad to be in the air with Clyde, glad to be rushing into the Arctic darkness; he closed his eyes and sucked the cold into his lungs.

"We have this timed," Clyde said, "so you'll see a little bit of daylight."

Wilson looked at Clyde. "Daylight?"

"It's far enough south that we'll get a little bit of light—a couple of hours." Clyde's puff of breath was red from the panel lights. It was hard for Wilson to picture the sun—this night that he'd grown used to seemed impenetrable—no sun could wedge itself into this dark. He looked at a web of red-stained frost on the window. Beyond, in the starlight, he could see the far stretch of tundra—even in this faint light; but the frozen polygons, the meandering tracks of rivers like the sutures of a skull, were invisible.

They passed through Windowledge Pass, the Brooks Range stretching away on either side, and Wilson could feel the mountains kinesthetically, in his arms, as if he'd raised his arms and stretched them beyond sight into the dark. The cabin was very cold. Wilson felt the frost forming on his eyelashes, catching at his eyes when he blinked. The Piper hummed around Wilson and when they were through the mountains Clyde suddenly whooped. "Damn if this ain't a treat," he said. "Better'n ridin' around in a pickup on a hot Texas summer night. Ain't it?"

"Better."

"Better'n crackin' heads in a bar."

"You a big head-cracker, Clyde?"

"Me? Well sure," Clyde said. "It comes to that ever so often."

"You know, that first night we went drinking I thought for sure you were going to crack that old man's head."

"What old man?"

"The one that hit you with his cane."

Clyde laughed. "Oh, him. Nah. Not him."

"At least break his cane over your knee or something."

"Well, there always seems to be some real basic decision to make about all that." Clyde paused and puffed a great cloud of his red breath into the cabin. "Just about any man I meet I could jump either way on...I could hug him or break his fucking arm. *Any* man."

"What makes the difference?"

"Damned if I know," Clyde said. They flew on for a long while over tundra and benchland and mountains and deep cuts of valley, all dim in the starlight. And then, though it must have come about slowly, Wilson suddenly realized that the sky was light. All but the brightest stars had disappeared and off to the left, beyond Clyde's bulbous profile, the horizon was a pale red.

Wilson looked down and he saw a file of caribou moving along a frozen stream. The caribou began to run, the line grew ragged. Wilson thought it was the plane that scared them but a few moments later he saw an arc of smaller animals at the rear of the file of caribou. Wolves, he realized; one end of the arc was moving fast, completing a circle, a single caribou—one of the stragglers, either old or young or sick—caught in the center. Wilson pressed his face to the glass, turning to watch behind the plane, but the animals were gone.

Later the Piper was following a river. Wilson thought he could see water moving in the cracks of its surface ice. Clyde was watching below more carefully now, craning his neck. He looped the plane to the left and Wilson faced the bright horizon. The red there was intense now, a color from a steel mill furnace. Wilson looked closely at the center of the color just at the rim of horizon; he stared hard and then his breathing stopped, he sensed the sun just one beat, two, before he saw it—a spot of fire there. Then it widened, rose, Wilson's eyes began to hurt and he glanced away briefly only to look back again. Against the reference point of the horizon, he could see the sun's movement, its curve prominent, the circle beginning to shape. He looked away once more and then back. He was drawn to the sun with the same fascination he might have had for a dead body in a city street—as a focal point for some momentous act beyond human control. As with the dead body, he expected this sun—in vain, he realized—to yield its secret if he could only look at it closely enough. As Wilson's eyes began to ache again, Clyde looped away. Wilson closed his eyes and he was aware of the hammer of the Piper's engines, aware of the curves of metal and glass around him. He felt confined and his limbs grew restless.

Then the plane dove down. Clyde said, "There they are."

Wilson kept his eyes closed until the plane flared out and he felt the skis touch and skim, the engine cycling rapidly down. He looked outside and a flat, white field raced by, slowing; in the distance was a stand of pine and a sawtooth of low mountains beyond. The Piper swung around and now Wilson saw the huddling of shacks, two made of logs and small, one large and made of lumber of varied colors, with one side-wall of corrugated metal. The larger house seemed scrounged, like the shacks, along Highway One leading to Saigon, that had walls of uncut Coke cans. But these had roofs full of snow and behind them was an outbuilding with a mound of snow before it, perhaps a buried plow. Beyond was a larger stand of trees. At the front door of the main house a figure had appeared. Clyde taxied toward the house until Wilson could see the eyes of the man in the doorway and then Clyde cut the engine.

Outside, as the man—thin-faced with a wispy beard—left the doorway and approached, Wilson realized that he himself had no clear reason for coming here. He had no pretense even, to answer the man's most obvious question. But Clyde intercepted the man, shaking his hand.

"Howdy," Clyde said. "We were flying on up to the North

Slope and I was looking for a cache of fuel I have along the Koyukuk. We saw your settlement and decided to come down and see how you're faring.''

Wilson had drawn near to the man from the house and he could see his gauntness even though he had on a heavy coat. The veins corded his neck, his Adam's apple hung in his throat as slack as a testicle.

The man said, in a low, passionless voice, "Did you bring any food?''

"No,'' Clyde said. "None to speak of.''

"I'm Luke,'' the man said and as Clyde and Wilson spoke their names Luke turned and began to walk toward the house— not from rudeness but from a kind of distraction.

As Wilson followed, he looked up and started. The windows were full of faces—faces made ageless, sexless, by the same sunken pallor of Luke's face. At first Wilson thought the faces had been watching him and Clyde. But the eyes were all focused out further. Then Wilson realized they were staring at the sun.

"You folks seem glad to see the sun,'' Wilson said.

Luke stopped and turned. But his voice kept its flatness. "We don't see so well at night anymore,'' he said.

Clyde's eyes slid toward Wilson, his mouth tightened. Wilson looked back at the faces pressed to the windows, the sun's reflection burning there in the panes of glass, giving color now, from this angle, to the pallid faces.

Inside the door Wilson was stopped by smells that pressed him back: piss and old bedding and wet lumber and semen and propane and sweat and Wilson could not move any further than the doorway. He watched Clyde walk into the center of the room and look carefully around.

The bodies at the window were turning. But slowly, the interest in the sun and the interest in the strangers in an almost equal balance. The children were the first to turn. They were scrawny, except for the smallest, a girl whom Wilson saw watching him from a shy tuck of her head; she had a bit of a pot-belly. The small children also were the first to turn back to the window as Luke motioned for Wilson and Clyde to sit at a wood-plank table.

Clyde crossed to the table at once; Wilson took very small breaths, tried to force his mind off the smells and he followed Clyde. A woman with a long braid and an acquiline nose joined Luke. Wilson and Clyde sat side by side on a bench across from Luke and the woman, who said, "I'm Sarah."

"I'm Clyde Mazer and this here is Mr. Wilson Hand. We're from the North Slope."

Luke and Sarah folded their hands on the table and seemed to be waiting for more. Wilson glanced back to the main room. The others—half a dozen women, half a dozen men, eight or ten gangly children on the verge of teenage, and a few smaller children were huddled quietly in the litter of the room piled with mattresses, cardboard boxes, magazines and newspapers scattered as if by a great wind—or they were back at the window watching. The little girl Wilson had noticed was sitting beneath the windows, her back against the wall, her hands clutched in her lap. There was no sound from the room.

"How long you folks been out here?" Clyde said.

"This is our second winter," Luke said.

"We just lost our horse," Sarah said.

"He's frozen out in his stall." Luke turned his head toward the back wall as if he could see through it to where the horse lay.

"But we'll get by," the woman said. "We've got a fine feeling here." Her voice rang in the room and Wilson heard a stirring behind him and then stillness. "It's not a giddy thing, this feeling," she said, suddenly glaring at Wilson, as if she read his thoughts—the thoughts he was unconscious of, for yes, he'd felt the quiet behind him and wondered about how such a fine feeling could produce the inertness of this group, the lethargy. She said, "The two winters especially have brought us close."

Luke's face did not change but his arm went around Sarah's shoulders and his Adam's apple jumped. He said, "It's the feeling of community, you see. The hardships are...a positive thing."

"Well, lookit here, son," Clyde said and his accent was the thickest Wilson had ever heard it. "Your kids over there might use a little..."

"What do you want here, Mr. Mazer?" Sarah said, cutting him off, and Wilson felt a vague relief at the strength of her voice. Her face was drawn and plain, dominated by her nose which only accentuated her thinness; she thrust her face forward toward Clyde, and Wilson almost smiled at the thought that the Texan had his hands full with her.

"Why, nothin' special, little lady," Clyde said with elaborate and patronizing courtesy.

Wilson expected the woman to at least flinch at this, but her face withdrew, Luke squeezed her closer, and she said, "You from the state government or something? We on land we're not supposed to be?"

"No, nothing like that," Clyde said.

"Then please leave us alone," Sarah said quietly, and she laid her head against the point of Luke's shoulder, as if she were very weary.

Clyde rose and Wilson followed his lead. Luke came around the table and preceded them to the door. Wilson glanced toward the little girl, still sitting under the window, but she did not look up. Beyond her, sitting on a mattress, two of the older children were leaning against each other. Their hair was long and Wilson did not know their sexes, but the two children held each other as if in a thunderstorm.

Outside, Wilson blinked against the light. He felt the abatement of the cold on his face—as comforting as actual warmth—and he looked briefly at the sun. It was just free of the horizon now but he knew it would go no higher—it was a little past noon. He could not keep his eyes on it for more than a few seconds and he watched Luke's back—hunched forward though the air was calm. At the plane, Luke turned and said, "I'm sorry. Our community here has room for only so many." He paused and then added, "Even for a brief time."

Wilson glanced at Clyde and found the man's gaze fixed on

Luke. Then Clyde said, his voice thick, "Well, Merry Christmas, hear?" and he turned to the wing to begin his pre-flight checks. It shocked Wilson: he'd forgotten that it was Christmas day; the house drew near in his mind, the children lay dead. Wilson shook the thoughts off but he would not look at the house. He stepped forward and offered his hand to Luke who grasped it with both his hands, the mittens taking any feeling of human contact out of the gesture.

Luke remained standing nearby as Wilson got into the plane and Clyde started the engine and taxied toward the woods and then swung around. Wilson took a deep breath and as he let it out moved his eyes slowly toward the house. Luke was still standing alone where the plane had been; and at the house itself, now that Wilson knew what to look for, he could see the faces at the windows. The Piper's engine raced—Clyde cranked it up high for the short takeoff—and the plane bolted forward. Wilson watched Luke, motionless, whisk by and Clyde lowered the flaps and the Piper leaped up sharply and trees flashed underneath.

Clyde pulled the plane up high over a frozen stream and then looped back, a turn exactly to the rear, and he dipped the nose. Straight ahead Wilson saw the house and, fifty yards in front of it, the dark strand of Luke's figure against the snow. Clyde dipped the nose further and Luke was rushing up, the engine raced, and Wilson gripped at the arms of the seat. Luke was facing the dive of the plane and as Clyde rushed at him Luke seemed suddenly to realize what was happening. Wilson could see Luke's face and the man twisted his body, fell prone as Clyde buzzed by, pulling up the nose of the plane and climbing again. The plane rose straight up and looped back and Clyde was diving for another pass. Luke was struggling to his feet and Wilson saw him look up and see the plane and stagger, his front covered in snow. Then Luke fell straight backwards and the Piper swooped down and Wilson gasped, sure they'd slam into the ground, burying their propeller in Luke's chest. But Clyde pulled them up and there was only sky before them and the press of gravity on Wilson's body.

"Shit, Clyde, what are you doing?" Wilson said.

"The fucking bastards are starving to death," Clyde said. "The crazy fucking bastards."

"So you're going to kill this one first?"

The plane looped out of its climb and came around and Luke was running now toward the house; he fell once, scrambled up, arms flailing, and he disappeared inside before Clyde could buzz him again.

"Why don't we just dive into their roof," Wilson said, angry at Clyde, though he felt no real sympathy for Luke. "You can take out a dozen of them that way, you crazy son-of-a-bitch."

"Don't talk like that, boy," Clyde said, a slow, serious threat. "I'll let you out to walk."

"I'm not scared of you, Clyde. Just get me back to Moonbase."

Clyde did not reply and the two men did not talk again. They'd soon flown out of the sunlight and the darkness pressed in like a fainting spell. Wilson thought of Marta, wished she would be in her room when he returned. He felt uneasy with Clyde. He didn't understand Clyde's rage, didn't really care about it, and he resented being compelled to consider it. It was just more clutter.

They landed at Deadhorse. It was nighttime and a haze had crusted over the stars. The wind whipped the loose snow around the plane and the two men still did not speak, even after the engine was off. Wilson pulled on his wool mask and put his mittened hand on the door handle.

"Take care, boy," Clyde said in a near whisper.

"You too, Clyde," Wilson said; he felt very tired and yearned now to curl up on himself under the covers of his bed.

Finn sent for Wilson a few days later and Wilson was afraid the man would challenge him over his inactivity. Going down the hall and out past the reception desk Wilson rehearsed scraps of explanation, ranging from "I'm very close to a breakthrough but I can't talk about it" to "Yes I said fuck the investigation long ago, and now that you know, I want out."

But when he was standing before Finn's desk the man stood and smiled and said, "How are you feeling now?"

"Okay."

"I hope you're doing the right thing, letting these attempts go on..."

"Let me handle it."

"Yes," Finn said. "Of course." Finn paused and looked at Wilson carefully, his eyes waiting, inquiring. Since Thanksgiving Wilson had been expecting the man to ask him about his presence at the chapel—if he was one of them or not. But Finn finally sat down and motioned Wilson to a chair.

"There's a reporter coming up here soon after New Year's," Finn said.

"A reporter?"

"Yes. From The New York Times."

"You think he's heard about the thefts?" Wilson said.

Finn said, "Oh, no. Nothing like that. He's coming up for...I don't know...Some profile of the oil industry."

"What's it got to do with me?"

"Well, you are still the p.r. guy up here. At least officially. If you want to keep up the pretense at all, you should meet him."

Wilson thought he'd like to talk to someone from New York. Briefly at least. "Okay. Yes. I'll see him."

"Very well."

Wilson rose and moved to the door.

"Wilson," Finn said.

"Yes?"

"God bless you."

Wilson didn't know what to say; he dipped his head and left.

On New Year's evening Wilson passed Marta's door on the way to the cafeteria. He stopped as he'd done several times before and listened. There was a fullness to the silence this time, as if someone were about to speak. He waited and then on impulse he stepped to the door and knocked. Almost at once the door opened and Marta stood before him.

"You're here," Wilson said.

"I just arrived."

"You're back early."

"I...wanted you."

Wilson embraced her. They moved inside and closed the door. For just a moment he looked about her room and its bareness led him out of his recent uneasiness as if he were a snake slipping out of its old skin. The hairbrush was by the TV again; the only change in the room was the disappearance of the stack of newspapers; the desk was empty. Wilson and Marta rushed through buttons and zippers and their clothes collapsed wildly together in the middle of the floor.

The first words spoken between them in the room came hours later, after midnight, when Marta woke Wilson and said, "Put just your pants and shirt on."

They rose and Marta dressed too and she led him by the hand out of the room and down the hall, along the balcony and down the stairs to the glass doors opening into the swimming pool. They pushed through and the lights were dim; the surface of the Olympic pool quivered and there was no one in the place, the tile tracks around the pool were dry. Overhead was a bubble-glass ceiling, the size and shape of the pool, looking up into the night. Marta stripped off her slacks and sweater and stood naked at the edge of the pool, her toes curling over the rim of tile.

"Marta," Wilson said.

"No one ever comes in here," she said. "No one wants to swim after twelve hours out there." She bent forward slightly at the waist and raised her arms as if to dive. The stretch and quiver of her breasts cut off his breath. He wanted her to wait, he wanted to strip quickly and come up from behind and bend at just the same angle against her, but she dove, her buttocks flashing like a sudden memory in him and then she was swimming under the water where she could hear no words.

Wilson stripped and dove in, too, the water warm, and he

closed his eyes and stroked beneath the surface until his lungs ached and he arched his back and kicked up into the air. The chlorine burned in his eyes, his sinuses, and he treaded water, looking for Marta. The surface of the pool was empty; he looked in all directions and he waited. She did not appear and he looked to the side, began to think about leaping out, finding her, but just then, far down the way, Marta's head came up from beneath the water. She shook the water from her face, a hand rose and pushed her hair back and she looked in Wilson's direction.

They began to swim toward each other and Wilson could hear the wind rushing outside, even above the splash of water about him. Marta came nearer and they drew up and kissed lightly and Wilson arched his body, brought his legs up and began to float on his back. Marta disappeared but Wilson stayed on his back staring up through the bubble of glass into the Arctic night. The water held him weightless and he felt a coolness, from exposure to the air, on his face, on the center of his chest, on a spot on the shaft of his penis. He floated and he listened to the wind pounding by and he saw a spray of snow, then just the darkness, a swirl of white, then the black; he followed this abstract dialectic with no thoughts, no feelings except an awareness on the surface of his skin that Marta was moving somewhere in the water.

He felt, for a moment, a sense of sufficiency. Floating here in mild water he watched the darkness and he waited for this naked, quiet woman to glide near. Thinking of her made Wilson want to tell her about the attempts on his life; and the recollection of his near-death sharpened this moment, heightened its sufficiency. Then water broke beside him, Marta appeared and rose and floated on her back.

Above, the wind blew, the darkness began to ripple in his sight, as it had on the night of the first attempt on his life. Then there was a fragment of the dark, ripped and flung across the sky. Another.

"The ravens," he said.

"Have you seen them cry?" Marta said.

"No."

"When they speak they throb up and down with each sound, like a black cock coming."

Wilson let his legs drop, he dove under the water and stroked hard farther into the deep end. He kept his mind closed. He felt a stuttering in his chest, his groin. Marta had been part of the moments of suspension, of calm, but it had been a lie. The silence was simply the failure to speak the foolish, cluttered thoughts that were there. He swam to the surface, broke into the air. A foolish thing, this...what? Jealousy? In his mind he cursed himself, cursed Marta. It was easy for her to take a man into her body. Those were words he'd forced from her. He saw her floating still, where he'd left her. He was erect and he swam to her and grabbed her and they spun and sank. He touched her breast, but aware only of the water against his face. She grasped his penis, squeezed it and she broke away, swam off toward the shallow end. He swam after her, catching her where they both could stand and she fell back, under the water, tugging at him and they held each other and he entered her under the water—difficult, tight—and he began to stroke. But inside her it felt crusty, clenched; under water it felt as if he were moving in her with her loins absolutely dry.

His breath was running out and they stood, still joined, her legs hooking up around his waist. She kissed him and her face was wet and hard, her tongue was a pushy maiden aunt. He wanted only to have this over with.

11.

From the balcony railing Wilson saw Finn bent over the pool table, pumping the cue, slower and slower, sighting the shot. Ronnie stood nearby, his cue upright beside him. Seeing Finn reminded Wilson of the investigation that he'd abandoned. His irritation at Clyde, his anxiety with Marta, now this man who was a silent rebuke over Wilson's failure to do his job—all this made Wilson grip the balcony railing very hard, made his breath quicken.

Pool balls clacked, Ronnie laughed, Finn straightened from his shot and Ronnie bent over. Finn turned away from the table. He looked up and saw Wilson. He nodded at Wilson, a slightly exaggerated nod intended to carry up to the balcony. Balls clattered and careened behind him and Finn motioned for Wilson to come down.

Wilson obeyed, though he was still having trouble breathing; he felt clenched. At the table, Finn shot and then rose up to greet Wilson. "Mr. Hand," he said with a faint smile.

"Finn."

"The New York Times reporter is scheduled in day after tomorrow."

"All right."

"If you're at my office at two, it would be about right. His plane is supposed to land at one-thirty."

There was a moment of silence, Wilson wanting to bolt, Finn glancing away, his face going solemn. "That reminds me. Your friend...Mazer."

"Yes? What about him?"

"He's missing."

Wilson touched the rim of the pool table with his fingertips, his face grew warm.

Finn went on, "He took off from Anchorage, I believe yesterday, and didn't arrive at the place he was heading for."

"Clyde's dead?" Wilson grasped the rim hard now, wanting to sit down, wanting to let go and fall down.

"Don't know yet. They're looking for him...Bush pilots have been known to walk out of these things."

"Was he heading here?"

"No. It was lucky they knew where he was going at all. He wasn't doing business for us and Mazer almost never files a flight plan. But he'd mentioned to somebody in Anchorage what he was doing. He'd bought about two hundred pounds of food and was flying it into some little settlement up along the Koyukuk."

"Hippies."

"What?"

"Nothing," Wilson said. He felt cold. He glanced past Finn and saw Ronnie crouched beside the table, lining up angles for his next shot. Wilson's hands rose, clenched, he began to tremble with anger. He was ready to dive across the table and pummel Ronnie. Raise that cue, Wilson said to himself, letting that be the final act of provocation. Stand up and raise the fucking cue like you were going to make a fucking shot.

Finn's voice, shaky, said, "Shall we say a prayer now for him?"

Wilson turned to Finn and the man drew back, his eyes widening. Wilson read the fear in Finn and that focused his anger on him. Wilson's fists clenched tighter, he felt his lips curling open. He could sense Finn's fear pawing out at him, he could sense the fear in the soft inside of his nose. He wanted to grab Finn by the throat, but he saw Clyde going down, Clyde's plane falling, the ground rushing at him and he wanted to be there, too, and his anger shifted one more time, to Clyde. Dammit Clyde, take me with you. But his anger would not hold on Clyde, it dissipated at once and he was left weak in the legs, in the arms. He looked at Finn and at least wanted to curse at the man but Wilson just turned and moved off.

Wilson took the chair away from the window of his room and he crouched down in the dark. He put his back against the wall, below the window, and he hunkered down there in just the same way as he'd sat in the shack in Vietnam. Come, he thought. Come. He drew his knees up, bent his head, closed his eyes and felt the wall against his back. Come. And the images swarmed into him, jumbling together, each vivid but falling into each other—the sunlight, the stretch of a hen, motes of dust, the oval blue spot, a patch of stars, a palm frond. As he sat now in his dark room groping consciously back to that week, he expected to find an answer. With Clyde lost, with Clyde leading him to the great act, to death, Wilson thought he was close to an answer. Yes. Death. He sat there in that shack and it was the terror of death that moved outside, that dipped the palm, that found its shape in the stars in the window. That's what kept him linked to those few days nearly a decade and ten thousand miles away. Wilson pressed toward this answer. Resolve it now. Come. But it was a lie. Death was not the final point. Even now the images settled. The swarming was over. He sat near the window of the shack and the heat pressed against his face, his head lolled back against the wall and the dust floated down the shaft of light, prisms, catching the light. Death sat across the room, rubbing itself with linseed oil.

Wilson heard the wind outside. The cold wind. He rose now in his dark room. He was confused. This edge, this risk had something to do with the answer. Go out again, he thought. Provoke them again. Face them. Not passive this time. Wilson went out of the room. He strode down the hallway in an unthinking fervor. On the balcony he looked both ways. There was no one in sight and he looked both ways again. He felt driven and he was conscious of that. He chided himself: he was trembling toward this exposure to peril like a flasher crouched behind a bush. But he could not stop the tremor. He went down the steps and on toward the back corridor and the chapel, the last place where they'd tried.

Two men were at the end of the corridor but they disappeared into a room before Wilson drew near. He could not tell if they'd seen him. He slowed at the door of the room and he heard a ripple of laughter inside. Wilson moved on. A light showed in the crack under the chapel doors and Wilson pushed through.

Standing at the lectern was Eli Marcus, a Bible lifted, his other hand sliding forward at the end of a gesture; in the air was a residue of words, silent but unmistakable. The chapel pews were empty.

Eli looked at Wilson and slowly lowered his hands, as if Wilson were holding a weapon on him. The preacher smiled and said, "You're the last person at this camp—perhaps in the world—that I'd like to have catch me rehearsing an...effect." Eli paused a moment and then he said, "Given our last conversation..."

"I understand," Wilson said.

"Do you?"

"You just tell your congregation..." Wilson didn't want to go on with this. Coming to the chapel to provoke another attack seemed suddenly foolish: the place had nothing to do with it. Wilson felt his sentence dangling; he knew he could simply turn and leave—he felt no real need to appear cogent to Eli Marcus— but instead he just plugged in words. "You tell them what they want to hear."

"Not at all," Eli said, with vehemence. "You haven't been listening."

"Oh shit," Wilson said under his breath. He thought, Now he'll make a big thing out of all this.

"You haven't heard a word," Eli repeated, his voice gentle now. He came down from the platform and as he approached, Wilson felt his own desire for another attack draw off, curl up in the corner to wait. Eli carried an aura with him and Wilson waited for it to touch him.

Eli stopped before Wilson, the Bible still in his hand. "I try very hard to look at all this with fresh eyes. The questions are too important for us to ignore them just because the ways we talk about them tend to be...overworked."

"Look, you don't have to do this..."

"I think it was Karl Barth who said that you can't talk of God by talking of man in a loud voice..."

"Eli," Wilson said sharply, to shut him up. He did not need to say more, for Eli smiled, a half-smile, self-deprecating, and he seemed to understand.

"I'm sorry," Eli said. "I was preaching to you like I'd preach to anyone. You don't need that."

"Am I too far gone?"

"No. Not at all." Another half-smile crept into Eli's face. Wilson was reminded by it of the coyness the man himself had condemned about crucifix Christs.

"What are you doing here?" Wilson asked.

"Tomorrow's Sunday."

"You're on the circuit."

"It's Moonbase's time," Eli said.

"Do you ever feel like your words are just...clutter? Not for others. I'm not talking about your work. For yourself." The point came out unexpectedly. Wilson thought Marta would do this man some good, stop him from talking so much.

"Of course I do," Eli said. And he said no more. The man waited and Wilson waited and then Wilson heard a stirring inside him—from the corner, from the desire for peril—he had to go now.

"Good-bye," Wilson said and Eli nodded. Wilson turned and pushed through the door and the hallway was empty. Wilson was beginning to feel frantic again. He played over the last time in this hall. He wanted the two men in masks. He'd fight this time. But he'd end up out in the dark, alone, like Clyde, like Beth, nearer to a resolution. It occurred to him that he hadn't spoken to Eli about Clyde. Clyde was why he sought this now. He felt a quick draining in his chest. "Shit," he said, low, without any clear motive. He felt the phoniness of this drive once more. He'd learned this lesson already, after his last, week-long attempt to provoke an attack.

He walked along the hallway, his legs heavy, stiff. The chlorine smell of the pool flickered in him—he thought of Marta, of being inside her soon—but it was an idle thought, unable to lighten his legs. Two men were circling the billiard table, a ping pong ball pattered somewhere. Wilson climbed the steps, moved along the balcony and entered his own hallway. He passed by Marta's door for now and he stopped at his own, unlocked it, stepped into the darkness of his room, and closed the door.

Wilson was clamped around the chest, his arms pinned, and a shape loomed up before him. He gathered his strength to start to fight, to drive his heel up and back into the groin of the man who held him but then he felt the point of a knife touch him in the throat and he froze. The knife was from the shape in front of him, a man who said, "Don't move at all, Mr. Hand."

Wilson held his breath, felt the knife point denting his skin, wanting to break in. His mind cleared, he could smell the flannel of a shirt, he could feel the ridge of wrist-bone against his chest.

"We've been arguing about you," the man with the knife said. "Some of us who think we should kill you. We gave you a couple of scares first—sportsmanlike—but we kinda want to get the job done."

The man paused, clearly for effect. The voice was a little nasal and undistinguished. Wilson could not place it, could not be sure he'd ever heard it before.

The man waited another beat and said, "Then there are the others who'd rather just buy you off. We've gone round and round arguing."

"I hate to come between friends," Wilson said. He paused briefly and then said, very calmly, "You shithead."

Wilson felt the tensing in the man through the faintest vibration of the knifepoint. Wilson thought he could feel a tiny nick in the blade, the beveled edge.

The man said, "If my side had won, that remark would have made this very pleasant."

"If your side had won," Wilson said, "you wouldn't have bothered to say a word."

"Under the agreed plan, I can still get my chance...Okay, smart guy. Here's the deal. We'll give you fifteen hundred bucks if you just get off our backs. Life's hard enough up here without Anchorage hassling us over a little bit of pleasure."

Wilson, caught off guard by this, nearly jerked his head. But the knife held him and his eyes widened instead.

The man went on, "If you want to maybe give us a hand, we can talk further and make it really worth your while. We could use another briefcase..."

"Hey," Wilson said. "Are you guys talking about...what? Drugs of some sort?"

"What the fuck kind of game are you playing?" the man with the knife said. "Look, my alternative plan is to stick you. I don't like you acting stupid, like we're a bunch of idiots. If you don't want to play ball..."

Wilson felt a laugh rising in him. Of course, he thought. Of course. Finn had said drugs were his biggest worry up here. An investigator comes up, everyone's involved in drugs and paranoid about it, and they think he's after them. Wilson's contempt for the investigation he was doing was validated—he hadn't made any progress after all; and the laugh actually began to shape in him and then he grew afraid of the effect a laugh would have on the balance between knife-point and throat and the laugh dissipated. "Listen to me. I'm not after a drug ring up here."

"What are you talking about?"

"I don't give a shit what you guys are smoking or snorting," Wilson said. "Beats the fucking doughnuts when you come in from the cold."

The man behind laughed at this and his hold on Wilson loosened slightly.

Wilson said, "I'm up here to find out about some missing

documents. There's some exploration reports that've been stolen from the records center and Anchorage is nervous as hell about it. That's the only reason they sent me up here.''

"Are you shittin' me?" the man said.

"No I'm not. Keep your goddam money. They just care about fucking Arabs finding out all the big oil reserve numbers up here.''

Wilson saw a motion and he knew the knife had been drawn away, though he still felt the knifepoint on his throat, the spoor of near-death. He realized how close death had been—waiting for a stranger's anger or whim or twitch—but it did not move Wilson anymore.

"Fucking documents?" the man with the knife said.

"Fucking documents," Wilson said.

The arms around Wilson loosened further and then fell away. The knifepoint was fading and Wilson waited. The man before him said, "If I get even a hint this isn't true, I'll kill you.''

"It's true," Wilson said.

The two figures moved away; the door opened but Wilson did not look at the faces. He kept his eyes on the spot beneath the window where he'd crouched earlier. Then the door was shut and it was dark again.

He raised his fingertips to his throat, touched the spot where the knife had lain. His hand was steady and he felt like a bored lover.

As much as Wilson hated to see Finn, the next morning he went to the man to ask him about word on Clyde.

"There's nothing," Finn said.

Wilson nodded and went out of the office. His irritation at Finn was soothed only because he'd had a chance to penetrate the drug ring Finn was concerned about and had refused.

Wilson felt bitchy, jittery. What kind of grief is this? he demanded of himself. He passed by the reception desk, along the balcony, and the lights were dim, the ceiling was too low, the walls drew close. Wilson's breath shortened, the air grew thin.

In Marta's room he could breathe again, in the dark, the only sounds the sounds of zipper and flap of cloth. Wilson, naked already, waited for her. At last she was against him and they began to touch and lick and nibble and he keenly felt their efficiency and she moaned lightly and turned her face and his own coming began and he simply noted its occurrence and withdrew and he lay on his back. Marta tucked herself into the crook of his arm, laid her leg along his thigh and his head buzzed, he sensed the walls around him. All the idle words he could not speak to Marta gabbled in his mind. Then he thought of Beth. They sat in a truck-stop restaurant in the crotch of an interstate. Outside, beneath the gull-wing light standards, the cab of a snub-nosed truck was tilted forward, cracked open to expose the engine. Beth sat across from Wilson in a booth by the window and she was turning a pocketknife over and over in her hands. When they'd come in she'd stopped at once by the cash register where a glass case held novelty key chains, sunglasses, flints, pocketknives. She bought a knife—nickle alloy trim, stagged handle, high-carbon steel blade. She opened the knife and laid it on the table. With her fingertips she touched the blade, the stag on the handle, the silver shackle. She began to talk about a television show she'd seen, a nature special about fish that lived deep in the sea, a mile and a half deep where there was never a flicker of light, a world of absolute and eternal darkness and yet the fish were brilliantly colored. For whom? she asked. For what? The fish where no light could go, no creature could see—the bodies of the creatures were extravagantly hued like sunsets and auroras. Wilson remembered later: after she'd eaten biscuits and gravy and home fries and sausage and four eggs and toast she said she'd awoken that morning thinking she might be sane. And he could feel again the regret he felt at that moment. He regretted not being able to reach her, to help her, to love her in the way she must have needed, in the way that baffled him still. Beth talked on in him, the words indistinguishable in the memory, but she talked, her hands moving in the air between them. And she bought another knife as they left because it had a different handle, a bird inlaid in mother-of-pearl.

Wilson sat up abruptly in the bed. Marta stirred and he turned to her. In the dimness he could see her arm laid across her forehead. He wondered who was in her thoughts. The other men who'd touched her crowded into the room, he knew her fingertips remembered them all, he felt her fondling them in her mind now, turning them over, stacking them against the walls.

"Who are you thinking about right now?" he said.

"What?" Her arm fell.

"Who's in your mind. Which of the men?" He could feel her recoil. All right, he thought. Let's get it done with.

"What do you want?" she said.

"I want to know how many men are in this room. I feel crowded."

"You want names?" she said, her voice hard.

"I want to be here alone with you," he said.

"Just at Moonbase," she said, "there are Ralph, Bill, Gabe, Henry..."

"Stop it."

"You stop it." She sat up now, pulled her legs underneath her. "What the hell is wrong with you? If you start this kind of shit with me...With *me* of all people. You made me tell you, goddamit. I started to trust you a little. Christ, I thought, a man who really can handle it."

"Please stop."

"A man who won't twist me against myself...Wilson, you son-of-a-bitch." Her voice dissolved, she was beginning to cry. He was stunned. She'd seemed to him invulnerable. This was impossible—tears; and so quickly.

"You son-of-a-bitch," she said and she was shaking and she let him draw her to him.

"I'm sorry," he said and he held her close and she put her arms around him as if he hadn't been the source of this pain.

The *New York Times* reporter looked like he had his down-parka on underneath his white shirt and herringbone sportcoat. He was a large man and his body seemed to be straining to be larger still. Only his ears and his eyes were small—parts of a much smaller man being carried along, frightened. He had a bib-shaped beard the color of a collie and he moved into the office with a headlong wariness—rushing through the door, withholding his hand—that linked Wilson back to New York City. Beth drew near, but for the moment her presence was vague, undemanding, as if she'd just idly taken his arm in a park.

Wilson was glad his meeting with the reporter would be without Finn. This faintly wheezing, narrow-eyed man with his tie askew brought New York too clearly back to Wilson for him to tolerate Finn's soulfulness. "I'm Wilson Hand."

The man finally offered his hand, briefly. "I'm Paul O'Dell."

He sat down acoss the table in the same physical relationship to Wilson as the records center employees Wilson had interviewed. Wilson felt he had an advantage; he nearly smiled but kept it in.

"Listen, Mr. Hand, I've talked to people from your department in New York…"

"What's that?"

"New York. I've talked to your corporate p.r. guy, Hegler."

"I'm not going to interfere with you, Mr. O'Dell."

The reporter stretched out his chest; he straightened his glasses with both hands. "And I'm not an adversary, Mr. Hand. I'm very interested in what you're doing up here—that is, what we're doing. I understand the intimate link between your fortunes as a company and our fortunes as a country."

He paused as if he expected Wilson to plug in the next few statements of what they were supposed to agree on. But Wilson knew O'Dell was posing and he waited a moment more and then said, "You don't believe that bullshit, do you, Mr. O'Dell?"

O'Dell adjusted his glasses with both hands again, this time with an air of examination. This obviously sounded like no p.r.

man he'd ever heard. After a moment, he seemed to decide that Wilson, instead of being a straight-talking potential ally, was in fact a particularly dangerous enemy. He lifted his jaw, as if daring Wilson to yank the squared-off beard. O'Dell said, "Well, I guess you'd be in a better position than me to judge that."

"On the contrary. Only people like you are objective enough to decide those matters. Don't you think?"

"Well, I didn't really come all this way to...ah...discuss the philosophy of journalism."

"What *do* you want, Mr. O'Dell?" Wilson felt in control, the way he'd always felt in his little service in New York; and here was a New Yorker, the voice hard-edged as a subway rail, a vague scruffiness about him, and a crackle of intelligence, and Wilson had him off balance.

O'Dell said, "Look, I'm not really challenging your need to charge a lot of money to get all this oil out. The President's pushing it like crazy but I've got an open mind. Personally I do. Forget the things our editorial pages harp on. I'm a news writer." He raised his jaw again and his beard jutted out and Wilson thought about jerking it down like a paper towel in a public toilet.

"So I still don't see what a news writer is doing up here," Wilson said, making his voice brittle. "You don't find *news* at the wellhead. Up here you do feature stories. Right? Arctic night. Hardhats. Drill bits and bitter cold. That's not *news*."

O'Dell went to his glasses again. Again Wilson wanted to smile. O'Dell shifted in his chair, twisted his head as if he had a crick in his neck. "I like you, Mr. Hand," he said. "You seem like a straight sort of guy."

"Mr. O'Dell, you're not here to make friends."

The visible parts of O'Dell's face—his forehead, the knobs of unbearded cheek—turned red. Wilson wondered where this man's flash-point was. O'Dell's mouth opened and closed without a sound coming out and Wilson thought for a moment that this was it. But O'Dell twisted his head the opposite way and made his voice very formal and he said, "We're working on something big at the moment. I want to see the oil field, get an overall...sense of the place. If that seems odd or...featury for a news writer, so be it. But you *will* let me look around, won't you?"

Wilson sat back in his chair and waited for a long moment. This time O'Dell's hands stayed on the table, his face was still, his eyes did not move away. "I'm sure Mr. Finn will show you what you want to see," Wilson said.

"Good. Yes. Thank you." O'Dell rose. He paused as if he expected Wilson to rise with him. Wilson sat where he was. He clasped his hands behind his head. O'Dell adjusted his glasses. He nodded his head abruptly and left.

For a moment Wilson felt smug. Beth, who he realized had been at his shoulder all along, bent to him, began to whisper something, but withdrew. O'Dell and the New York that clung to him lingered for a moment in the air but then began to rise toward the vents to be sucked out, and Wilson was alone. O'Dell had said he was working on something big. As detached as Wilson was from the investigation, he still paused to wonder if there were a connection.

Wilson and Marta lay that night together side by side. Wilson held her hand and her silence felt even less penetrable than before. He knew she was troubled. He thought of his foolish questions of the day before, and thinking of his foolishness simply stirred up the feelings once again. The names rang in his head. Ralph, Gabe, Bill...one other that he couldn't recall. And he'd cut her off. How many men here had lain like this beside Marta? Ralph, Bill, Gabe...One of them sounded familiar. But not familiar enough to make a connection and Wilson was glad of that; he forced his mind away. It was odd, he thought, feeling a retrospective jealousy over Marta at a time when their love-making had settled down, had become ritualized and thoughtful. Jealousies surely came in the first rush of passion when the rutting instincts stirred the deepest. But maybe this wasn't really jealousy. Wilson could see Beth's apartment stuffed with objects; there were never enough things to own. Marta's men felt the same to Wilson.

"Wilson," Marta said.

He started at the word. He had not expected to hear her voice at all tonight. "Yes?"

"I'm going to take my week off this time. Away from Moonbase."

She did not add "Away from you" but Wilson understood it. "Yes?" he said.

"I don't know when I'll take it, exactly. I've got some compensatory time put by. I just want you to know. Be prepared. One day I might be gone."

Wilson waited. He felt she wanted some acknowledgement but he didn't know what to say.

"But I'll be back," she said. She squeezed his hand and he felt a rush of gratitude that surprised him.

The sound of a small plane woke him—the engine pitching high, drawing near, buzzing past—very close. Wilson thought for a moment he was dreaming. He rose up. Marta was gone to work already. It was morning. He heard the faint bratting of the engine, circling out invisible in the dark, and then coming near again, driving hard. Wilson moved to the window and he could see nothing for a moment, but the engines raced and then the bright landing lights came down before him—straight down, it seemed—and rushed at him, the ravens flashed past in panic, and the plane spanked by overhead.

"Clyde," Wilson said, low. He dressed quickly and went out to the reception area to wait. He stood at the doors and time passed; he carefully watched each man who entered and the wool masks turned to him and then away and Wilson did not even look over his shoulder at the men. They weren't Clyde; he would know Clyde. He waited and his knees began to stiffen; a long time had passed and he began to feel clammy, his face grew warm. It hadn't been Clyde after all. "Shit," he said softly.

A large figure was at the door, going out. Wilson turned and saw O'Dell. Ronnie was with him. "So long, Mr. Hand," O'Dell said, a faint trace of a sneer in his voice.

Wilson was angry at Clyde for not showing up, for crashing, dying, without him, but even as he realized this, the anger shifted to O'Dell. Wilson said, "You got what you want already?"

O'Dell shrugged and began to push out the door. Wilson took a step toward him and said, "When should I look for this big story of yours?"

O'Dell pressed on through the door without acknowledging Wilson's words. Ronnie trailed past. Wilson realized the reporter had not gotten all that he had been looking for. As he watched O'Dell and Ronnie recede into the darkness, a van pulled up and a figure got out and though the man's back was turned and his parka hood was up, Wilson knew it was Clyde. The man faced the doors. He wore no mask. Clyde saw Wilson and grinned. He came up the stairs trying to saunter but favoring his right leg slightly. He came in through the first set of doors and then the second and Wilson strode to him and put both his hands on Clyde's shoulders and shook him like a child.

"You old fart," Wilson said. "I thought you'd left me behind."

Clyde's hands rose and spread and Wilson's hands fell to his sides and Clyde reached out and rapped him on the arm. "No way, boy. Just a dry run."

"You went down."

"Ran into a cloud with no bottom...Well, almost no bottom. Put down hard on a glacier and walked out."

"You walked out?"

"Most of the way." Clyde grinned. "Hey, you've got to let me make this sound good. They didn't know where I was, but I did. I went down pretty far south and I had some daylight and then an almost-full moon. I was only ten miles from a settlement. Wasn't pleasant with a gimpy leg and a half-dozen cracked ribs, but I been in worse scrapes, boy...You didn't miss nothin' at all."

Back in Wilson's room, with Clyde's whiskey bottle sitting between them on the desk chair, Wilson asked, "Where were you heading?" He knew the answer but he wondered how Clyde would reply to the question.

Clyde ignored it for a moment, lolloping three fingers of whiskey into a water glass. Then he picked up his drink and said, "Just routine stuff. Going up north with some supplies."

Wilson waited a moment to see if Clyde would say more, but he did not. "You were flying food to the hippies," Wilson said.

Clyde swirled the whiskey in his glass, watching it. "They were crazy sons-of-bitches," he said, low.

The two men fell silent for a long time, drinking steadily, and one more question slowly shaped itself in Wilson. Finally he said, "Clyde, what was it like at the moment you thought you were going to die?"

Clyde grew still. He put his glass down. Then he said, "I was scared, boy. I just wasn't ready."

Wilson was surprised at the man's fear, surprised that he'd expressed it. He felt Clyde's fear stretch out like the man's large hands and settle on his shoulders. But Wilson said no more. Neither man spoke again until much later when they decided to arm wrestle.

Clyde left the next day to recuperate in Anchorage and only after he'd left did Wilson realize the man had flown all the way to Moonbase just to have a few drinks with him over his escape. Two days later Marta was gone without a word, as she'd warned, and Wilson sat in his room, in the chair under the window, and he wondered how long all this would go on; and to what end. He stripped and slept a nearly dreamless sleep and when he awoke, his conscious mind remained as dreamless as his sleep. But there was no feeling of expiation or release or peace in all of this. The rotation of his life, the tilt of its axis, had simply taken him into a temporary darkness. When a rap came to his door he rose up and he looked at the clock and was surprised to find that it was noon.

He slipped his pants on and opened the door and found Finn. The man said, "I need you right away."

"I'll get dressed."

"Come to the records center."

The records center was empty except for Finn. He was watching a video terminal and Wilson approached and stood by him. On the screen, words were scrolling up, marching line by line to the top and disappearing, each line that blinked off the top being replaced with a new one at the bottom of the screen. Each line had a sequence of letters and numbers and then a few words, geographical identifications. Beechey Point sectors 50-75, Beechey Point sectors 75-100, Drew Point, Point Franklin sectors 1-25. Wilson looked at Finn.

"It's all been printed out," Finn said. "This is one of the directories that's been printed out. There's more. From all over. And there was an analysis run. I don't even know what all is involved."

"Stolen?"

"Of course stolen." Finn looked at Wilson. "Where the hell have you been? Aren't you here to prevent this?"

"When did this happen?"

"In the last twenty four hours."

Wilson thought of O'Dell rushing out the door three days ago. Wilson could not face Finn now or Gordon James or even his room. He had to put Finn off and get away from Moonbase for a time and still keep his options to return and he found the solution in a stroke: O'Dell. Wilson said, "I know what's been happening."

"You do?" Finn said, serious, his brow furrowed, ready to trust.

"I have to work quickly now. I have to go to New York City. The New York Times reporter is the key figure."

"The reporter?"

"Yes. Tell James to get me passage to New York. Tonight. O'Dell's the key."

Finn's mouth tightened into a thin line. He squinted and nodded in a comradely way and moved quickly off.

Wilson puffed in appreciation of what had just happened. He felt a rush from having made the right choices without thinking. A few days back in New York would give him a setting to renew his feelings for Alaska. And as the idea settled into his mind, he began to think there might indeed be a connection between O'Dell and the documents. As in the most basic investigative work, all Wilson had done was wait for something else to happen. O'Dell rushed out, unsatisfied. But he'd set something in motion up here and now it had yielded what he wanted—maybe information for that big story. It seemed plausible to Wilson. He would go to New York. He thought of Beth's picture, her bare feet on the front page of a newspaper—he thought of her feet broken down now, burned into ash and scattered on the East River or sitting on her mother's mantle in a Chinese vase or in the earth, mixed into the earth on the peak of a bluff along the Hudson. Wilson would fly to her, too. And to the sun.

12.

Above the cloud-cover Wilson was able to see the sun. But strapped into the jet, the land invisible, the thin whine of a child two rows up louder than the engines, Wilson had no feeling for it. And he was waiting for New York. He slept and woke and slept again and at last the plane began its descent and still there were clouds. When the plane broke through, Manhattan was off to the left. The buildings were crystal growths on a cave floor, crowded, leaving no place to step. The air was full of snow that was as unobtrusive as motes of dust. Wilson shivered. The island crept past beneath the plane and he felt cold.

He bought the afternoon *Post* in Times Square and he was conscious of the act—the last one he'd bought had Beth on its front page. But he needed something to hide behind and he folded the paper under his arm and waited on a triangle of concrete in the midst of the confluence of Seventh Avenue and Broadway and he waited for the light to change. The other New Yorkers moved a pace or two into the street, pressed right up to the edge of the traffic, could have wiped the dust from taxi doors with the slightest bend of their knees. Then they crossed against the light like matadors in a crowd of bulls, moving lane to lane among the random rush of the cars. Wilson stood on the sidewalk and waited, though just a few months earlier he too would have been crossing in the midst of the chaos, dodging through it, becoming part of it. But New York roared at him, jostled him, burned his lungs. The sidewalks swirled with people, swirled and lunged and Wilson drew into himself. The light said "Walk" and he crossed, going west on Forty-third and he saw, mid-block, a digital clock thrusting out from a building with simply the word "Times" in Gothic script over it.

He approached the *New York Times* building on the opposite side of the street and sat on a standpipe diagonally across from the front door. The building was massive, white-brick, and all along the front were large blue garage doors, some with the snouts of delivery trucks sticking out. The opening for people seemed ridiculously small—two cramped revolving doors—and Wilson hunched his shoulders against the cold air. He was very uncomfortable and he thought to leave. But he wanted Alaska; he was yearning again now, and he knew that if he used O'Dell in order to find the leaks at Moonbase, his job in Alaska was secure. If he failed, he'd have no way to return to the North Slope. The digital clock said four thirty-five. The lights were already burning on bar and deli and transient hotel down the block.

But he did not have to wait long. O'Dell emerged and began to move east and Wilson raised the paper. **RAPE VICTIM KILLS HUSBAND BY MISTAKE.** Wilson turned the paper just enough to watch O'Dell's back moving off, then crossing the street thirty yards down. Wilson rose and began to follow. O'Dell's size and his green Alpine hat let Wilson hang behind a bit further than he usually would. But the man never looked back, never showed a trace of suspicion, and he crossed the intersection moving from the west side of Seventh over the island at Times Square Plaza and on to the east side of Broadway, with Wilson beating the light just behind him. Hot dog stands, poster shops, spinning trees of postcards, windows full of cameras and calculators gabbled in Wilson's mind, made him grit his teeth. His purpose was accomplished already—he knew he could not stay here, he wanted to be in Clyde's plane flying over the tundra. O'Dell was moving south on Broadway, approaching Forty-second Street. But Wilson felt uneasy about Clyde and his plane: where could they fly that would stop this yearning? Just to fly was not enough, just to escape all this. Overhead, a three-story face blew smoke rings, across the street a billboard teenage girl stretched out along the whole width of a building, her ass high in the air, crowned with a designer-jean label like a nipple on a breast.

The walk-light was flashing "Don't Walk" and O'Dell was too far ahead, half-way across the street. Wilson shook himself out of his thoughts and sprinted, juking around two men, an old woman, and then out into the honks of taxis chafing as the light changed green with him in the way. O'Dell had turned east on Forty-second and Wilson was on the sidewalk, glad the man hadn't looked around. Wilson moved after him along the store-fronts.

On this block a marquee, framed in running lights, offered a triple bill of "Splits," "Beaver Hop," and "Take a Licking." O'Dell slowed. He passed under the marquee and his head turned for the first time—toward the box office and the inside posters. Wilson moved to the outside of the sidewalk. Ahead now was a string of movie houses and magazine stores and another marquee touting live nude sex acts, mixed couples, all your fantasies on stage. A sidewalk loudspeaker blared a disco song over a window full of velour sportcoats and Barcelona hats.

O'Dell slowed further. Wilson did too. And then the reporter stopped, looked at a window that said, "Live Nudes 25¢" and went in. Wilson hesitated. O'Dell could have stopped near the door. A middle-aged man in a business suit approached the door, opened it, and Wilson stepped near, shielded by the businessman, and he saw O'Dell's back, receding.

Wilson entered the shop, moved along the outer display—a wall full of rubber phalluses with nodules that made them look like the cocks of Martians and a magazine wall full of faces and organs, the smell of their slick paper strong in the air.

O'Dell lingered up ahead in a dim passageway of peep show booths. He was reading a film description by the door of one of the compartments. Wilson turned and faced a booth on the opposite side of the passageway. The photo had a woman and a large dog and Wilson did not look too closely. He concentrated on the periphery of his vision and O'Dell was turning again, moving deeper into the shop.

The dim passage led to a staircase lit in red and O'Dell went down another level, down to the 25¢ live nudes. Wilson followed, and the downstairs area held a row of doorways that curved at each end, a horseshoe of compartments surrounding an implied space. Above each door was a pair of lights, one red, one green. O'Dell was disappearing into a doorway with the green light lit overhead. The door clicked shut and a moment later the red light came on.

Wilson hesitated. Men jostled past and Wilson thought to return to the street and wait. But a doorway in front of him was ajar; the light was green and he stepped in. He shut the door and the walls of the room were tight, the air was close and smelled of sweat and vaguely of semen. A disco tune was thumping beyond a translucent plastic panel and Wilson dropped a quarter into a coin box on the wall and the panel rose with a faint, electric whir.

Inside was a platform with a bed and a large space curving along the windows. Two naked women were moving in the space, a third was sitting on the bed, rubbing a cream from a jar into her loins. Wilson could see other open windows on the legs of the horseshoe, men's faces wide-eyed there, one window whirring down, a flurry of movement under the falling shade, and then the window rising again and the face—a very young man with a blond mustache—settling into its frame again. One man reached through the space with a dollar bill and a tan woman with tight, small buttocks and straight black hair down to the middle of her back came and took the dollar and let the man reach through and begin to stroke at her breast, gently twist at her nipple. The other woman in the space also had a fistful of dollars and she stopped at the window next to Wilson's and took a dollar from a hand. The arm came out and the hand eased up between her legs and nestled into her crotch, and across the way the hand had finished stroking the breast and also connected into the woman's loins and held still. For a long moment there was no movement at all. The woman on the bed had stopped rubbing, had let her head loll back, had closed her eyes in a moment's dream of someplace else; the two women stood quietly at their windows; the arms stretched through, the hands were still. Wilson thought he heard a faint whine of anguish but it was the electric motor in his booth and the panel descended. But the sense of anguish and futile yearning remained and his eyes felt hot, his contempt for O'Dell was gone, the compartment pressed in on him and he could not draw a breath.

Wilson pushed open the door, went up the steps, along the dim passage filled with a metallic flutter from the movie projectors that sounded like the flight of tin birds, on through the bright walls of faces and phalluses and out into the cold air. He sucked in the cold and he felt Alaska inside him, briefly, but this air grated in his lungs and he moved to the edge of the street, leaned against a delivery truck parked there. His breathing settled after a time and he turned, empty, not knowing quite what to do, and O'Dell came out of the shop and walked off and Wilson followed him.

On the corner of Sixth Avenue, O'Dell went down the steps into the subway. Wilson paused at the top step and then descended. The corridor was newly refurbished in bathroom tiles and it stank of urine and the trains howled below. O'Dell was far away now, walking fast and Wilson's legs felt heavy. But he thought of what it would be like upstairs alone—the streets of New York and no link to the job that might keep him in Alaska. He hurried, jogged when O'Dell disappeared at a turning, ran hard toward the corner, fearing at the last moment that O'Dell would be standing there waiting, a trap, blowing Wilson's cover, but the corner neared and Wilson did not slow down and he came around it and saw O'Dell beyond the turnstile, descending the downtown steps. Wilson followed. He kept his mind on his work, remained coolly professional, followed O'Dell to his exit on West Fourth and up into Greenwich Village and along a narrow street of brownstones. O'Dell went up the steps of a building of red brick and he unlocked the door and went in.

Wilson was left alone. He imagined O'Dell entering his apartment. It had a cat, bookshelves of plywood and brick, a stack of *Penthouse* magazines. The man would cook for himself, go to bed, masturbate and sleep. Wilson was alone in the streets after all. He could go back now. Back to the airport and back to Anchorage. But that would be the end of things. He'd never be able to return to Moonbase. He'd allowed another theft, a major one, and had nothing to report. He would come back here tomorrow morning, but first there was the night.

A woman brushed past. Wilson smelled her perfume and turned to watch her recede, not seeing her, hearing only the rush of traffic, seeing the sprays of neon at the end of the street, feeling Beth, but feeling her by her absence. She was far from him here. She was gone from here. Only her absence was clear in New York. He thought to go to her mother, to find where Beth's ashes were. But he didn't want to know. The whole city knew she was dead. They'd seen her bare feet, months before the life was gone, the confusion in her face. The leaper died at last. The leaper was dead.

He lay in his hotel room. The traffic hissed past below the window and the nightstand lamp glared in his eyes and burned on his cheek. But Wilson left the light on to hold off his reverie. He was afraid of his memories in this city, afraid they'd be shaped by the place. But the fleurs-de-lis on the wallpaper, a woman's laughter in a distant room, the rush of cars in the street, would not hold him in suspension. He had no choice and he rose from the bed and switched off the light and then he lay back down.

Beth came to him at once. A cloudy summer Sunday a year into their marriage. The first image Wilson had was of himself sitting on a bollard at the end of an abandoned pier in the Hudson River. The river was the color of tarnished silver, the same color as the sky; and river and sky were separated by a thin strip of industrial shapes on the far Jersey shore. Beth stood beside Wilson and held his head beneath her breasts as if she were comforting him, but he could feel the faint spasms in her, he could hear her weeping. A moment earlier they had stepped inside the crumbling container terminal and the expanse of the floor was filled with objects: broken glass ground so fine it hardly crackled underfoot, and wood slats from packing cases; foam mattresses and spikes and pipes and newspapers and shoes and excelsior; bottles and doorknobs and springs and tires; a grocery cart, a bicycle frame and an old woman standing out in the center of the floor naked. Her hair was shaggy and matted, her body was stained like the walls, she turned her face to the intruders and folded her hands across her crumpled breasts and began to curse. They could hear her still, faintly, as they clung together beside the water. They could hear crashing, clanging, objects hurtling inside the terminal building. But Beth would not let the two of them flee. She stayed here at the edge, listening and weeping. Wilson wanted to take her away but she held his head tightly against her. Even now, even lying in this hotel room with Beth gone, he wanted to take her away, he yearned to take her in his arms and fly with her back to Alaska. Alaska was full. But not on its surface. Deep inside the earth it was full. That's why he wanted to return. He had not drilled quite deep enough but he was in the right field, the domes and the stratigraphic traps and the migration were right—and he wanted Beth to be filled too—he wanted her to find the peace he knew was close now. But he could not picture her. He could not focus on her face. The door burst open, he heard the flutter of the chickens in the yard and his eyes were dazzled by the sunlight and the dark shape there raised a rifle and the room was filled with a sound too fast to catch up with, too fast, too fast, he thought he was dead, he thought he was the target, his chest, his face. Was he dead? Was there no pain after all? Was he out of his body now? Was there a continuance after all? Bodies flew around the room. The dust swirled. There was stillness. His chest was heaving, heaving. He was still alive. His chest heaved. He lifted with it, fell, lifted again and then Captain Fleming was crouched beside him. Come on, Fleming said. You're free. The captain touched

Wilson's arm and Wilson jerked it away. The gesture surprised Wilson as much as Fleming. Why? Wilson asked that now, rising up in his bed. "Why?" he said aloud. "Why?" he shouted. Why had he felt a separation at that moment, as he was freed from his captivity? Not a rejoining but a separation, a clear separation. I got you back, Fleming said. No, Wilson said. "No," Wilson repeated in his motel room. He spoke the word softly, barely audible above the sound of the traffic.

He waited an hour the next morning, sitting on the stoop of a brownstone across the street and down the block fifty yards from O'Dell's building. O'Dell came out at last. He was carrying a small suitcase and Wilson followed him to Sixth Avenue, closing the distance between them, watching the suitcase. O'Dell passed the subway entrance and stepped off the curb and raised his arm to hail a cab. Wilson turned at the corner and moved with the traffic, watching over his shoulder as a cab stopped for O'Dell and then hailing one for himself.

Wilson followed O'Dell out to JFK and into the American Airlines terminal building. O'Dell paused inside the sliding doors and looked at his watch. Wilson moved off to the side and picked up a brochure at the currency exchange window. He opened the brochure and looked toward O'Dell. The man had entered a line to check his bag. The check station was at the end of the row and beside it was a wide metal scale. Wilson waited until O'Dell leaned over the counter and then he crossed to the empty space near the scale. He stood to the side and a pace behind O'Dell and he heard the clerk say, "That's seat 29A. It'll be boarding at about eight-thirty at gate forty-four."

Wilson turned and walked briskly away. He stopped at a flight screen hanging near the currency exchange and looked for gate forty-four. He found it. A nine o'clock departure to San Francisco. His fists jumped up before him. "Yes," he said, low. One of the little pleasures of his job rippled through him. It was still plausible: O'Dell could be going to San Francisco to get the stolen reports. The place was a reasonable compromise for both him and his Moonbase contacts. Wilson glanced over his shoulder. O'Dell was gone. Wilson went to the American ticket counter and bought passage on the nine o'clock flight to San Francisco.

Wilson watched only the taxi ahead of him. He knew the hills and the pastel houses stacked there, the bay and a bridge and wheeling gulls all were passing outside. But there was a hard, sculptured center of ice in him, a cold spike of Alaska lodged there, and he could not focus now on anything but the man up ahead who could be the key to returning to Moonbase. Wilson had been lucky in this matter. He'd done nothing on the investigation, had pursued only his own vague interests, and it was likely that he'd stumbled onto the solution anyway. And that would give him the credentials to go back. The two taxis moved through the city, and downtown, near the end of the cable car line, two blocks off Union Square, O'Dell's taxi came to a stop before a hotel with a heavy-marble, porcelain-faucet kind of elegance, an elegance so far out of phase with the atriums and bronze glass skins of new hotels that the place seemed a little scruffy in spite of its standards.

Wilson followed O'Dell up the steps and through the door. Wilson stopped and shrank back. The lobby was vast and full of people, mostly Japanese in groups, cameras slung from their necks. Around the circumference of the lobby were arrangements of filigreed chairs and settees and claw-footed tables holding lamps with shades the shape of pagoda roofs. The inner facades had friezes of mythical beasts and off the lobby was a sunken bar bounded by thick marble columns. The place scrambled Wilson's thoughts, made him anxious. Too many objects, too much clutter. But he had to stay with O'Dell now or he'd never be able to escape just such places as this. O'Dell did not head for the registration desk, as Wilson expected, but went down the steps to the sunken bar. Wilson moved to a column and looked around it and saw O'Dell sitting at a table near the steps. The suitcase was at his feet; his hands were folded on the tabletop. He was waiting for someone.

Wilson could not go into the bar because O'Dell was watching. Wilson looked around the lobby. The entrance to the bar faced the elevators across a wide, empty space. Against the dim side wall between elevators and bar was an arrangement of chairs and a table. Wilson crossed to it and sat in one of the chairs. He could see the entrance to the bar but he could not see O'Dell. He could not depend on recognizing the Moonbase contact; indeed, the documents could have changed hands since the theft on the North Slope. He decided to check each time anyone entered the bar.

He waited and tried to concentrate on the front doors of the hotel, waiting for the contact to appear. But the swirls and eddies of people, the decorative profusion of the lobby, still plagued him. Then a tall, slender man in his mid-thirties came through the front door. His hair was thinning and he had a sandy wiriness that Wilson associated with the men at Moonbase. The man wore a tweed jacket over a work shirt and was slipping a notebook into his coat pocket. Wilson tensed. The man seemed aimless for a moment, looking around the lobby, and then he glanced into the sunken bar and descended the steps. Wilson rose and moved quickly forward.

He expected the two men to be greeting each other, but he was wrong. O'Dell was still watching the steps and Wilson pulled back quickly. The angle of his approach had kept him out of O'Dell's gaze but he'd nearly been exposed. He looked past the edge of a row of man-sized plants and he could see O'Dell watching, waiting. The thin man had passed on into the bar without a pause. Wilson waited a minute and then another to see if this were just a cautionary maneuver of the two. But it finally became clear that the Moonbase contact had still not arrived.

Wilson returned to his chair and sat down. A group of young Japanese—the women with brightly colored socks and high heels, the men with Dodgers and Giants warm up jackets—approached the bar, went down the steps. Wilson did not rise. He knew O'Dell was still alone. Wilson waited, sensing the man just out of sight, knowing the correspondence of their feelings, waiting.

The come and go of people at the elevators behind Wilson stayed on the very periphery of his awareness. But a figure went by, moving from elevator toward bar, and Wilson saw the tall man, the silver hair, and his breath snagged. Eli Marcus.

The preacher went down the steps and Wilson rose. He crossed to the plants, looked around, and Eli was standing at O'Dell's table blocking the reporter from Wilson's view. They were talking, but Eli was making no move to sit; he had no documents with him. Wilson knew they would go to Eli's room. The elevator would be a problem, with both men able to recognize him instantly. He had to find Eli's room another way.

He crossed the lobby to the registration desk. There was a house phone on a stand and within his sight was the wall of numbered pigeon holes with room keys and slips of paper scattered through. Eli's room was empty at the moment. He would call the room and when there was no answer he would try to get the room number from the operator. If that failed, he'd leave a message and watch the clerk put the slip of paper into the hole on the wall. Wilson picked up the house phone. When the operator answered, Wilson said, "I'd like to speak to Eli Marcus, please."

"Just a moment...I'll ring."

The phone rang and Wilson thought he'd give it five rings before asking the operator's help. It rang again and then there was a click and a woman's voice. "Yes?"

The word hung for only a moment before Wilson knew that it was Marta. He sagged against the phone stand.

"Hello?" Marta insisted.

Wilson found himself removing his handkerchief, placing it over the phone. He lowered his voice, roughened it, and he said, "Sorry. This is the front desk. When are you checking out?"

"Day after tomorrow," Marta said.

Wilson's arms felt so weak he feared he could not keep the phone to his ear. But he focused on Alaska, Alaska, getting back. He had to nail O'Dell to do that the way he wanted. "And your room number is...what?"

"My room?"

Don't think about it, he shouted to her in his mind. "Yes."

"1857."

"Right. Of course. I have it here. Thanks." He hung up and put his handkerchief away. He drew his wrist across his forehead. He was sweating. What was the surprise? he thought. She said herself how easy it was for her to take a man to bed.

Wilson turned and looked across the lobby. O'Dell and Eli were entering an elevator. Wilson quickly put his back to them, allowed time for the doors to close, and then he crossed to the elevators himself.

On the way up, he let himself understand Marta's part in the theft. Details. The stack of papers—*The New York Times*—with energy stories circled. O'Dell's stories, no doubt. And the names she'd mentioned of the men she'd slept with at Moonbase. One of them had sounded familiar. Gabe. Wilson hadn't interviewed the man, but he felt certain he'd find the name on the list of records center personnel. One of the ones he'd never bothered to talk to. He was her contact inside the center, the one who actually made the computer run.

The elevator stopped at the eighteenth floor and Wilson stepped into the corridor. The doors closed and the hallway was silent. Wilson had to make a decision now. He thought to barge in at once, catch them all together, in the middle of exchanging the information. But the timing was delicate, he thought. They might sit and chat or drink or pray or whatever first, and if he burst in when the information was still concealed, things could get awkward. Especially with three of them. Marta spread her legs in Wilson's mind; Eli gaped. Wilson clenched his fists, tried to force his mind back to the documents. He'd pick off O'Dell outside the room or down in the lobby. Wilson felt a sticky restlessness spreading in his limbs, in his groin. Marta and Eli.

"Shit," he said aloud. He looked at a panel on the wall and

followed the arrow toward 1857. He turned a corner and approached the doorway and paused. He was conscious of his posture—the angle of his head, the slope of his shoulder—it was the same pose he'd held a dozen times outside Marta's room at Moonbase, listening for her movements, imagining her naked inside. He heard voices now. Eli's. O'Dell's. There was laughter. The voices approached the door.

Wilson was not ready for a confrontation. He moved further down the hall, away from the elevator. The room doors were recessed and he pressed into one, pressed flat, not quite hidden but at least not conspicuous. They would have to consciously look this way to see him. The voices were outside the room now.

"Okay," O'Dell said. "You've got..." The words blurred.

Eli began to speak and Wilson heard him say "no trouble" and "very big thing" and the rest was garbled.

Then the door clicked shut and Wilson heard a receding swish of cloth. He stepped out from the doorway and saw O'Dell at the far end. The transfer of information was complete and he swung the suitcase that was filled now with numbers. The man turned the corner and disappeared. Wilson moved after him but he slowed by the door of Eli's room and there were no voices. Only silence inside. Wilson's face burned. Then he heard a ping, far off. The elevator. Wilson ran hard, around the corner and down to the elevators, but O'Dell was gone and the doors were all closed.

"Damn," Wilson said, punching the down button. "Damn." He tried to hold himself still as he waited. He kept his back very stiff and straight and he listened to the lazy slip and clack inside the elevator shafts. Then the ping, loud, one elevator to his left. The doors opened and he stepped in and punched, "Lobby."

The elevator went straight down past fifteen, ten, five, but on four it stopped and a middle-aged Japanese man bowed his way on and Wilson suppressed a curse and the doors closed and he waited again. Three, Ballroom level, Lobby. The doors opened.

Wilson dashed across the lobby and O'Dell was not in sight.

Wilson pushed through the front door and pumped down the steps and there was no taxi in sight, not pulling away, not available for pursuit. O'Dell had his story and had gotten away.

Wilson took a deep breath. He could go to the airport. O'Dell would surely be there. Wilson could call the San Francisco police. There was criminal theft involved here, surely. But even as he thought about these options, his mind grew sluggish. The silence behind the doors of the hotel room gnawed at Wilson. The palms of his hands prickled at the imprint of Marta's body there, her naked body lying exposed to Pastor Eli now. Then his feelings careened off. He laughed aloud. Pastor Eli fucking Marta, his hand groping into the nightstand, raising the Gideon Bible as he came. Wilson laughed. There was time for the airport, for the police.

Wilson went back up the steps, across the lobby, into an elevator. At eighteen he stepped off and moved along the corridor, took the turn, slowed and stood at the door of 1857. He did not wait to listen. He knocked at the door.

He heard a rustle and then Eli's voice say, "Who is it?"

Wilson feigned breathlessness, taking all the tone, the timbre, out of his voice. "O'Dell," he said. Then Wilson put the palm of his hand firmly over the peephole. He felt there was a good chance Eli would open the door.

"Just a minute," Eli said.

A pressure began to build in Wilson's chest, his arms grew strong. He waited and then there was the rattle of the door chain being disengaged and the door opened just a crack and Eli's face came around it. Before the face could even register surprise, Wilson stepped back and then threw his weight against the door. The door flew in, Wilson lunged into the room and stopped in its center and Marta was sitting in the bed, the sheet covering her to the waist, her breasts bare, the nipples erect, her eyes wide.

Wilson turned to Eli who was coming into the room, his face pale. Wilson felt all his strength rush into his right arm, his right hand, he drew back and then struck straight out catching Eli on the point of the chin and the man flew back into the wall and slid down.

186

There was only silence in the room and this surprised Wilson. He turned back to Marta. She was watching him, her face blank. She had pulled the sheet up over her breasts. She still said nothing. Wilson looked at Eli who sat quietly on the floor, gingerly working his jaw. Eli's eyes rose to Wilson and the man also remained silent. Wilson squared around to Eli and the preacher said, "I won't fight you, Mr. Hand. I don't believe in it. You'll have to pummel me while I'm down here on the floor."

Now Marta was beginning to cry. Wilson heard her but did not turn. He felt suddenly weary. There was nothing of any real concern to him in this room. He just wanted to go back north, dig deeper.

"I know what you two have done," Wilson said, though he still faced only Eli. The man's chest had a tiny silver patch in its center. His pants, hastily pulled on, were unclasped at the top.

"Do you?" Eli said.

"I'm going to go now and have the police stop O'Dell at the airport."

Eli's face jerked as if he'd been hit again. Then he composed himself. "You'll let them perpetuate the lies?" he said in his richest pulpit-voice.

"Look, this is my job," Wilson said, and he hated the lameness of the remark, wished he could answer Eli effectively.

Eli said, "The truth is in Mr. O'Dell's briefcase right now and you should be aware of what you'll be doing if you prevent its coming out."

Wilson thought to just step over the man and out the door. The door was closed, he noticed. Eli must have consciously closed it before he'd been hit. To keep this all contained and quiet. To reason with Wilson. And Wilson felt quieter now.

He turned to Marta. She was still weeping softly. Wilson wanted to speak to her, to soothe her, but he could not shape any words and it occurred to him that she preferred it that way.

Eli's voice was moving now, tugging at Wilson's attention.

Wilson waited until Marta's weeping quietly snubbed to a stop and then he turned back to the preacher. Eli was talking about the President, about the Energy Independence campaign. "And it's all a lie," Eli said.

"What are you talking about?" Wilson said, pieces of Eli's speech beginning to fit together, beginning to agitate him, like grit in an eye.

Eli pulled his knees up and his voice pitched low, loosened a bit, but without losing its intensity. "Look," he said. "The fact of the matter is that there is no oil."

Wilson took a step toward Eli. "What do you mean?"

"I mean Alaska's almost empty...I won't draw any parallels for you. I don't need to preach to you. But the big lie is that we've got all the oil we need if we just decide to produce it. O'Dell's suitcase is full of the proof. They've been drilling dry hole after dry hole in Alaska. The known reserves up there are being sucked away. Inexorably. Do you know what those total reserves amount to?" Eli paused, waiting for Wilson to answer.

Wilson felt suspended. The words Eli was speaking seemed important but Wilson didn't know how to react to them.

"Do you know what the reserves amount to up there?" Eli repeated.

"No."

"Not quite nine billion barrels. Does that sound like a lot?"

"I don't know."

"It's a thin slick of piss, is all it is, Mr. Hand. The country uses five and a half billion barrels of oil every year."

"The exploration..."

"It's all going bad. Beaufort Sea, North Slope, down-country...all of it. And if a miracle happened and they doubled the reserves—found every bit as much again as they now have—it's still only a three-year cushion. But they're nowhere near doubling us. Nowhere near. It's all dry. Dead. Barren...That's the reality, Mr. Hand. That's the truth in O'Dell's suitcase."

Wilson felt suddenly weak, his legs trembled, he felt as he had in pump station one; he'd been right. The chasm opened again and he crouched beside Eli. The preacher's face looked older now, nearly old enough to fit his silver hair. "Are you sure?" Wilson said.

"I'm sure," Eli said. "We've had experts look at the reports. I'm sure. The ride's over."

The "we" in Eli's statement turned Wilson's face toward the bed. He could not see Marta from where he crouched. He rose up and Marta was lying flat, the sheet drawn up to her throat like a shroud, her eyes on the ceiling. Wilson's mind felt cracked in half. He still couldn't quite take this preacher's second-hand report for the gospel it wanted to be. And yet, his feet felt the trembling of the pump station floor, he heard the keening of the oil passing into the Arctic night. He thought of Artie Phillips out somewhere on the tundra, drilling in the dark, huddling in his van and thinking of God. Wilson knew he must find Artie. Go to Clyde and fly off to Artie. Artie was the point man out there. He would know the truth.

Marta's face had turned to Wilson. Her face was drawn down and Wilson couldn't tell if it was from fear or from sadness. He moved to her, bent to her, kissed her closed eyes and he felt them moving under his lips as if she were a dreaming cat. "Goodbye," he whispered.

13.

Wilson let go to the numbing crawl across time zones; the clouds were thick below and he tried to sleep, tried to keep himself in suspension until he could verify what Eli had said. But already he felt he'd gone too far, he'd stripped away too much. His mind felt barren. He turned to the window and he was startled, as if by his own face in an unexpected mirror: out in the center of the sky was the sun, and nearby, falling with it toward the horizon, were two sun dogs, burning coldly in their pursuit, never catching the sun, never falling behind. Watching them, Wilson felt his mind stir, the barrenness fill. The suspension persisted but now he sensed things moving out of his sight, a feeling like standing before Marta's door, listening to her silence within. Why was she involved in this? And Eli? Eli, he understood at once. All this fit his view of the world. Radical humility. That was part of the man's theology. Wilson saw Eli's vision for a moment: the earth, the earthly life we cling to, dote on, was empty. Proving that to the world was a bold but logical move for Eli. The *Times* story would be his sermon. But Marta? Wilson didn't let himself think too closely on the sexual hold Eli might have, his silver hair, his need. But she'd warned Wilson she wasn't loyal. To people, to places. She feared Alaska and now she had some power over it. The wells had been sucking at God's tit, she'd said. She knew now that they'd sucked it almost dry. He felt her draw near; her silence held a secret. She stretched out inside him. Her eyes were closed, her face was still; then she was gone.

It occurred to him that he'd not made the phone call to stop

O'Dell. He'd not thought the decision out and he wondered briefly what was behind it. He realized he would have had to expose Marta. But that hadn't been in his mind at the time. He'd just not thought to do it after hearing what Eli had to say. If what the man had said was true, then it didn't matter anymore. Wilson couldn't go back to the North Slope if it were true.

Wilson stopped his thoughts now. He kept his eyes on the sky but he concentrated on the periphery of his vision, watching the sun dogs, projecting the clutter of his mind out there, letting the cold fire burn it away as he waited for Alaska.

Wilson found Clyde's Anchorage address in the original packet of Gordon James's material. Wilson gave the address to the taxi driver at the airport and hunched into the chill darkness of the back seat. The early nightfall had come to Anchorage and Wilson was thankful for that. He could not bear the look of the city at this moment and he lowered his eyes to avoid the random run of neon outside.

He felt a slow flutter inside him, like the wings of a Moonbase raven lifting into the sky. He wanted to still this feeling even before he could identify it. He fixed on Gordon James, whose face remained in Wilson from having gone through the brown envelope, and Wilson thought of the man and the production numbers. James doesn't know what's in the production reports, Wilson decided. That's why he had been puzzled about who would steal them. The executive vice-president, the man whose deep concern James cited, obviously did know. Wilson snagged for a moment on why the top men at Royal were so afraid of the truth being known. Then he understood. Prices were high already, based on the exploration effort. A sudden lack of faith in oil as a future fuel would prompt massive fuel switching and hasten the search for alternatives before Royal and the other companies in the club could get rid of the oil they had and could develop ways to benefit from the future panic. Something like that. Wilson pinched at his forehead, kept his eyes in the shadows of the back seat. Though this all had some sort of logic to it, Wilson had a keen sense of his own indifference before it. It wasn't the fate of the world economy or the solar industry or the family automobile or plastic bags that moved him. Indeed, the thought of these issues made his shoulders sag, his mind balk.

He saw Artie's face in the van, the wind pounding the walls, and he remembered Artie starting to talk intensely, getting technical. But a clear phrase tumbled through: the earth's big secret. And another: tough to crack. Was Artie talking about the oil then? Was he saying he couldn't find any? The fluttering began again in Wilson and he channeled his anxiousness into a thought of the next hour. Could he find Clyde? Could he fly to Artie out on the tundra tonight?

Wilson glanced through the window to get his bearings and a high cyclone fence went by and, behind it, snow-covered rows of concrete pipe, orange in the sodium lamps. Wilson closed his eyes and waited, listening to his blood pumping deep in his inner ear.

At last the taxi stopped along a row of storefronts and Wilson paid the driver and carried his bag into the tiny lobby of the Klondike Hotel, where an old woman was sleeping by a switchboard. He went up a staircase and along a corridor with a bare bulb. Wilson found room 4B and knocked.

He waited and knocked again and Clyde opened the door. The two men looked at each other for a moment and neither face flickered; the lips, the mouths, the brows were still.

"I expected it would be you," Clyde said, low, without a trace of accent.

"I've come for you," Wilson said.

Clyde made a faint nod.

"Clyde?" A woman's voice, nasal, grating, came from inside. "Clyde, who is it?"

"You want me to fly tonight?" Clyde said to Wilson.

"Yes."

Clyde's mouth shaped, as if he were about to speak, but he did not. He turned, leaving the door open. "Clyde?" the woman's voice said and it was full of fear.

Wilson stepped inside. There was a kitchenette, another bare bulb hanging from a cord, a tattered couch and chairs crowded onto a tiny rug, a doorway framing the foot of a rumpled bed. Wilson heard the voice of a woman from the bedroom, cursing at first, in a loud whisper, then weeping softly.

Clyde came through the door, his parka over his arm, and he stood in the center of the rug. "There's bad weather up-country," he said.

"We have to go now."

Clyde nodded and they went out.

By the time they reached the airport a fog was creeping in, gathering against the earth. Clyde and Wilson stood outside the hangar door and watched the Piper, fifty yards away, fade and then vanish.

"The time's not quite right," Clyde said.

"Is there a place here to wait?"

"Inside."

They stepped back into the greasy dark of the hangar and moved off to the far side through a door with frosted glass. Clyde switched on the light and they were in a cramped office with a desk full of papers and engine parts, a wall covered with mimeo sheets and magazine nudes. There was a swivel chair behind the desk, a wooden chair near the door. Wilson expected the chaos of the office to bother him, but he knew the plane was nearby, knew the fog would inevitably lift and they would fly off, and he found he could step into this room with only a faint quaver. Clyde bent to a quartz heater on the floor and Wilson crossed to a coffee pot and hot plate behind the desk.

Wilson switched on the hot plate and he heard the wooden chair squeak behind him as Clyde sat down. But Wilson felt small inside and he did not feel like facing Clyde yet and the Texan stayed silent—the two men had not spoken at all on the way out here—and then the coffee was hot and Wilson poured two cups. He turned and Clyde's eyes were on him. Wilson crossed to Clyde and gave him the cup of coffee and Clyde took it with a nod of his head. Then Wilson went behind the desk and sat in the chair and the two men sipped their coffee in silence for a time.

Finally Clyde said, "Can I ask you where we're going?"

"Can you find Artie Phillips?"

"Yes."

"I want to go there."

"All right."

"The weather's bad, you said."

"Up north. Yes." Clyde paused, then added, "North Slope's the worst. We can get to Artie okay."

At the mention of the North Slope, Wilson stretched out to put his coffee cup down. He was very conscious of the movement of his hands to the table, the scrape of cup on desktop, the little sounds, the creak of his chair, the clicking of the quartz heater. He thought of the North Slope. If Artie said there was no oil, then what was the North Slope to Wilson? For a time he'd thought it would mean nothing anymore. But with this room clamped about him and Clyde waiting and the wind keening outside, he knew he would go back, he must go back.

"I think there's no more oil up there," Wilson said.

Clyde lowered his cup slowly, waited.

"The stolen documents," Wilson said, "are in the hands of The New York Times. There will be a story saying that the reserves we already know about are all there is...I let that story go forward. I had a chance to stop it but I didn't."

"No one will notice," Clyde said.

Wilson said nothing. Clyde's words had no meaning for him.

Clyde examined Wilson's silence and read it wrong and said, "Whoever wants people to think the other way will just trot out some different numbers and the whole thing will be forgotten—both sides—like yesterday's ball scores. People believe what they want to believe."

"I don't care about that," Wilson said. "Will you fly me?"

"Yes."

"I might want to go to the North Slope."

Clyde paused only for a moment and said, low, "I've always taken you wherever you need to go."

After that, they said no more. But the silence was not strained. They watched each other settle in the silence and then sleep. Wilson woke to find Clyde snoring, his head sharply angled against the back of the wooden chair. Wilson rose up and went out of the office, through the hangar, and he looked outside. The Piper sat on the pad, the taxiway lights stretched out to the runway. The sky was thick and low but Wilson knew that Clyde could fly in this. He turned back, moving through the hangar and he stopped. He felt the shapes in the dark, the torn-down planes, the engine blocks and hoists. They leaned against him and Wilson hurried on; he opened the frosted door and stepped in.

"It's time," he said. Clyde opened his eyes and Wilson said, "It's time."

Wilson and Clyde went out to the plane and when Clyde turned over the Piper's engine, the sound rushed into Wilson, thrummed in his hands, his chest, his eyes. The plane moved out to the runway and as it lifted into the air Wilson felt the slow flap of a raven's wings inside him.

For a time they flew above the clouds, the stars as precise as numbers, and then the clouds hunched up and Clyde dove down through them and flew near the earth. Wilson became conscious of hard, square turns, the intervals between them very regular. Wilson tried to shape in his mind the grid pattern Clyde was flying as he looked for Artie.

Then Wilson saw a tight web of light off to the right of the plane. Before he could speak, the plane banked toward the lights and dove down, made one pass, circled back and landed. The engine stopped and Wilson looked toward the vans. Backlit by orange service lights, a dark shape moved toward the plane. Wilson pulled on his wool mask and mittens and opened the door.

The wind pushed him and he leaned into it and went down the wing. The figure arrived and motioned him to follow. They walked across the snow and above the wind Wilson heard a hum. He looked off to the right, toward the derrick-rig. The hum sounded slick, dry, a false impression, he knew, because it was simply the generator, but he wondered what the derrick was touching now, deep inside the earth. Rock and ice and maybe carbon residue. He remembered Artie wanting to leap down in the hole.

Inside the van he shed his parka and mask and the figure who led him was John, the Eskimo. The man said, "Mr. Hand, isn't it?"

"Yes."

"Artie will be glad to see you."

John stepped aside and Wilson went into the tiny office. Artie stood up from behind his desk and leaned far forward to shake hands. "Wilson," he said. "I didn't expect to see you again."

Wilson sat in a chair opposite Artie. The wall of topographic maps—all that earth—nagged at him—the pads of color there were layers of scum on a stagnant pond.

"Did you catch your thief?"

"Yes. I did." Wilson hesitated. As much as he liked Artie, liked his eager, pliable face, liked his seriousness, Wilson had no tolerance for indirection now, he wanted only to ask his question and leap from there. "I learned something, Artie."

"What's that?"

"From the stolen documents...They say that Alaska's going dry. They say the reserves we know about already—enough to cover our full usage for only a year and a half—that's all there is. I want to know if this is true."

Artie's face—its constant, subtle motion—stopped still. His mouth slowly grew tight and then he said, "Maybe in the sea there's more...I only have experience with the land...This part of the land..."

"Artie. Do you think it's true?"

The man leaned back in his chair. He closed his eyes briefly.

"I'm sixty-three, Wilson. My eyes go dry. I can't blink them moist sometimes. My joints freeze up. I move slower now. My breath can grow...very short..."

"Is it true, Artie? Is the earth going dry?"

"I've always expected some compensation," Artie said. "Some greater...sensitivity...Like I could feel the oil down there. I'd get old and I'd lose the edge of some of my senses, but the closer I'd get to going into the earth myself, the more I'd know about it...I'd find oil, Wilson. I'd find oil and they'd bury me down the drill hole, stuff me down there with all the dinosaurs and tropical ferns and I'd just float down deeper and deeper. I'd find that ocean of oil in the center."

"Artie."

The man paused. He leaned forward and laid his hands palm-down on his desktop.

"Do you think the oil is gone?" Wilson said.

"What you say doesn't surprise me." Artie put one hand on top of the other. "I believe it. Yes."

There was a burst of cold air, a clomping, out in the entranceway. Wilson rose. He expected to be weak, but his legs were strong. Only the confines of the office plagued him now. The office door opened and Clyde stood there and Wilson said, "We have to go."

Clyde's eyes moved to Artie and then back to Wilson. "North Slope?" Clyde said.

The North Slope drew him; empty now, stripped down, he'd have some time alone, sitting in the dark—there was still no sun up there, wouldn't be one for ten days or more. He took a step toward Clyde. "Yes," he said. "Now. Please."

Clyde dipped his head almost as if he were shy. He nodded once. "All right, boy."

Wilson heard Artie rise behind him. "Bad weather up there," Artie said.

Clyde looked at Artie and he smiled faintly. With his Texan twang, Clyde said, "This is what I been doin' for twenty years. I been in lots of weather."

Wilson turned as he heard Artie coming around from behind his desk. Artie reached out to Clyde and the two men shook hands. Then Artie put his left hand briefly on Clyde's shoulder and they hugged, pounding each other on the back, their craggy faces—similar enough to be brothers—side by side.

Outside, Wilson sat in the Piper's cabin and waited and he felt calm. He did not examine the feeling but he knew it had to do with going back north. Artie had confirmed Wilson's sharpest fear, but Wilson still felt calm. He leaned forward and peered into the dark. Clyde unwrapped the engine and filled the gas tanks in the wings and then he went into the van and came out across the snow carrying a gasoline heater. He opened the cabin door and put the heater behind the seats. Wilson turned full around and Clyde, pulling back, paused. He looked at Wilson and his features were blurred in the dark.

"Playing it safe?" Wilson said.

"Not very," Clyde said. "There's nothing to eat in here, nothing to build a shelter..."

"Do you want us to wait this out, Clyde?" Wilson tried to keep his voice neutral, but the thought of waiting, the thought of staying away from the North Slope for even another day, roiled his mind. New York was dead, Beth was dead, his week of captivity had ended, Marta was gone; but they all kept their shape inside him, they whispered to him, touched his eyes, and he knew they did not persist on their own, they did not preserve their own lives. And he knew the force that gave them life, held their shapes, moved even him, quickened even him, made him yearn, drove him months ago to Alaska and called him back now, called him to understand.

Clyde had backed out of the cabin at Wilson's question and then re-entered and sat down in his seat. He shut the cabin door. "I've been flying most of my life," he said.

"No bullshit, Clyde. Please. What do you want?"

"I want to fly tonight. Wherever you want to go."

Wilson faced forward. His own breath plumed before him. Outside the window of the Piper, snow was dashing by in the wind. Beyond was only darkness. "You'll regret tonight, Clyde. You'll regret."

"Not me, boy." Clyde turned over the engine, the snow swirled away from the window and the engine cycled up, the Piper moved out, away from the vans, turned and without a pause Clyde raced the engine and the plane slid along the tundra and up into the darkness.

14.

The plane groped its way low over the tundra and after a long while Clyde began to draw the plane up higher and higher and then he said, "Lookee there."

Wilson leaned forward and above them were stars. Wilson turned and Clyde was grinning. Wilson wondered how frightened Clyde had been. The man's grin blazed in the cabin. Wilson leaned forward again. The stars were scattered, random; there was no mountain of stars there, no shape at all, but there were stars and Clyde began to whistle and Wilson leaned back in his seat and he was glad for the stars; he would reach the North Slope tonight, he thought. And then he slept.

Wilson was falling. Into a deep hole in the earth he fell and he woke and he fell, the plane dropped, its skin whining. The stars were gone, Clyde's arm vibrated at the controls. Wilson squinted into the scene as if he were detached from it. But the hole, the deep hole—that was detached, that was the dream. He knew he was awake now. He knew the plane fell and Clyde quaked and Wilson's arms floated and the plane's motor grew soft as Clyde throttled back. They fell and Wilson had no breath, could not breathe, the falling clenched its way up his legs, his chest, his throat and then he was pressed into his seat and the plane lifted hard, the cabin clanged, the air punched into Wilson's ears and the plane rushed up. Outside, the stars were gone, a spew of cloud dashed over the wing. The plane lost its upward momentum and leveled off and Wilson grew conscious of the engine again, its pitch normal again; level, even flight.

Wilson turned and Clyde glanced at him. Wilson expected the

man to smile, to joke now that the danger was passed. But he said nothing.

"Downdraft?" Wilson said.

"We're in thick now," Clyde said. "We're near the Brooks Range and we're in thick." Clyde pushed forward and the plane's nose went down and they began to dive.

"Is there a bottom?" Wilson said.

"I hope to hell there is."

The plane dove and the engine pitched higher. Wilson watched ahead and only their lights were before them, filled with the swirl of cloud. Wilson gripped the arms of his seat and he tried to picture the cloud opening up; he shaped the image again and again, waiting for the cloud to respond, waiting, and then waiting to die, waiting to slam into a mountain, and this thought clutched at him, clawed at his face; not yet, he cried in his mind, not yet.

The plane lurched down, the tail fell, the plane dropped flat. "Shit," Clyde said.

"Not now," Wilson cried. His head filled up with furniture, traffic, horns honking.

Wilson jerked down, the plane lifted, soared up, Clyde throttled back and the plane rose up very fast, updrafting into the heart of a cloud. How far from the flanks of the mountain, how far; Wilson tried to squeeze his mind dry with the thought of the mountain rushing at him and then he saw a jagged ridge up ahead, looming up and crested with stars. Wilson thought for a moment he'd died, the moment had come and this was a last vision, but Clyde whooped and the plane shook and leveled, released from the updraft.

Clyde throttled up and the plane rose and turned and flew parallel to the range. The weather held. In the starlight Wilson could see the mountains stretching far ahead and the clouds following them, off to the right, a long, silver-flecked hedgerow.

"The pass should be here pretty quick," Clyde said, his twang heavy. Wilson grew uneasy now, uneasy at Clyde's impulse to chat, uneasy even at the sudden placidness of the flight.

Up ahead the clouds were beginning to curl in toward the mountains, filling the gap between, but before the plane reached the place, it banked left, turned into the mountain and climbed toward the pass. The stars had vanished ahead, the sky was black and the shape of the mountains disappeared. Clyde switched on the landing lights and Wilson could feel him tighten. They entered the pass, rock faces slipped by; Wilson felt wedged in by them and then a spume of cloud suddenly tumbled into the lights, swept over the plane, rushed through the pass to meet them.

"Shit," Clyde said and the plane jerked down in a mountain wave. He fought the control wheel, throttled back, Wilson sensed the crags—invisible now—leaning into them, reaching out and then the cloud broke and he saw a rock face rushing for the plane and Clyde yanked the controls, dropped the flaps, and the lights showed a long, wide ledge, snow, the plane slammed down, Wilson's jaws snapped together, his bones squeezed, metal tore and he lunged forward into silence.

A moment later his head swirled like the cloud and then cleared. His neck ached, his body tingled, and then in the first moment of full awareness, when he knew the plane was still, was sitting on the ledge that had only briefly flashed in the lights, he felt the seat move under him, a crack of rock and the plane settled, canted backwards a few degrees. Then the plane grew still again.

Wilson turned to Clyde and the man was hunched against the controls. His hand was pulled up, splayed over his ribs. After a moment he pulled back from the wheel. He opened his mouth, mute, and then he seemed to compose his face—red from the panel lights—and he turned to Wilson.

"We don't have much time," Clyde said. "Get as much out of the plane as you can."

They put their wool masks and mittens on and Clyde opened the cabin door. The wind slammed in and Wilson felt a movement in the plane, downward, his hands gripped hard at the seat.

He sensed the deep drop to his right, a thousand feet into darkness, farther, much farther.

Clyde shone a flashlight out his door and then switched it off. He reached behind the seat with a small bark of pain and picked up a large gasoline can and the gasoline heater.

"I'm going to start the fuel tank draining," Clyde said. "Get everything you can. Even the seat cushions." Clyde lunged into the dark and Wilson rose up and turned to kneel on his seat. He grabbed three blankets—two wool, one down—and he found a canvas packet of tools. He scrambled sideways to the door, hitting his shin on the throttle. The bite of pain focussed him on his body. He was all right. Nothing was broken. He wondered about Clyde's ribs. He pushed against the wind, drew his leg from under him and stepped out onto the wing tread. He could see Clyde rising from behind the wing.

"Out here," Clyde shouted, his voice whipped into faintness by the wind.

Wilson went down the wing.

"Throw it," Clyde shouted. "Quickly."

Wilson threw the tools off the plane and they dropped out of sight into the snow. Wilson held up the blankets; the wind would carry them off if he threw them. "Clyde," he shouted.

Clyde looked up and came to the edge of the wing and took the blankets in his arms. "Move," Clyde said.

Wilson turned. His body was stiff in the parka. He'd dressed the warmest he could, he thought, as he went back up the wing. Rubber boots, down pants, layers and layers underneath. As he'd grabbed the objects in the plane, he grabbed at these little fragments of hope. His body was sound. For the moment he was warm enough. He leaned into the cabin and he fell forward, a crack, the plane lurched a foot and stopped. Above the wind he heard Clyde's curse. Wilson wanted to back out but he knew there were things inside that they'd need. Things. He reached in without moving his body and pulled the seat cushion off the far seat; carefully he transferred it to his other hand and tossed it off the wing into the snow. He took off the nearest seat cushion and tossed it after the first. He paused.

"Sleeping bags," Clyde said, just behind Wilson. Wilson looked over his shoulder and saw Clyde crawl out on the wing. For weight, Wilson realized, to help keep the plane from falling into the chasm. "Move carefully," Clyde shouted over the wind.

Wilson turned his face back to the cabin. The red panel lights still glowed and he felt a clutching in his chest, his arms wanted to flail, he wanted to jump back and leap off the plane. Let it go. He felt the suck of the chasm.

"Move," Clyde shouted. "Move."

Wilson thought he heard a deep running crack, through the wind the crack ran, but he moved now. He laid his knee in the center of the pilot's seat and let his weight ease forward onto it. The plane shuddered, the wind pushed at him, tried to push him farther in, faster. Cloud-spew swirled in the red lights. Wilson looked into the rear of the cabin and he saw two cloth bundles. He leaned sideways against the back of the seat and stretched out his arm, stretched far but he could not touch the bundles. His reach was a foot short and he slowly drew his other leg into the plane. Another shudder, another faint increment of tilt, he turned slightly, leaned over the seat, put his hands on the two bundles. There was a third bundle underneath and he scooped deeper, held all three in the loop of his forearms. He lifted them slowly, moved slowly while the wind rushed around him, swirled around, cried for him to rush, to follow, to fall.

Wilson drew back. He was unbalanced in the door. He heard the running, cracking, he staggered and lurched against the door frame and the plane moved, a snap, metal screamed. Wilson fell back, twisted around, he staggered up onto his knees and he saw Clyde scrambling and Wilson's legs moved, he raised a knee high, touched the wing with his toe, the ball of his foot, and his body rose, tensed to jump. Deep cracking, the wing slid out and he pushed off, his arms clutching the bundles, he flew out and the snow came up and he heard the cry of metal, felt a vast lifting behind him and he heard a heavy scrambling, a clang and then another, fainter, and then the wind, only the wind.

Wilson lay still for a moment, listening to the wind, waiting for the earth beneath him to split and fall away. Then he grew conscious of his arms squeezing tight; his muscles ached in their strain and he loosened his hold. He sat up and looked back. The plane was gone.

A column of light stretched out to the place—Clyde's flashlight—but there was nothing left, just a jagged sheer of rock and the wisps of cloud and Wilson saw the beam of sunlight filled with motes of dust, saw it now like a double exposure, laid on top of this beam of light against the black; dust and cloud swirled together, and Wilson looked at the place where the light dissolved and it was empty. Wilson was cut off again and he heard the rocks cracking like the popping of a chicken's neck outside, out of sight, close now. Close. And he felt the tightness in his arms disappear. He sat in the snow, the wind pounding at his chest, and all his fear was gone.

The light moved. Clyde's flashlight slipped to the left, downwards, and it lit the gasoline can sitting in the snow, where the wing of the plane had suckled it moments before. The light moved to the heater and the blankets laid beneath it, and then the beam moved to the cliff-edge again and Wilson saw the light wavering. The column of light quaked and Wilson followed it back to Clyde and he could not see the man's face but he knew Clyde was afraid, he could hear Clyde's fear, it whispered to him as if he sat with him in a quiet room. People crowded into Wilson now, Beth came in, Clyde stayed but Beth was there, too, her face crimped in fear, her hands trembling forward, clutching at Wilson's arm just as they clutched at the railing on the balcony; and the Viet Cong with the blue mark on his face came in, too, oblivious on the surface to the meaning of the mark but frightened inside. Wilson saw the fear in his captor's eyes, even at the moments of the man's keenest hatred for Wilson the fear was shining there. Wilson had seen it from the first. Now, sitting on this rock ledge, he was fully conscious of it, he stretched out to touch the spot, heal it, and the man was just out of reach and Marta came in, silent in her fear, passionate in her fear, and Wilson knew he himself was not afraid. And then this frightened him. He felt the cold creeping into him and he was afraid he was letting go already and he rose up from where he sat. The beam from the flashlight was on empty snow, trembling; Clyde's face had lowered.

"Clyde," Wilson shouted against the wind.

Clyde's face snapped up; he turned and then raised the flashlight, aimed its beam beyond Wilson. Wilson turned and watched the column of light moving along first the rock face and then the ledge, moving out along the gouged path the plane took in its crash landing. The cliff rose up sheer from the ledge and Clyde's beam wavered again. He moved past Wilson, he began to move forward along the ledge, not running but with a clear edge of panic. Wilson followed, stumbling on the surface of the rock. He moved after Clyde and he saw the ledge narrowing, veering in. "Clyde," he shouted.

The man was moving more slowly now, as the edge pinched in. Then he stopped. Wilson stood just behind him and looked over his shoulder. He followed the beam of light another thirty yards to a cornice of rock, a wide overhang. Beneath it, snow had drifted deep onto a broad shelf. Clyde lowered the light to the ledge between the overhang and where they stood. It was narrow and uneven but wide enough to hold them.

Clyde turned around and he said, "We have to make a shelter."

"From what?"

"We'll dig a snow cave in the drifts under that cornice...First we'll move all our things back in there. You got a packet of tools out?"

"Yes. First thing I threw down from the plane."

"Good. Now take it...easy..." Clyde's face was hidden behind his wool mask but his head grew still, his words stopped; the head lowered, wobbled.

Wilson put his hand on Clyde's shoulder, then gently cuffed him on the side of the head and the man drew up straight.

"Take it easy," Clyde said. "If you work up a sweat, you'll die. Your clothes will get wet and they won't dry out and there's nothing we could do to stop your freezing to death...Slow and easy now."

Wilson nodded and they returned to the place where the plane was lost. Clyde passed on to the patch of snow where the tools fell. Wilson knelt by the gasoline heater and he held down the blankets with his hand before lifting the weight. He picked the blankets up and he thought to take the heater as well but it was heavy and he knew it would make him awkward along the ledge. He rose and Clyde joined him with the packet of tools. Clyde raised his flashlight and switched it on and the two men stared at each other for a long moment. Wilson wondered if Clyde was still afraid. Then he turned the question onto himself and he felt irritated, standing here with his arms full of blankets, but he was not afraid. They made their way to the last thirty yards of ledge, near the overhang. Clyde swung around to Wilson and said, "Follow me very closely."

Clyde led him along the ledge. Over the man's shoulder Wilson could see the light flitting out, coming back, tracing the rim of rock at their feet. Wilson grew sharply aware now of the lunge of space two paces to his left. The cloud, the darkness, blotted out any sight of the deep drop but Wilson knew it was there; it nibbled at him; his left side, his left arm, his left hip knew the drop was there.

Clyde stumbled. Wilson's free hand went out, touched the man's back. Clyde leaned against the rock face. Wilson heard Clyde's voice, very faint, being carried off at once by the wind. Wilson bent closer. "What?" he said.

Clyde did not raise his voice, did not turn. Wilson strained and could hear a tiny litany of cursing, fuck, fuck, fuck this, fuck.

"Clyde," Wilson shouted. "Clyde, move on now."

Clyde straightened up and the woolen mask turned over his shoulder; the eyes there were bright, even in the dark.

"Hang on, Clyde."

The Texan turned and the light went out to the rim of rock, the open space that had swallowed the plane, and then the light quickly darted to the center of the ledge, the path to the overhang. There were only a few more yards to go. The ledge pinched in, narrowed to less than a yard, then to little more than a foot; they moved slowly. The wind pummeled them, angled their steps abruptly. This last foothold had to be accurate, right in the center, and Clyde pulled back.

"Step now," Wilson shouted.

Clyde started forward, pulled back again, and then stepped out and strode across the narrow ledge and under the cornice of rock. He stood up to his calves in the snow and he stumbled farther in and then squared around and shone the light on the narrow stepway. Wilson looked down at it, waited for a gust of wind and then as the wind peaked and fell he stepped forward, his foot touched and he swung on and into the snow. He stumbled in his haste and fell to his knees and rose up at once, panting, his heart racing. Stay calm, he thought. Sweat and die. If Clyde were afraid now, they'd be lost; Wilson knew he wouldn't be able to cuff him out of it, for his own fear scrambled up inside him, barked in his head. He looked back the way they'd come. He'd have to return, he knew. The heater, the gasoline can, the cushions, the three bundles. Their possessions. The metal and plastic and cloth that would keep them living for a while longer.

"I have to start the cave," Clyde said, close by.

Wilson turned and Clyde's eyes would not hold still in the mask; their focus darted from spot to spot on Wilson's face and Wilson's fear pushed into his own eyes, eager to see this other man's fear, like a dog straining at another dog through a fence.

"I have to dig the cave now," Clyde said.

Wilson suddenly feared the ledge; now that he'd left it he feared it with a fear that made him want to grab Clyde by the throat for his cowardice. But he fixed on the man's fear; he knew the man was worse off than himself. He squeezed his mind shut and shaped the words, forced them out: "All right. I'll get the other things.''

Wilson took the flashlight and faced the ledge. He felt stronger now; he was glad now that Clyde would be able to stay under the rock and begin to dig them a hole. Clyde would be safe there for a time, would get his courage back. Wilson flashed the light on the narrowest spot of ledge and he moved the light slightly to the jagged fall of rock, the darkness that scattered the light. Wilson shone the beam back on the ledge and he stepped forward.

He moved quickly—too quickly, he realized—and he slowed to keep himself dry, and after a while, in three trips, his lungs burning in the thin air, he transferred the gasoline can, the cushions, and, finally, he began tossing the three bundles, one at a time, over the narrow step before going across himself. Two of the bundles were the sleeping bags Clyde had mentioned. The third turned out to be a parachute. After tossing the parachute, Wilson was about to follow when he thought of the heater. He paused, his breath quickened. No more, he thought; but they had to have the heater and he went back; he followed the scar of the crashing plane once more, wondering at the narrowness of the ledge, wondering at Clyde's skill at crash-landing them here. And that appreciation of Clyde's skill changed at once into an ache over the man's clear fear of death. Then Wilson approached the heater. He tried to lift it. It was very heavy and awkward, heavier than he remembered it. He was growing weak. He carried it by the top handle with both hands, back a last time along the ledge to the narrow crossing.

''Clyde,'' he called.

There was no answer and he shone the light into the recess. Clyde was bent into a snow drift that curved high over his head against the rock. A short-handled shovel was in his hand and he looked toward the light.

''Clyde,'' Wilson shouted. ''I need help.''

Clyde hesitated a moment, like an animal caught in headlights on a country road. But he put the shovel down and came out of the recess.

Wilson tried to lift the heater to show Clyde the problem and Clyde said, "Easy with that."

"How?"

Clyde glanced out over the rim and then said, "Come near and reach it over to me."

Wilson pressed against the rock face and eased along the ledge to its narrowest point. Clyde came closer, also pressing his back to the wall of rock. The heater was to Wilson's left, the side farthest from Clyde. He lifted the heater by its handle with both hands; he pulled it across his body, wobbling; he faced the chasm now, his feet stretched out to the rim, he pressed back against the rock wall, the wind whined in the heater's grill and Wilson's arms vibrated, his groin crawled. He could pitch forward easily now, he could pitch down and fall after the plane. He remembered the cry of metal. He moved the burner on across his body and then he had to hold it by one hand, his right arm tensed and he let go with his left hand and the heater sagged down but he fought it; he brought his hand back against the rock face and the heater sagged still, he tried to raise his arm but he couldn't. He looked over to Clyde. The man was reaching, too, but he could not take the heater. Wilson turned his face to the front, squeezed his eyes shut; he pressed hard at the arm, pressed hard and he barked into the wind, howled into the wind, and his arm rose, quivering. He knew how weak he was in the thin air, even as he pushed himself on, he thought how weak his body was, how foolish, and the heater jerked and the weight was suddenly gone and it unbalanced him, he lurched sideways, he went down, his hip hit rock, his left leg shot out, his shoulder hit the ledge and he felt the pull on his chest, his left foot went out into the emptiness, an emptiness that sucked at him, climbed up his leg. No, he cried. His left hand found the rock-rim. He held it, then it gave, it broke, his hand too went out into nothingness and he hunched his back, drove his weight into his right side, and he was still. He drew his foot back onto rock, his hand back onto rock; he lay motionless there, his eyes closed, the wind sweeping over him, and he did not want to move again. Let me die here, he thought.

"Wilson." Clyde's voice was faint, shouting into the wind. "Wilson. You all right?"

Wilson opened his eyes and looked at his position, lying sideways on the ledge, and he slowly raised his torso, sat up, and scooted farther back along the ledge. Then he got to his feet. He turned to see Clyde still clinging against the wall, the heater beside him. Clyde motioned with his hand to come over. This would be the last time, Wilson thought, and he didn't let himself think it out. He found the flashlight still burning on the ledge; he picked it up, shone it on the path, made two steps and was across.

Wilson and Clyde moved together deep into the recess and the air grew much calmer; only the eddies of the wind came in and Clyde showed Wilson what to do and they began to dig their cave, working slowly, ultimately even opening their parkas. Wilson worked in a half-conscious, heavy-limbed trance and when they were done he had no idea how much time had passed, though it was at least two hours. In the large drift they had dug a tunnel sloping downwards and then they had scooped out the inside, making a domed room with a level floor. They dug two ventilation holes, one as straight up as possible, coming out near the place where the snowdrift met the cornice of rock; the second was dug by the door. Clyde entered the cave and Wilson handed in their possessions one by one. Then Wilson crawled down the entrance and into the cave. He could just barely stand straight in the room and he lit the flashlight.

The room was circular, perhaps ten feet in diameter. The heater sat in the center of the floor; the seat cushions made a sleeping platform beyond the heater, a sleeping bag spread out on it; the other sleeping bag was on this side of the heater and was laid on the floor. Against a wall were the packet of tools and the gasoline can. The blankets were piled nearby and the parachute had been unpacked and lay folded on the blankets.

Wilson shone the flashlight on Clyde. The man peeled off his mask. "We'll take turns sleeping up on the cushions. It'll be a little warmer up there." Clyde smiled; an act of will, Wilson knew, for the smile froze and became brittle and Clyde's eyes slipped away; he turned his face from the light.

"Talk to me now, Clyde," Wilson said.

Clyde made a sound in his throat but did not speak for a long moment. Then he said, "I'm sorry, boy. You always think you're ready, but you're not. I've been flying to this place for...a long time."

"What's our chances?"

"We won't freeze in here. Even after the gasoline's gone for the heater we could hang on for a long time. But it's dark out there. It's gonna be dark for ten more days and then there'll just be a tiny little window of daylight—open and shut—open and shut. Nobody knows where we are."

"Artie?"

"I go weeks without seeing Artie. Artie is off alone out there, isolated. It's going to take a long time for him to realize we're missing."

The light on Clyde's face quavered. Wilson tracked the beam back to his own hand, felt himself shrinking inside. "I feel very weak," he said.

"The air," Clyde said. "The cold...You're weak now. I am too. That's our problem. That's our real problem." Clyde was panting heavily. He paused, sucked in air, held it. His voice steadied and he said, "Somebody's going to miss us eventually. A woman or two. Artie even. And we're in a pass that the bush pilots use. But our plane's gone. We're buried in this mountain inside a snow drift. There's no trace of us out there." Clyde turned stiffly to the cave's doorway. He was beginning to breathe hard again. "With the wind and the snow and the terrain and what we've got to work with, there's no signal we could put outside to last. So in ten days we've got to be ready to go out there." Clyde jerked around, thrust his face at Wilson, the face passing out of the light of the flashlight and into shadow, the features fading even as they drew nearer. Clyde's voice trembled. "We've got to be ready to go out every day during the little bit of sunlight—every day for weeks maybe—and make sure we're noticed...But it's the food." Clyde's great hands grasped Wilson by the shoulders. "In this thin air, in the cold, no food for two weeks, that damn ledge, the wind...no food and our strength will be gone...We've fucking furnished our grave here..." Clyde's hands leeched against Wilson, they did not move but they drew at him and then they went dead and their weight made Wilson's shoulders sag, he felt he was being pressed into the earth.

"I'm not ready for this," Clyde panted, his voice squeezed into a whisper. His hands lifted away, he half turned into the cave, then turned back again. "I'm not ready," he said.

Wilson felt the room of ice closing in, Clyde's fear drew the room in, Clyde's fear tunneled into Wilson's chest, tunneled down at an angle, began to scoop out its own room, its own cold room inside Wilson. "Shut up, Clyde," Wilson said, low. "Shut up," he said louder, pushing Clyde. "Shut the fuck up," he shouted and he pushed Clyde in the chest, hard, and Clyde yielded, he staggered back and fell down heavily into the darkness. Wilson's flashlight hung at his side and he could not see Clyde but he heard the man's panting, and tiny sounds, sounds deep in his throat. Wilson thought to raise the light, illuminate the man, but he was afraid. He stood there waiting and finally Clyde's breathing grew quieter, it faded into the sound of the wind outside.

Wilson shone the flashlight on Clyde and the man looked into the light briefly and then lowered his head, averted his eyes. He said, "We should get as much rest as possible. Use energy only to stay warm."

Clyde's voice was calm but Wilson read as much humiliation into it as self-possession. Wilson wanted to say something to take the sting away for the man but he couldn't think of anything. His mind felt as weak as his arms, he could not lift a thought. He regretted this; he felt Clyde's hurt. But then Clyde insisted that Wilson take the first shift in the sleeping bag on the cushions and Wilson knew to acquiesce quickly; he knew Clyde was trying hard to act the way he'd thought for twenty years he would.

Clyde burned the gasoline heater for a few minutes to warm up the room. They sat in silence in the orange glow, stretching their faces and hands and feet into the areola of heat. Wilson existed in those few minutes entirely in his fingertips, the tips of his toes, the curve of his cheeks. He kept his face turned to the heat. Like the sun dogs—he thought of them—his face picked up the heat, the color, as if he had this flame in himself, his own center of warmth, a sun of his own, a fragment of sun sufficient in itself. From the angle of his head he could see the pile of blankets, the packet of tools against the wall, distant, three blankets, a parachute, tools— a hammer, screwdriver in there, a small shovel, a file—Wilson felt a clutching in him and he closed his eyes to these objects. He shifted his face and opened his eyes and he saw only the arch of the ceiling, beads of water there, the slick, empty surface rising and curving beyond his sight.

Then the heater was off, the blankets were spread out on the sleeping bags, the parachute was laid up against the wall, covering the entrance. The flashlight went out and Wilson plumped the down bag and he paused. He listened in the seam-less dark to Clyde moving, the scuff of his boots on the snow floor, the fluffing of the bag, the rustle of him climbing in, then silence. Clyde vanished.

Wilson was alone now. The wind rushed past outside but it sounded very distant, it blew on the surface of the earth and Wilson was deep inside; he was standing in a hollow in the earth, an icy hollow that he knew had hidden tunnels, tunnels that he'd had no hand in digging, and now he had to climb another layer down, a hollow inside this hollow. He opened the bag and he climbed in, he inched his body deeper inside, the darkness total, his eyes useless; dark inside the earth, all objects gone now, all clutter, nothing in this hollow but him and the hollow within him and an eye inside, an eye that fluttered now, awaking. Wilson drew farther inside the bag, his chest entered, his throat, he sank deep inside, deep, far from the surface, the wind grew faint and ceased and there was silence.

For a moment he was keenly aware of his body, as if he could count all his bones. And then his body dropped away, suddenly, like a fall into the chasm, and he watched as he fell, down the dark steeps of rock, down he fell and below, rushing at him, was the sun, three suns, the sun dogs were there, all three leading him, burning even in the tropical sky, in the window of the shack. He rose from the floor and his captors came and a rifle butt swung, his head jerked to the side, he landed hard on his bad arm, a face drew very near his, cursing in an alien tongue. Then another image. The first night. Silent. The sky cloudless, the palm fronds still. The guard shifted his weight, his heels scraped on the wood-plank floor. The man with the mark on his face. Wilson had spent the afternoon quaking in fear, the fear burning in him, but burning away, consumed now, gone now and he was surprised. He heard the man clear his throat, gently, and he heard the man's hand rise, heard even that sound; he heard the horizon then, humming, humming with hands rising, breaths being taken, these sounds sharp in him, and he was conscious that the fear was gone, he was filled with the sounds of the night, the shudder of a sleeping hen, the beating of his captor's heart, and Wilson heard Clyde moan in his sleep. Wilson turned his face in his sleeping bag. Clyde had moaned but there was silence again. Wilson knew that just before the moan he'd come up against a feeling that had hidden itself for a long time. He saw the rock wall springing at the plane just before they'd crashed. Wilson turned his face back and lay flat, lay stretched out like Marta in the hotel bed, like Beth, dead in a coffin, laid out before dissolving in the fire; he saw Beth's body lifted high into the air, the sun coming down, lighting her body, the body vanishing in a lick of flame. But the night fell at once. The night, the first night of captivity; he'd known briefly then what he'd felt. And he knew it now again. Joy. He'd sat in the room in the night, stripped of the world, his life yanked away, and he'd been filled up, he'd heard and seen and felt more sharply than ever before and he felt a joy at this, unmistakably a joy; he was dead in that shack, he was dead, he knew, dead to himself and yet there was something left, something much clearer; he knew all this, but as soon as he did, the feeling changed, the joy dissolved in the form he'd just known and his ears heard nothing, his hands grew numb, he turned his face and he knew his captor was crouching there, the man's face tingled, the man's death was worn there in an oval mark, the man's rage made his hands tighten, his chest quake. Wilson wanted to reach out in the dark and then Wilson was lying on the floor, the same face bending to him, in sunlight, the face was cursing, the dark eyes widened in rage, Wilson's arm throbbed and he saw the oval mark again and he reached out. But this time, in Wilson's mind, deep in the earth, he touched the mark and it disappeared, the man's face softened, his eyes filled with tears and Wilson was sitting again, alone, the motes of dust falling in the sunlight; he watched them tumble there. And then he rose up. He walked to the door of the shack and he opened it and he stepped out onto the front porch. Up the rutted, dusty road, passing from sunlight to palm shade to sunlight again, was a woman, drawing near. She was naked; her face was lowered; she came up the road and the chickens scattered away and her bare feet and legs were covered with dust. She came up to the porch and she stopped before Wilson and she raised her head and it was Marta. Wilson touched her face in the same spot as he'd touched his captor's face. She took his hand and kissed its palm and she vanished. Now there were two people coming up the road. He knew from their walk that they were his mother and father. He waited on the porch for them, waited and he heard no sound, felt no breeze on his skin, no warmth, no cold; he had vision only—he could see the eyes of his parents, filled with tears. And they drew near, their clothes covered with dust, and they stopped before him. His hands went out and he touched their faces and he felt the warmth of their skin, he felt the tiny fretting of wrinkles there, he moved his fingers and made the skin smooth and they vanished. And Clyde moaned again, a stuttering moan, a sob, and the dusty road, the palms, the hot sky vanished and it was dark. Clyde cursed in a garbled, diminishing sing-song and then he fell silent and Wilson heard the wind, far off, moving over the surface of the earth. He heard Clyde's pain in the wind, heard it keening there, keening like the sound of the oil as it flowed from the earth, a wound, the blood flowing from the earth, emptying the earth, but he was deep inside and again something remained, something that had been covered over before, something lost, something lost but moving always, flowing beneath or passing over, like a cloud in a mountain pass, Beth's face fluttering there for a moment, the steam from the car's engine passing over her, and beneath the almond trees Wilson saw her at the moment of her death, even then, even before her face was frozen and replicated a million times, confusion there on her face, her bare feet waiting for the flame. Wilson stood in Beth's apartment. He stood in the center of the floor and Beth was before him, her back to him, on the balcony. Around him on the floor all the objects were stacked, the unpacked boxes and the chairs and the books and the lamps and the clocks, and he raised his hand and they vanished. He wanted to speak now, wanted to tell Beth to turn, to look, to step onto the bare floor, to step within the empty walls, to wait there, to accept it, to listen, to wait for what would happen, but he could not speak and he knew she was afraid, she moaned and he knew she didn't have the strength. She stepped forward to the railing and he tried to move but he couldn't, he tried to reach out but already she had lifted herself and then she was gone. The sky beyond the balcony went black, the room went black, and Beth's voice keened in the dark, the wind keened and Wilson heard Clyde cry out in his sleep.

Wilson blinked at the darkness. It did not disperse. Beth was gone, dead, beyond his touch; his parents were gone and Marta was gone; the man with the mark on his face was dead, had died at the very moment of Wilson's release from the room. Wilson felt chilled, deep within, he felt chilled and he was conscious of the layers around him, cotton, wool, fiber, down, layer over layer over layer. Clyde whimpered and Wilson's face turned. He could not see the man in the dark. He could not reach out his arm. And his touch could not help Clyde, he knew.

Food. The man needed food. Clyde was not ready to die and he needed food. Wilson stirred. He raised his hands and pulled the sleeping bag down from his throat, his chest, he drew himself out of the bag and sat up. He turned and put his feet on the floor. Wilson stripped off his wool mask and the cold bit at his face. He waited a moment and he concentrated on the air. It was very cold now in the cave. The sleeping bag had been large and loose-fitting and he'd kept his parka on inside it. He unbuttoned and unzipped the parka and took it off. He dropped it on the floor. He bent and took off his rubber boots and stood and removed his down pants. He was very cold now and he moved more quickly. He stripped off his woolen shirt, his flannel shirt, his wool pants, his wool socks. The surface of his skin was crawling now, burning in the cold. He felt light, but the fibers of his underwear scraped at him, filled his mind with a thrashing, bird wings, mechanical birds, rows of them arranged along an apartment floor. Wilson ripped open the front of his long underwear, he stripped it off, his penis shrank into him in the cold, he burned, he ached, he burned and he sat down and took off his cotton socks and flung them into the dark. Softly he said, "Eat. It's finished." He lay back naked and the flames licked along his body once more and then there was no feeling at all; he heard only a humming at the far horizon.

About the Author

ROBERT OLEN BUTLER is the author of seven critically acclaimed novels—*The Alleys of Eden, Sun Dogs, Countrymen of Bones, On Distant Ground, Wabash, The Deuce,* and *They Whisper*—and a collection of short stories, *A Good Scent from a Strange Mountain,* winner of the 1993 Richard and Hinda Rosenthal Foundation Award from the American Academy of Arts and Letters as well as the 1993 Pulitzer Prize for Fiction. He lives in Lake Charles, Louisiana, where he teaches creative writing at McNeese State University.